Chicago

Chicago

A Novel

David Mamet

HARPER LUXE

An Imprint of HarperCollins*Publishers*

This book is a work of fiction. It is compounded of historical fact, myth, and imagination. Received chronology, having been, at some points, an impediment to narrative, has been jostled into a better understanding of its dramatic responsibilities. References to real people, events, establishments, organizations, or locales are intended only to provide a sense of authenticity, and are used fictitiously. All other characters, and all incidents and dialogue, are drawn from the author's imagination and are not to be construed as real.

HarperCollins books may be purchased for educational, business, or sales promotional use. For information please e-mail the Special Markets Department at SPsales@harpercollins.com.

FIRST HARPERLUXE EDITION

ISBN: 978-0-06-283593-2

HarperLuxe™ is a trademark of HarperCollins Publishers.

Library of Congress Cataloging-in-Publication Data is available upon request.

18 19 20 21 22   ID/LSC   10 9 8 7 6 5 4 3 2 1

To the memory of J.M.

370th Infantry 1917–1919
St. Mihiel, Soissons

Chicago Police Department
1924–1953

. . . Til upon thine Inland Sea
Stands CHICAGO great and free;
Turning all the world to thee,
Illinois Illinois.

—CHARLES H. CHAMBERLIN, 1898

Chicago

PART ONE

Chapter 1

Parlow and Mike sat quiet in the duck blind. A camouflage screen of marsh grass and twigs had been set before them; the blind itself was five feet deep, dug into the soft earth, and lined with discarded lumber. The day was dry, and the blind was dry.

Parlow and Mike half-rested against the blind's lip. Parlow was by far the better hunter; Mike came for the company and a day in the air.

Parlow faced west, and Mike east. The wind was out of the west, but the chances were even: they might come in on the wind, or they might turn into the wind to land. Fifteen decoys bobbed in the marsh before them. "No, they might come from anywhere," Mike thought. It was a joy for him to be in the winter sun.

"I am jealous, yes, of others' success," Parlow said, "but I never envied anyone's achievement."

"Uh-huh," Mike said.

"Some swine made more money than I," Parlow said. "Sold a story to *Harper's,* fooled a critic—there are *those,*" he said, "who fall with the right side up, and, thereverafter, whoever *sees* them, thinks, that fella looks like 'Heads.' *You* know them names. Edmond Harper *Gaines,* Lucille Brandt Williams, anybody with three names. Read the review, choke down the prose, of what in the world was the Reading Public thinking?

"No, it's not impossible that culture is a *field.* Of good or bad potential, but capable, presumably, of bringing forth some fruit. What does it require to promote growth . . . ?"

"Shit," Mike said.

"It requires manure," Parlow said, "animal or vegetable."

"Write it up for the *Little Review,*" Mike said.

"I sent them my article on the Prairie school of architecture," Parlow said.

"And?"

"They wrote they were considering it, and I found myself ashamed. But fuck it; it all comes from the Japanese. Those who have seen that Land of Cherry Blossoms; who have inhaled the mixed, suggestive fragrances of that ancient land; for those, e'en the unquenchable longing to return is small price to pay for having witnessed it."

"The longing to return could, conceivably, be quenched if you got on a fucking boat," Mike said.

"*Who's* got the time?" Parlow said. "And then there's seasickness."

"What did you like best about Japan?" Mike asked.

"Diminutive women, reasonably priced," Parlow said. "What makes the world go round? The world's like a hamster wheel, revolves as the motive force runs against it. The world goes around, as everyone is running in the wrong direction."

"And, of course, over there," Mike said, "they've got the direction wrong."

"What a terrible thing to say," Parlow said. "Why would their direction be wrong?"

"Because they're in the Southern Hemisphere," Mike said.

"Japan," Parlow said, "lies in the same latitude as Cleveland. Didn't you read my book?

"That fucking book, *speaking* of envy, was on the *short* short list for a Most Prestigious Literary Prize," Parlow said.

"What impeded your reception of it? Evil forces?" Mike said.

"I attribute the injustice to a public gorged on accounts of the fire, the earthquake, the waterspout, and the tidal wave, now grown inured, and uninterested in the mundane but necessary work of reconstruction," Parlow said.

"You should have come home sooner," Mike said.

"My God, you're right," Parlow said.

Parlow had come home in the spring of '24. He'd taken a six-month leave from the City Desk and gone to Japan. Four days from the end of his leave the earthquake struck, and Parlow was the Man on the Ground. When the wires were, though intermittently, restored, he filed with the *Tribune*.

The competition, with several hundred journalists bidding for wire time, restricted Parlow to the barest facts. They would, he knew, be colored, shaped, and inflated by Rewrite. That was reporting, and that was his job. But he wanted to write not just the facts, but the story of the tragedy.

At the end of the earthquake, when the tally showed one hundred thousand dead, and, as Parlow said, "That's the score," most reporters came home. Many wrote magazine pieces and books. But Parlow stayed on through the first efforts of reorganization and rebuilding. He took the boat home one half year after the disaster. He assumed, correctly, that all would have heard the story of the quake; and he, himself, was sick of it. So he wrote about rebuilding, and sanitation, and architecture, which had been his study before the War. Nobody bought his book.

"That's the reason it didn't sell," Mike had said. "Here's what you *should* have wrote: A young naval ensign, call him Yoji, is in love with the poor but lovely daughter of a traditional Japanese craftsman. Let's make him a potter. The hills out beyond his traditional rice-paper shack, alone in all the soil of Japan, bear that clay, renowned through the ages, from which and which alone Japanese emperors have caused to have fashioned the ceremonial bowls, which . . ."

Parlow's eyes narrowed as he heard them. Mike squinted, and could just make them out: four of them, in echelon, coming left to right, low and fast. The left was Parlow's side. And Parlow waited, admirably, until, as Mike thought, the right instant, which was just before "too late." He stood, swung through the lead duck, dropped it, and dropped the second. Mike shot behind the third duck, then the fourth was flying away, out of range, and Mike shot again, knowing the shot was pointless.

Parlow's birds had folded up and fallen like stones. They were some forty yards out in the marsh. Parlow was already levering himself out of the blind. He passed the shotgun to Mike and waded out. "Well, he heard them first," Mike thought. "I lost my hearing to a radial engine; and he's a much much better shot. He's a good shot."

Parlow looked awkward as he waded out, the water up to his waist. He was of medium height, stockily built, round-faced and balding. He wore wire-rimmed glasses, smoked an ancient bulldog pipe, and affected in winter tweed, and in summer cream linen suits.

He and Mike were of an age, and of the same height, but any witness would have described Mike as the taller.

They walked back at sunset, along the Fox River to the Fox River Hunting Club. Outside the door Mike turned back.

"Ain't it grand?" he said.

"What?" Parlow said.

Mike waved one forefinger around the horizon, taking in the beautiful low vista, the marsh, and the lowering day.

The club was just a small cabin purchased and moved from a tourist camp. There was room for a woodstove and two cots. Every inch of the walls held hooks. The hooks were salvaged cast iron, wooden pegs, tips or racks of antlers, and nails. They held hunting gear, waders, coats, hats, shooting bags, game bags, dog leashes, duck straps. Strings of cheap, farmer-made decoys were hung on the walls. Two magnificent carved mergansers sat on a window ledge.

As Parlow and Mike entered the cabin, the local boy was tending the stove. He was a redheaded Pole, fifteen years old and broad as a barn. Parlow held up the duck strap and said, "You want to do eight?" The boy smiled and took the strap from Parlow. The ducks were threaded through the loops in the strap by their feet.

"Hang this against the wall," Parlow said, "and you've got a peachy painting by some Dutch guy, got sick of the rain, painted dead birds."

"Lot of people, loop 'em in by their *heads*," the boy said.

"I always thought that monstrous," Parlow said.

The boy took the ducks and started out back, to the shed, where he would clean and dress them.

"How many you want? One? Two?" Parlow called. "Keep two, you greedy son of a bitch, why don't you grow up?"

The boy had dressed the ducks, and wrapped the breasts in butcher paper.

The owner of the Tokio bowed Parlow and Mike in at the restaurant door. Parlow handed him the large brown-paper parcel and spoke to him in Japanese.

The owner accepted the parcel in two outstretched hands, and bowed his unworthiness for such a gift. He and Parlow exchanged a few ceremonial phrases. Mike said, "Knock it off, I need a drink.

"These son of a bitches," Mike said, "you can't help but love 'em, kicked the ass of the tsar."

"So what?" Parlow said.

"Well, they get credit for the win," Mike said.

The owner brought them a teapot and two coffee cups. The teapot was full of bad scotch. Parlow poured their cups full. A waiter scurried in from the kitchen, holding a tray. The tray held two small bowls of soup. He put the soup in front of the two men and bowed himself away from the table. He passed into the kitchen as a young woman was coming out. They exchanged a word, at which, Mike saw, Parlow smiled. The young woman passed their table, and all nodded their courtesy. She continued, through the small dining room, to her post at the cash, and the boy spoke to her again.

Mike pointed back at the kitchen. "What'd that kid say?" he said.

"Something in Japanese," Parlow said.

CHICAGO · 11

It was, of course, something to do with Parlow and the young woman. Her name was Yuniko, she seemed to be somewhere between eighteen and thirty-five. She had been Parlow's mistress since his return from Japan.

Parlow nodded in the direction of the girl, who smiled and hid her face behind her hand. "I believe," he said, "that, at some point, that point following close upon the conclusion of our meal, I will absent myself from Felicity awhile, and spend the evening with a friend."

"Who's this Felicity?" Mike said.

"No, I shall never kiss and tell," Parlow said. "But you, I know, are yourself not unacquainted with the Biological Imperative."

"Oh, my," Mike said.

"I have offended you," Parlow said. "*You* think that your love is pristine, while mine must savor of more earthly things. Is that it, is that the thing?"

"She's out of town," Mike said.

". . . The Irish girl?" Parlow said.

"The Irish girl, yes."

Parlow shook his head at the vagaries of an uncertain world.

"Well, there you have it," he said. "*Poor* fellow. Puts me in mind of the old tale, young swain, dying of love. Love is denied him, standard-issue cruel father, whisked her away. Young swain fashions her image out of straw—"

"Why'd he whisk her away?" Mike said.

"'Match unsuitable. Details to follow. Send collect.' Image made of straw. Spends his last few coins on finery, dresses the straw image up. He worships it. Girl? Pines away. 'How can you be so cruel, O Father?' Father relents. Brings the girl home, 'You want him so much, go have him.' They return. The young *swain* has just been beheaded for worshipping idols."

"Did this take place?" Mike said.

"Too good to check," Parlow said. "Also, where is your sense of poetry?"

"They took her," Mike said, "to Wisconsin."

"No, that's unfortunate," Parlow said.

Mike's girl had gone away for the weekend, taken, by her parents, to Milwaukee.

All knew she was too old to be forced into the excursion, but she went. And it was not necessary to pronounce the actual reason for her sentence.

Mike was lonely.

The City Room was quiet. The bulldog edition had been put to bed, and most of the men were down in the Sally Port, drinking from relief, or from fatigue, or from habit, or for the hell of it. Mike had decided "to make the Great Hegira," as Parlow had once put it, and join them.

The Hegira involved levering oneself away from the desk, the appurtenant bottle, and the company of the reporters, and descending those four stories to the Sally Port, there to imbibe much the same hooch, in quite the same company.

As he put on his coat, he gazed absently at a proof tacked to the wall. It read:

> . . . missing from the armory of the National Guard are seventy-five .45-caliber Thompson guns, two hundred fifty Colt 1911 .45 pistols, and twelve thousand rounds of .45 cal. ammunition. Packed with each submachine gun were: one instruction manual; two stick magazines, capacity twenty rounds; one drum magazine, capacity fifty rounds; a canvas carrying case, and a sling; and a rudimentary cleaning kit.

Mike muttered, "Yeah, *okay* . . . ," and started downstairs to the speakeasy.

He had often thought that the stories told at the bar were far superior to those printed in the rag. He had often expressed this view, and been hooted down for it.

"What do you think they're paying us for?" Crouch had said.

"Man bites dog," Mike had said.

"*Bullshit*," Crouch said. "Man bites dog is too interesting to be news."

"Then what is news?" Mike said.

"*News*," Crouch said, "is that which makes its consumer self-important, angry, or sufficiently whatever the hell to turn to page twelve, and, turning, encounter the ad for the carpet sale."

"I thought news was supposed to interest," Mike said.

"That's why your stories get spiked," Crouch said. "Interest City Hall, you get yourself fired. Interest Al Capone, you wind up dead as Jake Leiter. Interest Colonel McCormick, means maybe you've screwed the pooch, he thinks your name is more important than his, you're not only sacked, but unemployable. For, mark, lad," Crouch said, "there are forces alive in the land. We are not of them, but, rather, a distraction from the troubling knowledge of their presence."

He picked up the copy of the newspaper, folded, on the bench next to him. "See here." He read, " 'More Luxury Autos Disappear from the North Shore. The current spate of coach-built auto disappearances: Packards, Duesenbergs . . .' "

He turned the paper over.

" 'Public outcry over repeated thefts from the National Guard armory . . .' "

He let the paper fall.

"A *newspaper* is a joke. Existing at the pleasure of the advertisers, to mulct the public, gratifying their stupidity, and render some small advance on investment to the owners, offering putative employment to their etiolated, wastrel sons, in those young solons' circuit between the Fort Dearborn Club and the Everleigh House of Instruction."

"Well, fuck *you*," Mike had said, "as we said in the Great War." The company had tapped its glasses, and murmured approval. Some half-stood and said, "*Hear him.*"

"Fuck you, *too*," Crouch had said, "as *we* said in the Great War, in which, though debarred by age from fighting, many suffered not only regrettable casualties to our youth and purse, but the dull pain of disillusion and uniformly wretched quality of reportage."

"Those with the best minds were fighting," Mike said.

"And those with the best minds are fighting *still*," Crouch said. "Not on some forgotten field in France, no, not in Flanders's fields, obscured by those unfortunate 'poppies,' but here, *here*, my man, on the streets of our fair city, for the right to control territory, and routes and methods of distribution of that very substance we, in what I understood prior to this contretemps to be 'fellowship,' called hooch. This battle—"

Mike had stood.

"I have a confession to make," he said. And the bar grew silent. "I, like plucky little Belgium, and her noted nuns, have been getting fucked." There was some small applause, and Mike stilled it by raising his hand.

"I have been debauched by journalism, but. But. And here I ask you to restrain both your incredulity and, if it be, your contempt: I have come, in my shame, to a conclusion so foreign to the general understanding, that—"

"Get to the hook," Crouch said.

"I have decided *not* to write a novel," Mike said.

In the respectful pause, most signaled for another drink and waited. Mike lit a cigarette, still holding the floor. "Write for the rag," a reporter yelled.

"I shall," Mike said, "*but,* I shall not write about the small freshwater shark, abstracted from the best of aquaria, and placed in the pool of the Fort Dearborn Club; nor of the remorseful police captain who, one half hour from irremediable disgrace, attempting to blow out his brains in the confessional, shot, instead, an altar boy, though *not* him whose story was about to bring the penitent to ruin."

Murmurs of "Wretched judgment" and the like came from the bar.

"I shall not write of the poor but honest Jewish tailor—"

"Staple of our trade," a wag said.

"—who discovered, sewn in the lining of the coat given to him to be recut for a gentleman's funeral, those twelve one-thousand-dollar bills, nor of his struggle with his conscience, which urged him to keep them all; nor of his decision to bring the lot before Pharaoh (Mr. Brown), nor of Mr. Brown's generosity, in spiffing the guy fifty bucks and the promise of limitless custom.

"Nor shall I write of the bloated plutocrat *bitten* by the shark, nor of the attempts to hush it up, which, I have found, as have you all, is the most holy charge of our craft. My pen and whatever might be my small abilities will run to none of these reports, nor along the path which might elevate them, if not to the status of art, at least to that of literature."

"Why *not?*" Hanson said.

"Because he is in love," Parlow said. The reporters, variously, howled, applauded, or cheered.

"Love," Crouch said, "is as much the death of journalism as cooze is its analgesic. It is as the clap to fornication, or remorse to the adulterer."

"Who is the fortunate one?" Kelly asked.

"These lips shall not speak her sainted name," Mike had said. He sat.

Chapter 2

Her name was Annie Walsh.

At the beginning of their courtship Mike spent quite a bit of time flirting with her.

He was, as usual, conducting the operation with care, such care consisting, to his mind, in a fine assessment of that point at which his raging lust for her possession would overcome that which he understood as a decent respect for her youth and innocence.

"It's something like flying an airplane," he told Parlow. "It's designed to be unbalanced. The only way you can keep it in equilibrium is to make it *go* somewhere. It's in stasis only before or after it has gone somewhere, or when it isn't going nowhere anymore—"

"She's too young," Parlow had said.

"—as, for example, after the Hun has executed the

Forbidden Stitch upon your tailplane, and left you looking down for a good place to die."

"Save it for your book," Parlow said.

"Oh, it's all going in the book," Mike said. "One way or another. For it is *in* me, and, thus, must come out."

"Well, I'm sure that it was a traumatic experience," Parlow said. "For all that it was good, clean fun."

"Yeah. It was fun," Mike said. "That's the dark, sordid secret that us fighting men carry. A canker on our heart."

"You said you weren't writing a book," Parlow said.

"The heart is a fickle mistress," Mike said.

"The broad's too young," Parlow said. "*Also,* you fuck around, the Irish? Her father'll kill you, and that's not a metaphor."

"What if I marry her?" Mike said.

"*Oh* my," Parlow said.

"Well, people have gotten married for less."

"Does she even *like* you?"

"Everybody likes me," Mike said. "I'm a likable guy . . . I've got a *job* . . ."

"Did you say you *might* write the novel?"

"I can do both."

" 'A man cannot serve two masters,' " Parlow said. "Who said that?"

"*Lad: A Dog*," Mike said.

"What do you talk about with this kid? She can *talk*, right . . . ?"

"She don't *have* to talk," Mike said.

"You know what?" Parlow said. "You don't *even* fall in love like a nigger. You? Fall in love like a *hillbilly:* See the girl? Throw her, her two kids, and her banjo, back of the truck, and off you go."

"That's right," Mike said.

Mike had first seen Annie Walsh behind the counter at The Beautiful, where he had gone in pursuit of a hunch. The hunch came from a memory of his attendance at Mob funerals.

It struck him, when perfected, as one of those ideas so clear and simple the recipient cannot believe they have not been exploited before. For why, Mike thought, as does any blessed with true inspiration, would God choose him, a fool and a sinner, to receive this sign of Grace? But He had.

There, at the funeral, its honoree a representative of the South Side, one Alfonse Mucci, were the warring factions, convened in the usual performance of "peace at the waterhole." And there was Mike, and there were his colleagues, representatives of the City Desks of the other Chicago papers, each searching for a slant that would be evident to him but somehow opaque to his equally attentive competition.

Mike's survey strayed past the reposed-in-respect faces of Mucci's colleagues and assassins, and onto the floral tributes. Here he found the usual wreaths, crosses, and horseshoes, bearing the usual sentiments; and, wired to their wooden stands, upon each, a small card.

The crowd had left the graveside, and the gravediggers appeared, but Mike stayed on. He walked around the grave and toward the flowers. He bent to look at the small white cards and found them, each, to be a direction to the deliveryman: A. Mucci/Lakeside, two P.M. And each bore the logo of its supplier. The more elaborate displays had, in the main, been propounded by two enterprises: Flessa's, of 2331 Michigan Avenue, thus the supplier to the South Side, and "The Beautiful: Florists of Distinction," 1225 North Clark Street.

Mike had begun frequenting the two emporia as possibly productive of criminal gossip. He had not been disappointed.

Of the two, the management of Flessa's was more garrulous, and happy to regale a customer, for Mike posed as such, with tales of the great, spicing the potentially dry recitation of business with the gossip, overheard by or indulged in with the proprietor, of the colorful vagaries of the Capone Mob. These stories, quips, anecdotes, or offhand comments, Mike threshed for facts, several of which were of sufficient accuracy to have earned him, on two occasions, polite warnings from, as they put it, "Friends of the Big Guy." The Big Guy, also known as Mr. Brown, was Al Capone; these friends had spoken to Flessa, who, through his new reticence, had made the edict known to Mike, who then curtailed his investigations of Flessa's.

Mike's response to the Call to Adventure, like that of many another hero, had cooled after this first opposition. The Call was repeated on a slow morning in May. He'd come in to take Parlow to lunch, and found him typing. Mike sat by the side of the desk and watched. "The rich the rich the rich make me sad," Parlow had said. "In this greatest land God ever had the native sense to bless. When any . . ."

" 'Elevator operator'?" Mike asked.

"Elevator operator, yes," Parlow said, "can rise to wealth upon the instant, by the mere possession of a *tip:* when those absent the understanding that the Lord gave geese can throw darts at a board, and pick stocks whose potential is limited only by the faith and credence of the American folk."

"Who do you know who struck it rich?" Mike said.

"My sister, or somesuch, undoubtedly had a friend at the beauty salon whose husband, boyfriend, bootlegger, lover, chance acquaintance . . . and I'll tell you what else."

"I'm listening," Mike said.

"I'm sick to death and want to turn my face to the wall over exposés. 'Here we find' "—he passed his hand over the pile of books on his desk—"review copies of, *what*? Exposés: meatpacking, railroads, telephone, the *stock* market, for the love of God, child rearing, every swinging dick with a typewriter is crafting an indictment of the American Way."

"Many of them are women," Mike said.

"I stand by the previous statement," Parlow said. "And there is money in that, *too*. 'An exposé!' the Consumer of Littacher exclaims: 'Oh my: how astute to note, and how brave to relate that we are all corrupt swine, rooting in the feces-nurtured loam of life.' "

"I accuse you. You've been reading in French," Mike said.

"And if I have?" Parlow said. "Is that not also a language, as you, no doubt, had noticed, in your sojourn there, amongst the antiquities, their outlines gentled by the wash of time, the German Big Berthas, and the Treaty of Versailles?"

"What makes you sad about the rich?" Mike said.

"That which makes everyone sad who is not of their number," Parlow said. "That they are better off than we; and *we* brave our unmerited poverty stoically, whilst they sail yachts, and indulge in God knows what depravities in boathouses."

"But do you not also hate the poor?" Mike said. "For they possess no money. Therefore what can they do for me, save impotently rage, because I, occasionally, sport a clean collar? Fuck the poor. Further, saving always the criminals, they have misunderstood the situation. For, how do they propose to raise their state? By appeal, finally, to government."

"Fuck the poor," Parlow said.

"And what about—" Mike said.

"I'm not done," Parlow said.

"What about strikes?"

"I'm not done," Parlow said. "And what is government but the nom de guerre of thugs and whores; of greed, which, were it practiced by those out of office, would result in their dismemberment. *Strikes* I approve of, as partaking both of bootless appeal to 'authority,' and crime. Thus, the weary brain might encompass them under two heads equally potential for copy."

"Is there a third head?" Mike asked.

"Yes," Parlow said, "its name is the lawful petition for redress of grievance."

"How shall that be addressed?" Mike said.

"Not by the *American*," Parlow said, "nor the *Daily News*, nor the *Tribune*, but by the clubs of the Pinkertons, hewn from trees grown for that purpose."

Parlow took the sheet from the typewriter and yelled, "Boy!" He put a fresh sheet in the typewriter, and began to type again.

"Stand them up against a wall," Parlow said. He looked up, and shouted, "BOY for the love of Christ!"

Mike took the typed sheet and waved it over his head. " 'Boy boy and there was no boy,' " he said. He lowered the sheet of copy and began to read.

" 'Page two: Of Civic Improvement. The parks, won by Abraham Lincoln for our perpetual use, are that transition area so beloved of architects. They do not encompass, but set off Chicago's beauty. See them from the east, as the eye and the spirit move from the wild of the Lake, to the subdued, the *urbs in horto*, of a twenty-six-mile-long garden; a pause, if you will, between Nature and Commerce, and on to the . . .' "

Parlow looked up for a copyboy. "Don't read that shit," he said to Mike.

"What is it?" Mike said.

Parlow stood. "*BOY* for the love of Christ, bleeding on the Cross!" he shouted. "Is there no one in this organization doing his job but fucking *me*?"

A copyboy came sauntering into the City Room.

"Where have you . . . BOY, you worthless *pig*," Parlow said. The boy began to run toward him.

"Yes, run. *Run*. You fucking *maggot*."

Mike held the sheet aloft, and the copyboy took it and ran off.

"And come *back*!" Parlow shouted.

"What is this shit?" Mike said.

"It is an article on beautification," Parlow said.

"Why are you writing it?" Mike asked.

"I am writing it as a favor," Parlow said.

"For whom?" Mike said.

"I'm not going to tell you," Parlow said.

"If you were, what would you say?" Mike said.

"I am writing it for the new young lady on the cultural staff," Parlow said.

"You whore," Mike said.

"I'm doing it for money," Parlow said.

"She's *paying* you?"

Parlow raised a finger to his lips.

"*Why?*"

"Apparently, she can't write," Parlow said.

"Anyone can write," Mike said.

"She's had a sheltered life," Parlow said. "Nepotism,

that great equalizer, has gotten her a job, but, faced with her first deadline, she'd come down with the fantods. I need a drink."

"Let's get a drink," Mike said. "You can buy."

Parlow shook his head and continued typing.

"Okay, when you're done," Mike said.

"No, I need a drink *now*," Parlow said.

Mike opened the desk's bottom drawer. The bottle was there, but it was empty. Parlow shook his head.

"Go on down," Mike said. "Go on, *I'll* finish it." Parlow got up. Mike slid into his place at the typewriter. Parlow kissed the top of Mike's head, picked up his coat from the hat stand, and started out of the City Room.

The page in the typewriter read: ". . . *our native Chicagoan love of flowers . . .*"

Parlow had gone down to get drunk. Mike was left with the unfinished article—his only (but sufficient) clue to its tone and content "our native Chicagoan love of flowers."

The previous copy had gone to the compositors, and Mike could only guess at the identity of those clichés still available for use. "What the hell," he thought, "screw 'em, let the copy desk figure it out."

After "*Chicagoan love of flowers,*" he typed, "*which,*" and stopped.

Did Chicagoans love flowers?

Women loved flowers, he knew. Men did not care. Chicagoans did not seem to love flowers any more than any other group, and probably loved them less, he thought, being more down-to-earth folk.

But *someone* loved flowers, or there would be no florists. Mike, like any writer faced with a stringent test or deadline, began to daydream. Who supported the florists? he wondered. Men looking to please a woman, women, the rich, and, he remembered, the gangsters; and thought on this slow day he might haul out his aperçu again.

Parlow found Mike in the News Morgue, reading a paper from '23. It was a photograph of a huge floral tribute.

"The florists," Mike said. "North Side."

"Yes, the Micks have the florists, and their entry to the North Side, its rich apartments, happily served by the delivery boys, 'Wait right here, while I go into my bedroom, young man, and fetch you something for yourself, dot, dot, dot,' where was I?"

"The florists," Mike said.

"The North *Side*," Parlow said, "widening their

commerce also to the selling of hooch, nose candy, opium, and the control of the speaks north of our Rubicon, the Chicago River.

"The Nation of Ausonia-in-Exile has to *their* credit: the Negro enclaves of the South and West Sides, *numbers*, girls, and the aforesaid analgesics. The *North Side* . . ."

"Nails Morton," Mike said.

"*Nails*," Parlow said, "yes, was, nominally, a florist. And he was the Hebrew ombudsman and *Jud Süss* to O'Banion and his merry band of horticulturists."

"*Nails*," Mike said. "Pulled in, in his youth, for the murder of this or that odd duck, various other juvenile pranks, including 'parsimony with lack of intent to share with the cops.'"

"Judge says, 'Stateville or France?' Nails chooses France. Comes home a hero. Grows rich as shit, yellow kid gloves. Riding his horse one day, Lincoln Park, horse throws him. Kicks him to death. You have to love it."

"The horse?" Mike said.

"The horse, munching his 'hay,' that night. O'Banion, his myrmidons bust in, 'rat tat tat.'"

Mike continued to stare at the paper.

"The horse," he said. "What did they shoot him with?"

"Where have you been?" Parlow said. "They shot him with the tommy gun. Have you no sense of *fitness* . . . ?"

"Old days, Roman times, they would have cut his throat," Mike said, absently.

"Time marches on. *P.S.:* they *left* the tommy gun, on top of the dead horse, discarding it, as it had been defiled by 'contact with the horse.' You've got to love it. Weiss, Teitelbaum, must have bemoaned the waste of four hundred bucks."

"I would mourn it myself," Mike said. He held the magnifying glass close to the paper.

"What are you looking at?" Parlow said.

Mike was looking at the photograph. He took the magnifying glass and held it over the inscription, spelled out in daisies, in the midst of the horseshoe. " 'All the Best Wishes from those who Wish you the Best,' " he read.

"Ah, yes, the language of flowers," Parlow said, "is 'the language of love.' "

"I'm working out a *lead*, alright?" said Mike.

"Is that what they call it now?" Parlow said.

"That's what they call it," Mike said.

Mike's repeated excursions to The Beautiful were decreasingly productive of information as his informant,

Annie Walsh, was the impossibly beautiful daughter of the proprietor, who, from his workroom, kept a constant and effective vigil upon her. And, as a demonstration of his fatherly concern, reduced his speech to monosyllables. This, while balking Mike in his attempts at useful conversation, did not prevent him from, silently, and irremediably, falling in love with the girl.

"What," he said to Parlow, "am I to do?"

"If you had what I will call 'your druthers,' what would you do?" Parlow said.

"I would walk into the shop and say, 'Get your coat,' and I would take her with me far away, and never let her out of bed."

But he had, as yet, even to speak to her beyond the ordering of just those flowers sufficient to excuse his presence in the shop.

Mike was not, of course, deluding the father, who, in addition to suspecting any man of any age, was especially attuned to the actual appearance, however disguised, of lust; neither was he fooling the daughter, who, like all women of all time, was perfectly aware of both the presence and the degree of men's interest. His only dupe in the charade was himself. And he paid not only by unrequited longing and by indecision, but by his unexamined but persistent dislike of any duplicity involving his love of the innocent girl. For was he not before her under doubly false flags, his dumb show as a customer masking not only his concupiscence, but his indeed more vile character as a spy? And might it not be argued, he wondered, that information elicited from her or her establishment might eventuate in their chastisement by the O'Banion organization? Which last consideration did not occur to him in his adventures on the South Side, where, had the question occurred to him at all, Mike would have considered himself as "bound to take his chances like the rest of us."

But not the girl. He did not wish to involve the girl.

To her he did not compose poetry but that prose, to his mind, beyond such, and more fitting to a newspaperman. These forays in prose began, in his imagination, as simple and therefore worthy declarations, but quickly devolved into her silent acquiescence, and his lifting her out of her clothes (the scene, in fantasy, being transported from the flower shop to his apartment on Wisconsin Street), and her introduction to the art of love.

Mike had discussed his floral inspiration with JoJo Lamarr, reformed, or, as he liked to say, "momentarily unapprehended," cat burglar and utility man.

JoJo's résumé included stints as a steerer for a bunco mob, a shoplifter, and a general purveyor of information. He had no particular affiliation, and when asked, described his ability as an independent contractor as "being the world's friend."

He invariably dressed in a shirt and slacks of tight-tailored nailhead denim. This, to those in the know, an allusion to his time spent in Stateville prison, and to his status there of one who, if not a boss con, was suggesting an acquaintance.

Over the denim he wore a knee-length coat of light-weight brown leather. The entire outfit, to those who could read, proclaimed: "This is where I've been, and this is where I'm going. For the moment, I am here: 'What's yours?'"

Mike had come late to meet with JoJo and proffered the writer's universal excuse of work; bolstered, in this instance, by the extraneous "I was at the florist's."

JoJo discounted the dual excuse, known to all who tread close to the line as a dead giveaway.

He filed the unexplored obfuscation away, and asked, "At work, what were you, running down the dodge?"

"Which dodge of many?" Mike said.

"Yeah, the *funeral* dodge," JoJo said.

"Why the funeral dodge?"

"Because you said you were at the florist's," JoJo said.

"'The funeral dodge,'" Mike said. "Enlighten me."

"The guy *dies*," JoJo said, as would a magician explaining to a neophyte the most basic of illusions. "He's dead, what does everyone do?"

"They go to the funeral," Mike said.

"You bet," JoJo said. "*While* they are gone, who's minding the store? At home?"

". . . Uh . . . ," Mike said.

"Precisely," JoJo said. "Nobody knows.

"Nobody knows. This is the beauty of death: that it leaves a hole in the accepted working of things. Everybody assumes somebody *else* is 'taking care of it.'"

"In this case?" Mike said.

"'It'?" JoJo said. "'It' is the house. Funeral director assumes somebody called a caterer. Caterer assumes somebody's bringing the flowers. Dress some broad up, appropriate to the neighborhood, waltz her in there with a casserole, who's going to question her? She? Cleans the place out. It's a naturally occurring windfall."

"What about—" Mike said.

"Yes, yes, yes, rich people, people in the know? They hire security. Sure. They've got a list. One, maybe you piece *them* off; or? *Two*, Aunt Mabel, comes in with a suitcase, out of town, just heard the news. Least she can do, she can't take the joint off? Case the joint. Too much protection? Either sign off, 'I'll go to the hotel,' come back *later;* or simply walk away. The least you have got, you've got some information. *Sometime;* things calm down. Family gets over it. Wife is off, fucking the gardener, kids are away at school. Maybe, weep weep weep, they go on vacation. Now: even though you walked away at first, the information you gained there is *priceless.*"

"How?"

"You *saw* the joint—huh? Mike? When you were Aunt Mabel, you said, to the butler, gardener, nanny, 'What is *your* name . . . ?'

"You come back, the boys come back in, possibly, 'I'm Forstairs's brother, I stopped by to give him a . . .' You know Forstairs is the gardener, you've got to be okay. Might buy you a minute, never know.

"*Also,* and more importantly, the Pinkertons, you come in during the funeral? What are they guarding? They back up against one wall? That's where the safe is, prolly. Information is gold, and will save your ass much more often than a Third Model Smith and Wesson, which, finally, is just going to get you in the soup."

"*You* carry one," Mike said.

"Wrong," JoJo said. "I've never in my life; yes, well, yes, when I was a kid. Before I went to college, yes. After that? I had a trade. I'd *never* carry a gun.

"Why? You kill somebody, they're more apt, some-body? Come looking for you; not only later *on*, but *now*, as it makes a noise. My trade, part of it, is, one: to *plan*, I don't *need* the gun. Part of the plan is 'IT GOES WRONG.' It goes wrong, I am not without resources; I've thought out an exit; a plan of escape; excuses, which may either extricate me, buy me time to attempt the same, *or* explain myself to the cops in such a way they might, on the way to the slam, offer me a drink instead of beating the shit out of me for my presumption.

"Guns, some guys? Use them to *threaten* people. All I know, the only thing they're actually good for, *shoot* 'em."

"You can't use them to threaten people?" Mike said.

"Yeah, you *can*," JoJo said. "Two choices: the mopes are either frightened or they're not. They're *not*, what good was the threat? They *are*, they might, unknownst, have a piece on *them*; now? They're *frightened*? Maybe they're fighting for their life, drag it out and shoot *you*. Yes yes yes," he said. "But that's my thinking.

"Would I, on the way to the chair, shoot the turn-key? How the fuck do *I* know. Probably yes, or I might just chin up and take my medicine. Am I constitution-ally incapable, shooting someone? *I* don't know. I'm not a *moron;* the other hand, I have no wish to hurt anybody.

"I like to help people," he said. "Here's one: because you never 'went away.' You never got an education. You had? First thing you learn there: What is trouble? We know what it is. It's *trouble.* Where's it to be found?"

"The least likely place."

"And, *Mike?* Let this be a lesson: the more innocent a thing is, the more *some* guy"—he gestured to himself as an example—"is going to find some way, get over on you.

"Popcorn. I was working in the carny selling popcorn—fill up the bottom of the bag, half inch of sand: *popcorn. Nothing* is on the up-and-up."

The true advance in Mike's education had come from observation of the girl, over tea at the Budapest Café.

The intimacy of the Budapest was a proclamation. Prior to that, Mike was allowed to enjoy her company only as the reporter following a lead.

The fiction served them both, and after three visits to The Beautiful, it was, in the main, forgotten.

Mike realized that there was information to be gained from attendance at funerals. He let the lead go at that, and spent his mornings in The Beautiful greenhouse questioning the girl, now and then, merely for form. The worth and meaning of the questions was understood by both as cooing. The girl appreciated his decent protection of a troubled chastity whose blushes, absent the neutral topic, would reveal itself past hope of recall.

In their talks at the florist's, Mike sat on the high stool and smoked cigarettes. Annie was dressed in a green work smock, which he thought the most graceful garment he had ever seen. She wore white cotton gloves, and pushed the hair back from her forehead with one. As she worked, the gloves dirtied. She searched the gloves, at first, for a clean spot, and as those became more rare, her forehead was streaked with dirt. Mike was entranced.

He retailed her secrets to Parlow.

"Did you know," he said, "that flowers can be scalded back to life?"

Parlow, as a reporter, could always be charmed by anything smacking of a dodge.

"Yes," Mike said. "You have to cut the stems *longwise*, on the diagonal, to allow them more access to the water. The water must be fresh and cold. You can then pour the *hot* water from the kettle on the new cuts; in they go, back in the vase, and you'll add a day or two to their effective life."

Parlow began to speak.

"*And,*" Mike said, "you never use scissors to cut the stems."

"Why?" Parlow asked, thinking himself the most useful of friends.

"As that compresses the stem," Mike said. "And you are, then, allowing the plant *less* water. Here is my favorite. It's florist's wire."

"Florist's wire," Parlow said.

"A super-thin gauge, inserted *through* the stem, up into the flower itself, correcting its drooping head. You take, for example, a rose. Past its prime . . ."

Parlow nodded in sympathy. "New cut to the stem, boiling water, *strip* the dead petals—leave the fresh, insert the wire, the head of the rose comes up, and you can sell 'em again."

"Again?" Parlow said.

"People buy flowers," Mike said. He saw Parlow's agreement and continued. "Where do they take them?"

"To their girl," Parlow said.

"Yes . . ."

"Or their mother."

"Yes, yes, and they take them to *functions*," Mike said.

"Yes, they do," Parlow said.

"They pay for the flowers, which are left at the functions. What happens to them at the function's close?"

"Someone takes them to hospitals for the poor," Parlow said.

"Henh," Mike said. "The house staff, cleaning staff, bellboys sell them back to the flower shops."

"I had no idea," Parlow said.

"*Well*," Mike said. "And you can paint flowers, you can dye 'em, you can, look here, you can, same old flower . . ." He moved his hands to indicate *after we have done the things to it previously mentioned.* "What draws us to it, for, certainly, it represents youth."

"Youth and sex," Parlow said.

"Not with one's mother," Mike said.

Parlow said, "Consider Hamlet," as Mike continued, "Youth. 'Dewy freshness.' "

"Oh, my," Parlow said.

"That glint," Mike said, "which only comes in youth. 'Though, over time, and with mutual support, of course, it may be replaced by a comradely understanding, which—' "

"Yes, alright," Parlow said.

"—the old flower, by the way, I'm speaking of the rose," Mike said, "and, if you place a penny in the tulips' water, that will preserve them. The rose, especially, stands for young love."

"I never doubted it," Parlow said.

"The capillaries of its stem—"

"I had assumed the stem itself was a capillary," Parlow said.

"It's not," Mike said. "As the stem ages, they collapse, they desiccate, less water reaches the bloom. The new rose, of course, in the display, is sprayed with water. What is more beautiful than that glistening—"

"Alright," Parlow said.

"But the old rose, however it is culled, wired, and stripped, its petals just won't cause the water to bead."

"It beads, no doubt," Parlow said, "in the new rose, as it is replete, and can hold no more."

Mike looked accusingly at Parlow, who performed ignorance of his affront.

"But the appearance of this freshness may be gaffed," Mike said, "by spraying the rose with glycerin."

The tutorials at The Beautiful continued. They were, one morning, cut short as Annie was directed to accompany the driver to the cemetery.

She got into the neat red van marked *The Beautiful.* Mike, as a matter of course, climbed after her into the van, which both silently agreed was but logical.

The red van drove through the stone gates of Waldheim Cemetery. The driver parked the van alongside the large equipment shed. Mike followed Annie into the shed.

They walked past the mowers and rollers. The groundskeepers were sitting at a table in the back. One of them hailed the driver, and led him to a double door. He opened the door. Beyond it were arrayed multiple floral tributes.

The more ornate bore symbols or sentiments; many bore both. There were the shamrock, the thistle, hearts entwined, the cross, and the names of family or official positions of the dearly departed.

The tributes were arranged into groups.

The driver preceded the groundsmen to the group he recognized as his own. Money changed hands, and Mike helped him and Annie load the tributes onto the van.

Mike and Annie rode in the back of the van. Each sat on a wheel well. The flowers, filling the van, came between them, and they peered through them and parted them as they spoke, every aspect of the rough ride a source of shared enjoyment.

Mike helped the driver unload the tributes at The Beautiful's back door.

They had bought back both the flowers and the stands and the easels upon which they stood.

On each of the easels was a small printed card: WALSH'S THE BEAUTIFUL, 1225 NORTH CLARK STREET.

Mike saw that the back of each had the name and telephone number of the purchaser. And he saw some
names which, when coupled to that of the honoree,
suggested a connection sufficiently corrupt to be worthy of investigation.

Mike pocketed the cards.

He could try to excuse himself, as the months went
by, with the idea that he was merely doing the job which
he had been pretending to do; but he could never accept the excuse as, before he pocketed the cards, he
glanced over his shoulder to make sure that he could
not be seen. He hated himself for the thefts.

Chapter 3

Mike had been courting Annie for the better part of a year.

Their courtship had begun with the exchanged glances and small talk whose true meaning was hidden at no depth at all. He was allowed, first on a night-by-night basis, then as a matter of course, to walk her to the trolley after work.

Mike had gone, first, to the shop, on business; and, his business concluded, returned to gaze at and to court the girl, who, as he knew in the first instant, was and would always be the love of his life.

And, so, throughout the summer and fall, he would walk her from work, most meetings taking place just around the corner from the shop and her family's disapproving eyes. For he was not of their ilk, not a Catholic, and only, as they well knew, interested in the one thing, which, absent the sacrament of marriage, meant damnation and disgrace.

She left when the shop closed for business; her father and brothers stayed on to tend the flowers, to make the day's last deliveries, and to shut the shop down for the night.

Annie was pursuing the secretarial course at the Armitage College of Business; and so was excused from the shop on school nights at five, where Mike, when not on a story, met her and walked her a slow six blocks down to the trolley stop.

Once, her brother had driven past, in the red van of The Beautiful. He had not noticed them, but Annie had seen him; and Mike, as a reporter, attuned to slight fluctuations in behavior, was impressed beyond measure to note that she altered not a jot, disdaining both concealment and assertiveness. He exchanged a look with her and her look said their courting had progressed to the point at which she could trust him with her deepest secret, which was that she knew and was proud of his love.

Rain, and, some months later, snow made it but prudent for them to wait for the car under shelter.

The awning of the Budapest Café protected them, and the café itself was just beyond the awning. Both were pleased with the unexceptionable choice of refuge. There were coffee, tea, cakes, Bohemian pastries, and light ethnic food.

The Budapest was a luncheon resort, sufficiently superior to a coffee shop or lunch counter to appeal to the genteel, the shabby-genteel, and those who enjoyed, or did not mind, their company.

The tablecloths were pale yellow; the tea and coffee cups were placed on paper doilies. The clientele was exclusively middle-aged women. Annie and Mike were content that the atmosphere effectively protected and restrained, and, so, advanced their infatuation.

Annie held, for him, the inviolable purity of the pregnant woman, the young mother, the young bride. He'd seen it in France, at the Front, in women whose only defense was their defenselessness and a reliance upon the understood inviolability of their state.

He'd thought it, likely, a function of a shared religiosity; for it needed no one to explain that those who touched the defenseless woman, virgin, mother, or bride, were damned to hell. The French and Belgians shared the Catholic adoration of the mother. The Germans did not.

Parlow suggested this might have been the impetus for their rape of Belgium, whose first victims, the myth ran, were the Belgian nuns. He, though a noncombatant, assumed the atrocity stories were myth, as he assumed most stories which inflamed or ratified the passions were myth, as indeed were most stories presenting themselves as news.

"If it were true tragedy," he'd said, "we would avert the eyes. And we might kill or rage, but I believe we'd tell no one—and most certainly not for money.

"As we do. All newspapermen loathe themselves."

Annie had asked Mike about the War. It seemed a safe topic: neither love, nor his work, and so he spoke of it simply, retelling or embellishing, though never inventing, the droll.

He took great care in his tone to have it understood that he felt his job was to amuse and to divert her, always lightly, for the time they spent together was the only meaning either desired.

As the weeks progressed, he saw that she took increasing care with her appearance. He was charmed, and thought that even the almost-deniable touch of rouge, and the merest touch of lipstick, could not diminish her shocking virginal beauty. Crouch and the City Room had noted his behavior, and had guessed its cause. But only Parlow knew the name. "There's only one cure for it," he had said, "but, unfortunately, no one knows what it is."

The fat Hungarian owner of the Budapest was good enough at his trade to spare the couple knowing glances, and smiles, and fulsome performance; Mike appreciated his courtesy. He wondered if Annie noticed, and concluded she had no need to do so. She was a convent girl, to Mike's eyes incapable of guile or sin. For good or ill, he would, if he could, mediate between her magnificent, sad reserve and a world by which, if he had his way, she would never find herself affronted.

It was unclear to Mike how their love might progress. He saw her gratitude for his restraint, and was delighted with himself for discovering how to make her happy.

One evening, having safely put her on the trolley, he found himself singing softly. He stopped, and thought, "Oh. I suppose this must be courting."

Chapter 4

Jackie Weiss, Mike Hodge wrote, had died of a broken heart, it being broken by several slugs from a .45.

His funeral was notable for the display of his widow's undergarments as she hopped down into the grave and upon his casket, whereupon she began to scream, "Jackie, don't leave me," and resisted the efforts of the chief mourners to haul her from the grave.

It was, Mike wrote, as formulaic as a Gypsy wedding, with its ritual attempt at abduction by the groom, and the corresponding opposition of the brothers of the bride.

On seeing the copy, Parlow had commented that Mike had the Irish girl on his mind, and if he desired to "tell the story of his love," he should ask for the sob sister column, and stay clear of the City Desk.

Also, he had said, if we believe the Viennese, the mind is controlled by various independent helmsmen, each at war with the rest; and chief of all was he who would fain scream to the world the secrets the others existed to keep hid.

Mike lit a cigarette.

"In *this* case . . . ," Parlow continued.

". . . Alright," Mike said.

"The fantasy that you are going to abduct the no-doubt-flaxen-haired blond child from her family, and the deeper fear that they are going to kill you for it. IT'S AN EMASCULATION FANTASY."

"Go grow a goatee," Mike said.

"Yes, yes, I have my foibles," Parlow said, "and, yes, my hobbies, too. One of which is the contemplation of that which I'll call human nature. For is man not the measure of all things?"

"I never knew what that meant," Mike said.

"No one does," said Parlow. "It is a mystery."

The woman in the grave had screamed for an amount of time nicely calculated to observe the obsequies, while holding just short of the mourners' tolerance for the February cold. There were fifteen Jews around the grave, five Irishmen from the Chez, two outliers. Two men in foreign overcoats stood just beyond the group. Parlow said that he didn't like the overcoats.

"Jack, Jack forged a *machine* in Chicago," she'd called out, "and he will create another *up there*."

Mike thought it *just* on the right side of the pathos-bathos line, and had included it in his tale.

Parlow objected.

"It was a close thing," Mike said, "but she did it well, and I thought she deserved some notice. What the hell."

He had omitted, in respect, the rabbi's aside that Jackie had not touched his wife for thirty years, save to occasionally beat her up. But Mike told Parlow.

"A sad thing," Parlow said. "Further, what is this machine he supposedly forged here below? He owned, if'm not mistaken, two candy stores and a piece of a speak."

"*If* that," Mike had said. For the speak, the Chez, though managed by Weiss, was nominally the property of the straw man, Morris Teitelbaum, and owned, in truth, as all knew, by the North Side, which meant Dion O'Banion. And no one save the widow, in her understandable grief, had ever voiced the notion that Mr. O'Banion ever shared ownership of anything with anyone.

"People, in fact, have died for that belief," Mike said.

"And they were right to do so," Parlow said, "for what is property?"

"Property," Mike said, "is theft."

The telephone rang on Mike's desk. "Excuse me," he said, and walked across the City Room, and answered it.

Mike Hodge and Clement Parlow worked in the Coffin Corner of the City Room of the *Chicago Tribune*.

It was known as the Coffin Corner, as it was the place where old stories went to die.

Its north wall was covered in cork, and the cork covered with many layers of news deemed insufficiently pressing—and human interest considered too highbrow—for dissemination to the Reading Public: the death of a polo pony, escaped from its North Shore stall, having fought its way into an antique store and been shot for its pains; its animal brethren, lost dogs, cats with the foresight to warn their owners of the risk of fire; twins separated at birth, reunited; luxury limousines disappeared from their garage and never found again; the odd weeping Madonna, pet ocelot, infant chess prodigy, and their like.

The reporters suspected that management kept the wall full to stand as an object lesson to the worker bees.

Parlow and Mike, however, had been in France, and prided themselves on an immunity to both innuendo and omen, and had adopted the ancient partners desk in the corner as their retreat and resort.

Parlow sat tilted back in the swivel chair, his paunch resting comfortably on his short legs. He took a kitchen match from the pocket of the old tweed jacket and lit it on the sole of his boot. He put the burning match to his pipe. The match went out, and Parlow fished out another. He shook his head and fiddled with the stem.

"It won't light 'cause the pipe's broke," Mike said.

"'Broken,'" Parlow said. "Broke is what you get after a night on the Levee. You know that . . ."

Mike, at thirty, looked a decade younger than Parlow, who was thirty-two. He watched Parlow light the second match on the worn sole of his jodhpur boot, a souvenir of his war, which he'd spent as a railroad dispatcher in Vesy-le-Duc. Mike, who had flown in France, thought the boots an affectation, and had told Parlow as much. Parlow now puffed the pipe alight, and gestured to Mike to begin.

"Jackie Weiss," Mike said, "made the classic mistake of confusing his *position* with his best interest.

"*For:* the guys come in the door, the correct response is not 'I worked my whole life for this business and I owe you nothing,' no, but 'Blam blam blam.'

"Jackie, however, paid for what seemed, to his mind, sound financial practice, but was found to be false economy."

"He *was* tight," Parlow said.

"He was tighter," Mike said, "than Wilson's asshole. I'll grant you that. And that contributed to the disaster. His *true* error, his *true* error was the lack of that business acumen which allows one to choose between two rotten paths."

"Those paths being?" Parlow said.

"Well, the choice was clear," Mike said. "He was either eventually going to have to pay the vig or eventually go with Teitelbaum to talk to O'Banion. There was no third choice."

"*If* he was behind with the vig," Parlow said.

"Why else would they shoot him? *So.* What does he think he gains, the two goons bust in there, launching into Voltaire, or whatever he thought it was, on the Rights of Man to run a supper club and the odd whore, without paying tribute? This eludes me. Fucking, for it *is* going to come to a showdown. *Alternatively,* if Jackie, and God rest his soul . . ." Mike lowered his feet from the desk to the floor. He leaned over to Parlow's side of the desk and took the battered silver lighter from the top of a package of Camels. He shook a cigarette out and lit it. He returned the lighter to its former place and returned his feet to the desk. "Alternatively, had he, scorning the craven counsels of indecision—"

"Who said that?" Parlow said.

"*Napoléon* said," Mike said, "that all that separated him from the lesser generals was this: he knew what to do with five minutes."

"And Jackie?" Parlow said.

"Goons walk in the door of the Chez," Mike said, "the bolder man goes to the riot gun behind the bar, 'blam blam blam,' continues on to Teitelbaum, drags him to the scene, shoots him dead, and blames the whole thing on *him*.

"*Now* his problem is not how to skim four, five hundred bucks a week he won't have to pay vig on, but how to deal with O'Banion. Which responsibility, it seems, Jack was unwilling to undertake."

"Understandably," Parlow said.

"Perhaps," Mike said. "But see the alternative. *I* don't know. Would *I* do it? I don't know."

"What do you do with the law?"

"*Come* on: the thugs? You hit 'em with the Winchester. You step over, you take the piece out, each one, from their no-doubt shoulder holster, you shoot up the back bar, break the mirror, you replace the guns in their now-lifeless hands, it's self-defense."

"And why do you shoot Teitelbaum?"

"Teitelbaum, alright, is Weiss's pissboy and O'Banion's stooge. You shoot Teitelbaum, throw him in the tableau vivant, what do we got? A guilty party. Goons bust in, it's *Teitelbaum* went for the gun, because *he's* the guy been skimming. Weiss is, thus, proved an innocent bystander."

"And now . . . ?"

"Now? Everything's hunky-dory, that foul excretion, that self-confessed thief, Teitelbaum, has been removed."

". . . The cops?"

"The cops don't care."

"It's fascinating," Parlow said. "Save it for the Sally Port. *Plus,* who knows Jackie Weiss was behind on the vig?"

"Then why'd they shoot him?" Mike said.

"Let us leave conjecture at the province of philosophy, as freeing as it is," Parlow said, "and submit ourselves to the tyranny of fact."

Mike sighed. He lowered his feet to the floor. He pulled open the top right drawer of his desk, and took from it two sheets of paper, leaving the drawer open. He squared the sheets and inserted them into the typewriter.

" 'Jackie Weiss expired last night in a hail of gunfire'?"

"Very funny," Parlow said.

Chapter 5

*J*ackie Weiss, last night, made the fatal mistake of confusing his position with his own best interest, the column read. *His position was that of restaurateur to the North Side's sporting set, his God-given right to continue as such was the rock on which he stood and died; the noted devotion to the principles of free enterprise being replaced, in his head, by two slugs of .45-caliber lead. He is survived by his wife of twenty-two years, the former Margaret O'Neil. Floral tributes may be sent to Congregation . . .*

But Lita Grey, née Berenice Mancuso, was interested neither in the direction of floral tributes, nor in the death of Jackie Weiss, which had not, to her, been news since last night's phone call, following hard upon the shooting. She was interested in determining those immediate steps most necessary for her continued preservation in a world made financially barren by the death of her protector.

Her review of her assets was brief and, to her mind, unfortunately complete. She had the use of her apartment through the end of the month, some ten days off; she had her jewelry, worth, she assumed, something in the neighborhood of ten to fifteen thousand dollars; she had a closet full of clothes whose housing and upkeep she could not, at the moment, afford; and she had the face and form of a Circassian concubine: ivory skin, violet eyes, and, at most, another half decade in hand to exploit them.

"You want to be careful of that newspaper ink on your fingers," Ruth Watkins said. Lita nodded, and took a tissue from the box on the cigarette table at her side. She wiped her hands and let the tissue and the newspaper fall to the floor.

"You want me to bring in the coffee?" Ruth said. Lita nodded.

Ruth shook her head in comment on the wretched state of a world ruled by the vagaries of both men and a God of, no doubt, the same sex.

"He could've *fucking* died," Lita said, "in a month that wasn't February."

"And in the beginning of the month," Ruth called from the kitchen.

"Well, that's the truest thing you know," Lita said.

"What about the car?" Ruth said. She brought in the small tray and placed it on the low table. She sat on the edge of the chair across from the chaise longue. Lita motioned to her and Ruth nodded her thanks, and took a cigarette from the silver box on the tray, and lit it. She crossed her legs.

"The *car*?" Lita said. "The whole *fucking* thing is in his *name*, and I am not sure that that bovine cunt of a *wife* does not have the right to send someone by to take the dresses and the *shoes*."

"Yeah. That's too bad, honey," Ruth said.

"It *is* too bad," Lita said. She stirred a drop of cream into her coffee with a minute silver spoon. She raised her eyes toward Ruth, who shook her head no.

"Fucking *men*," Lita said. This summation, it seemed, freed her from further self-pity, whose banishment she proclaimed by a squaring of her shoulders and the adoption of her "willing" smile.

"*Okay*," she said. Ruth, in response, sat up straighter, took a quick puff of the cigarette, and watched Lita as she walked from the chaise longue toward the windows.

Lita looked out on East Lake Shore Drive, now

sheathed in ice, the odd car swerving and crabbing against the wind.

"You going to sing tonight, honey?" Ruth said.

"I'm gonna. I am *going* to, I . . . ," she said, both understanding that whatever her decision, her fate would, as always, be in the hands of a man, the peculiarity of this particular emergency only her ignorance of that man's identity.

The situation, both understood, rested on control of the Chez, which, following Jackie's death, and in the short run, might mean Jimmy Flynn, the assistant manager. But the short run probably would not extend beyond the afternoon's marshaling of forces for the evening's entertainment, at which the various powers would declare themselves, the favorite being Teitelbaum, for his well-proven controllability, but bets on the widow as a long shot were still being considered.

The Chez Montmartre had been closed for the week of the murder, the investigation, and the funeral. It was called a supper club, which all understood to mean speakeasy. It purveyed edible food, and liquor which, while it was not imported as advertised, was sufficiently cleansed of poisons as to not induce either dementia or blindness. The freehold of the Chez was extended to its manager (the late Jackie Weiss) by the North Side, which is to say, by Dion O'Banion, said writ entailing upon the proprietor the license to run girls and dope in addition to the noted comestibles, and to provide the after-dinner diversion of some reasonably honest games of chance.

Jimmy Flynn perched on the kitchen prep table of the Chez. He was dressed in gabardine slacks; a light-weight yellow wool shirt, open at the neck; and a gray cashmere sport coat. His six tuxedos hung in the ward-robe in his office, and his anxieties ran from wonder-ing if he would ever wear them again professionally, to wondering if he would see evening. For he did not un-derstand what Jackie had been guilty of, nor of how far that guilt might be assumed to have run.

He had debated wearing a gun to work, flight, and a preemptive visit to O'Banion to exhibit either fealty or a swift and irreversible decampment if such were de-sired.

He had decided to wait. And he held the club's prep-aration for evening in abeyance as a sign of respect for the wishes of its new proprietor.

"The joint, we open up again," said the maître d', "is going to be hot: phone's ringing since noon; though what they think they're going to *see* . . ."

"The aura of Jackie Weiss," Jimmy said. "You got to keep up with the magazines."

The last of the busboys entered the kitchen through the alley door. Jimmy glanced reflexively at his watch, and then at the kid, who lowered his eyes. Eight people stood in the corners of the kitchen.

"Well, *fuck* it," Jimmy said. He stepped down, stepped forward, and pushed open the doors to the restaurant. He caught the low tone, and inferred the content of the conversation of three busboys, seated, smoking, across the room, on the stairs leading down from the foyer. They rose as Jimmy entered, and began to take down the chairs which had rested, overnight, on the tabletops. Jimmy motioned for them to wait, and they stopped and stood, waiting.

Jimmy looked toward the bar, in front of which Jackie Weiss had met his demise. He envisioned a line running from the foyer, where the thugs had stood, to Jackie's last stand, in front of the bar, and turned to continue the line to a spot just to the left of the kitchen doors, where, sure enough, three gouges in the plaster showed the bullets' former resting place—the slugs dug out by the police and safe, in envelopes, in the precinct's evidence locker, never to be disturbed.

"Where the fuck is Teitelbaum?" he said to the room, but there was no answer and he expected none. "Fucking kike is in hiding."

Jimmy shook his head. "Fucking Jackie, hit him

two times with a forty-five. Two slugs *through* him, and stuck in the wall. Fat as he was." His thoughts continued to the unpleasant image of this fat man on top of Lita Grey. "Well, *he's* dead," he said.

Pops was the handyman and stage door keeper. He was a black man in his sixties, dressed in blue overalls. Jimmy Flynn looked up and saw him. "What?" he said.

"We going to open up tonight, Mister Flynn?" Pops said.

"Whadda you got, some personal *interest* in it?" Flynn said.

The phone rang. The busboys turned their heads toward the maître d's podium. The phone rang again. Then it was answered in the kitchen. After a moment the kitchen doors swung and Alan, the maître d', leaned out, holding the door open, indicating he had work inside.

"Mrs. Weiss's guy, her '*lawyer,*' called. She would like the club closed, for the evening, in memoriam of—"

"*Fuck* this," Jimmy said. "And I don't *know,* anything in her name, in *his* name . . . ? Or belong to *who?* Some horse the fifth race Washington Park, the last twenty years. Lita the Torch Singer, the one *before* her, the front line at the Everleigh Club, the fuck do *I* know . . . ?"

"*Teitelbaum?*" Alan suggested.

"Teitelbaum blows his nose in his underwear. I didn't, anybody see him at the funeral . . . ? I got to get in touch with O'Banion."

". . . But if Mrs. *Weiss* is in control . . . ?"

"She's not in control. She *is* in control, she must, at some point, sell out to Teitelbaum, for O'Banion, or present the club to him, a peace offering, he doesn't go out and kill her children."

"*I* say she holds out, *meaning* it as a gesture of defiance."

"No doubt," Jimmy said. "Or as an homage to that fine conservative upbringing she received in the slums of Krakow.

"Let her *come* tonight, and *tell* me, she wants the joint closed, her and her lawyers, that we may demur, and be seen on the rational side of the argument. She *hated* the motherfucker. She wants to mourn, let her go gash her flesh. Call our broad, tell her she's going on tonight. Call the combo. Get someone to patch up that wall. Fuck it, we open up. Mr. O'Banion says otherwise, I'll blame it on *you.*"

Chapter 6

The old City Room hands' principle was "The story's a lemon: squeeze it dry."

The principle obtained in every aspect of the job. The publishers and the advertisers set the tone: trading ad revenue for promotions disguised as news. The reporters equally felt themselves entitled to whatever copy they could convert into preference, sex, or cash.

Mike, in his early days, had written the odd "marvel of science" half column about some new radio or refrigerator, passing off as news that which was obviously bribery.

The reporters shook down the stadium owners, trading good coverage of the local teams for tickets, and trading the tickets for cash. Likewise it was the reporters' vail to exploit and be exploited by the town's showmen. A supportive notice, or the promise of same, was always good not only for extra tickets to the show, but for an introduction backstage, to the chorus girls.

But the most fungible of all was the puff piece: advertisement passing as news, on the star's new car, beauty tip, favorite food. These valentines, as they were known, were not only good in trade, or as sexual leverage, but, correctly exploited, redeemable for cash.

The neophyte fenced with the public relations man, pretending virginity; the seasoned said, "How much?" and struck a hard bargain. The observed rule was "They *asked,* they've got to *pay.*" Reporters loved corruption. It was not only the game's rule, but its complete playbook.

All had heard of the fellow at the *American* who had, in fact, bedded a Very Famous Film Star on her trip west.

He'd been taking a walk and bummed a smoke from the bellman curbside at the Drake Hotel. The bellman dropped the name of the famous new arrival; the reporter called up to the suite and improvised his pitch.

He said he was writing a piece on Rags to Riches; his particular hook, how the star's discipline and virtues learned on the farm led to and sustained her success in the wider world of film. He knew it was thin, but he'd made it up on the spot, and he was hungry.

A woman's voice told him to come up. He assumed it was the maid, but it was, in fact, the movie star, drunk as a lord, and randy beyond even his wide experience.

He'd come to, sick as a dog, in her compartment on the Super Chief, at a whistle-stop in Ashton, Wyoming. He was awakened by the rough handling of two railroad cops, under the direction of her manager. They threw him off the train, with a caution that if anything of the escapade appeared in print he would be killed. But he'd retained his memories, the bragging rights, and the supportive evidence of two pair of her monogrammed lace panties.

All supposed he carried them, constantly, in the lapel pocket of his coat. But he needed to show no one. He had shown them once, and the respect of the community was, from his return, constant and sincere.

He'd been invited to her hotel room because of a lapse in her security. Her manager, a hophead, had been in the adjoining room getting fixed, and so unable to protect his charge from her proclivities. The manager missed the train, and the ensuing two days, then rented a plane and caught up with the pair in Wyoming.

All in the Sally Port agreed that the plane was hardly

sporting; Parlow bemoaned a civilization which, in addition to its undoubted blessings, carved out the leisurely heart of the past.

The *American*'s fellow possessed status unlimited and was, as Parlow had said, like unto those who, glorious in battle, see, when they speak, that all men must hold their tongues. Mike scolded him.

"That's the one quote of Shakespeare everyone knows," he said. "And it don't even fit. You disappoint me."

"I was using it ironically," Parlow said.

Status, in the Sally Port, was awarded for the exploit, for the quip, for the unpunished transgression against law or policy, for extortion, and, occasionally, for writing.

The award for writing was not given for reportage, which came under the heading of intuition, hard work, intrepidity, or luck. These Men on the Scene called it in; their stories were structured and rewritten by that group generally known as "those tin-eared time-servers and tools of the rich," the first being Rewrite men, and the latter editors.

It was the reporters' daily job to be brash and unfeeling, to steal the photo portrait of the slaughtered infant from the mother's bureau; to taunt the spouse murderer into an interesting outburst; to withhold pity for the youth sentenced to death. It was their job to be not only brave but foolhardy. Covering the shootout, the school fire, the flood, the train wreck.

It was the ethos that pertained in France. There, the fliers retold only those stories which reflected discredit upon them, their skills, and their courage. All escapes were ascribed to luck; the well-performed maneuver, kill, landing was confessed to've been accomplished with the eyes closed.

In the Sally Port, as in France, credit was awarded not for the feats, but for the worth of the attendant story. But highest status—equal to that of him of the Panty Raid, as it was called—accrued only to him who could actually write.

Mike had covered the All Saints Catholic School fire. Twenty-two schoolgirls had died, screaming, behind the barred second-floor windows. Two firefighters had burned to death, swinging their axes at the masonry. Mike had seen it all. He'd come into the City Room, his eyes red, stinking of smoke. He'd gone to his desk and downed half a bottle of scotch. Poochy had dropped his film at the photo lab and come up to the City Room, as he needed to be with someone who was there.

Mike had put a sheet in the typewriter, and was staring at it. Poochy was still in his overcoat. The hem of the coat was burned. It was still dripping water. He looked at Mike and shook his head. Mike handed him the bottle. Mike began to type.

Mike filed the story and it ran the next morning, on page 1, under his byline.

When he came to work, his way to his desk took him through the Compositors' Room. Work stopped as he walked through the room. Each man began tapping his composing stick against the desk.

Mike walked to his desk through the awed silence of the City Room. He sat quiet at his desk for a quarter hour and went home.

The papers had hit the streets and the newsboys were crying the fire headlines. Mike let himself into the apartment house door and climbed the two flights to his room. Annie was on the landing waiting for him.

Chapter 7

Peekaboo was of that color the age knew as high yellow. She had graduated, somewhere in the past, from whore to madam, and had run her house, the Ace of Spades on South Michigan Avenue, since the Armistice. In her wandering days as a whore she'd found it revenue-effective and appropriate to indulge in jack-rolling.

She'd abandoned the practice with her settlement in Chicago during the War, and now considered herself an honest woman, who gave value for the money. She was forty-eight years old, and dressed, as usual, in a simple gray cashmere frock.

She left the house kitchen and walked into the narrow hall, which, like the rest of the house, bore the traditional deep-flocked red wallpaper.

She glanced into the parlor.

There were two fellows, whites, as were all her customers, from, she guessed, the high South, perhaps Missouri, laughing too loud at some feminine remark or gesture, they having decided that the evening's theme would be the black girls' naïveté.

The three candidates she'd sent down were, she thought, doing well, as they should, having been selected for their affability.

"Good," she thought. She continued through the hall toward the back of the house. The front doorbell rang, and she turned.

Marcus, the houseman, looked up at her, meaning, *Are you here?* She raised one shoulder and a hand to indicate, *How would you expect me to know, until I know who it is?*

He took the rebuke in good form, unfolded himself from his chair, and stepped through the doors and into the vestibule. He closed the doors behind him. The doorbell rang again.

Marcus moved to the left side of the door. He reached with his right hand and opened the Judas hole, viewing the entranceway from the side.

Thus protected from a possible admonitory shot to the head, he saw a youngish man in an overcoat, in front of the peephole, stamping his feet for warmth.

He slid the wood panel closed, came around to the door's front, and looked through the peephole. "Hold on a minute," he said.

He opened the vestibule door and called to Peekaboo. "It's Mike Hodge," he said.

"In the kitchen," Peekaboo said.

Four of the girls were in the kitchen. One was actually sick; one was shamming, but Peekaboo had let her slide rather than endure the tears and protestations of mistreatment that would have followed a demand to work. The girl would have to go, and go quickly, but Peekaboo did not want to dismiss her when she was, though only notionally, ill—the unspoken threat of appeals to outraged sisterhood staying Peekaboo's hand, as the girl knew it would.

"Well, good," Peekaboo thought. "She wins one, *I* win one. Order is maintained, and what the fuck."

The two other girls were in working gear. They sipped their coffee out of chipped navy mugs, perched primly in the breakfast nook, careful of the drape of their gowns.

"How many times do I have to *tell* you," Peekaboo said, "to not sit in the kitchen?"

"We wanted a cup of coffee," the younger one said.

"You wanted a cup of *coffee*, all you had to do was *ask* for it," Peekaboo said.

"We didn't want to make extra work for Marcus," the younger one said.

"What *is* there about a whore," Peekaboo thought, "makes it impossible to tell the truth"—Mike came into the kitchen—"about any-fucking-thing whether or *not* . . . ?"

"Hello, old-timer," Mike said to Peekaboo.

The two on-duty girls nodded vaguely at him, and moved off with their coffee cups, toward the door to the back room. The two casualties lowered their eyes, the goldbrick actually clutching to her throat the collar of her nightgown.

"For the love of *Christ*," Peekaboo thought.

"You know what you bitches *need*?" she said. Her remorse at her broken vow of imperturbability added to her rage.

"*You* need, as in the *old* days, some *boss*-nigger with a stick to motherfuck your *no*-good, 'eat my food' black asses, to some semblance of gratitude, 'til you thank God for the roof over your *no*-good, *frowsty* . . ." She collected herself. "Get the fuck out of here, and wash your hair," she said. The two girls left the kitchen.

"Never criticize in front of strangers," Mike said.

"And *you* better stay away from that *Irish* girl," Peekaboo said. " 'Cause if *I* know about it, the whole world is waiting for the shoe to drop."

"World is waiting for the sunrise," Mike said.

"Yes, I know. I heard it on the radio. What're *you* doin' these days?"

"I'm looking for a line on who did Jackie Weiss."

"Well, that's *another* good idea," Peekaboo said. "Howzbout this: two Sheenies from Detroit, and I'll throw in the phone book."

"Certainly," Mike said.

"Then, what do you want a *line* on, who's going to run the Chez?"

"No."

"Then?"

"I want to know: why didn't he 'go' for it?"

"Why didn't he go for it?" Peekaboo mused. "Mayhap he was feeling secure and unthreatened in his native lair, or somesuch, and he felt . . . protected. You know, Mike, about the protective mechanism of, what do they call you, 'males'? I been hearing about it my whole life, 'cept when it's some girl you got tired of, some wife don't wind your clock anymore, or mouthed off, or she looked at you cross-eyed over the oatmeal. And you beat the shit out of her."

Marcus had walked into the kitchen, carrying a large camel-hair coat and a man's white soft-collar shirt. He opened the cleaning cupboard. "Ammonia," he said.

"Whazzit, *lipstick*?" Peekaboo said.

"It's lipstick."

She sighed. "I'm gonna, I swear to God, what *mindless* hussy, have I got to fucken *shoot* her, to remember: They *done,* you *paid*? They get *dressed*? They done with you, you done with them. *Don't* kiss 'em goodbye."

She took the coat from Marcus and examined it. It was a heavy, expensive gray coat, new-bought for winter. A small enamel shamrock pin was stuck in the lapel. It had a thin but quite noticeable smear of red lipstick on the collar. She nodded, and Marcus showed her the shirt, its collar similarly stained.

"Ammonia on the *coat,*" she said. "The collar, try alcohol first; do we have time to wash it, 'fore we send him home?"

Marcus shook his head. "Late already."

"Nice coat," Mike said. He looked at the label. "Marshall Field's," he said. "Camel hair. Lord Raglan."

"That's the sleeves," Marcus said. He pointed out the diagonal set of the sleeves.

"We got another spare shirt we can give him, or run out right now?" Peekaboo asked. Marcus shook his head.

He took a dish towel, saturated it with ammonia, and laid it flat on the kitchen table. He put the overcoat collar, stain down, over it; he looked up at the pots hanging over the worktable. Peekaboo nodded. He took down a casserole pot and laid it over the coat, to press the collar down on the towel.

"Coat going to stink," he said.

"Yeah, well, yeah, the coat's gonna stink," Peekaboo said. "The smart move, he want to be *sure*, is burn it with a cigar. Sm'by, at the club, in conversation, burned his coat."

"What about the shirt?" Mike said.

"*Alright*," Peekaboo said. She lifted the casserole pot, and picked up the coat. "Here's what he *did*, you see? He's coming back from the *Turkish* baths: wants to be fresh for his wife, what does he do . . . ?"

"He shaves," Mike said.

"Michael," said Peekaboo, "for a white man, you ain't *quite* so dumb as someone would expect.

"*Marcus*," she said. "You take your *razor* . . ."

"He won' let me," Marcus said.

"You tell him he *will* let you, r'he ain't comin' back no more, n'you *nick* him, the . . ." She looked at the coat. "The *right* side of his face. *His* right side, do you understand?" Marcus began to resent the insult.

". . . smarter minds than *you*, alright," Peekaboo said. "Listen and learn: *his* right side. You *drip* some of the blood: over the lipstick stain, his *shirt* collar, you drip some of it, over the stain, his *coat;* you pour alcohol *over* the cut, you pat it dry with a clean towel, you use your styptic pencil, you pat it dry, you cover it with a *court* plaster."

"Coat still stinks of ammonia," Marcus said.

"They *used* it, at the baths, try to get the *blood* out," Peekaboo said. Mike began to offer what he obviously thought was a wise suggestion.

Peekaboo held up a finger to forestall him. "Which baths he goes to?" she said.

"I think, *likely,* the Kedzie Baths," Marcus said. "Is where most of 'em goes."

"You find out," Peekaboo said. "We know the man there? The Kedzie."

"Yes, I do," Marcus said.

"Who is that?"

"George White," Marcus said.

"*Yeah—that's* right," Peekaboo said. "*Call* him, 'n' tell him what happened, what's there *in* it for him, tell him I owe him five dollars, the bloodshed he witnessed."

Marcus said, "Yes, ma'am," and took the clothing out of the room.

"*Who* goes there?" Mike asked.

"What?" Peekaboo said.

"Most of 'em go there, the Kedzie Baths, Marcus said . . ."

"The *Irish*," Peekaboo said. She pointed to the shamrock pin on the coat's lapel, as if demonstrating the obvious to a small child. "Yeah, the Irish—they all go there," she said.

"Would she call them, the wife?" Mike said.

"Man's wife? Would she call the baths?"

"Yes."

"His wife?" Peekaboo said. "She might. What does it cost to be prepared?"

"Cost you five dollars," Mike said.

"I'll pass it on," Peekaboo said. "Plus which, thing you don't *ever* want to do, get in the habit being sloppy."

"Well, but, you can't chase it down 'til the end of time," Mike said.

"You chase it down, to the limits," Peekaboo said, "your opponent's mentality. This bitch, now, she suspected her husband—and be sure she does—he says, 'I cut it shaving, at the baths,' she calls the baths, talks to some fella, all she knows, is some poor nigger, up from Alabama, too *dumb* to lie . . . she's content. Don't go no further. Why should she?"

"To find out the truth?" Mike said.

"She knows the truth," Peekaboo said. "She needs to be assured her husband is observing the proprieties."

———

Mike first met Peekaboo on Armistice Day 1925. Parlow had come into a small inheritance and Mike agreed to help him blow it. They were celebrating in an alcove table, in the small dining room of the Ace of Spades. A waiter stood at the table's end. Across the dining room, the large doors gave onto the parlor. In the parlor various white men, most middle-aged, most portly, some prominent, and all well-to-do, sat talking with the girls.

It was a custom of the house, Parlow said, to trust the madam with the choice of companion. Rather a courtesy, he said, like asking the chef to design the meal. Peekaboo had left the kitchen and was walking across the parlor, smiling at one and all.

"We'll start with a bottle of plonk and two steaks, please," Parlow said.

"How would you like them, sir?" the waiter asked.

"Black outside and pink inside," Parlow said. "Like Bessie Coleman's pussy."

Mike saw Peekaboo's welcoming smile go fixed and false as she turned and retired to the kitchen. The waiter's face became immobile. Parlow, drunk and oblivious, continued ordering. Mike nodded his agreement to the proposed meal, then rose and excused himself.

He knocked on the door to the kitchen and entered.

Peekaboo was seated at her desk. She had an account book open before her, and was topping off a glass of scotch and shaking her head.

As Mike entered she rose. "Sir, I must beg your pardon," she said, "but the service areas are in no shape which would add to what one surely hopes is the tone of your evening."

"Ma'am, my name is Mike Hodge," he said. "My friend is drunk, and spoke grossly and disrespectfully, both of women, and of one of your race who is particularly worthy of respect. I beg you to accept my apology for his crass comment, and can offer only this excuse: that he is drunk, and that he is more drunk than usual, this being Armistice Day. If you would have your people let me know what we owe, we'll settle up and get out of your hair."

"What do you care about Bessie Coleman?" Peekaboo said.

"I saw her fly. I was a flier in the War. I knew what I was looking at. She was superb," Mike said. He shrugged, then bowed his apologies, and turned to leave.

"*What's* your name?" Peekaboo said. Mike told her again.

"Please sit down," she said.

He pulled up a chair, and sat next to her at the rolltop desk. She raised a hand, and a black man in livery brought over a second glass, from the step-back dresser.

The dresser displayed several cut-glass "Bohemian" goblets, and three framed photographs. The largest was of Marcus Garvey. The frame was pressed gutta-percha. Impressed into the bottom were the words "Up, you mighty race, you race of kings—rise to your feet, you can accomplish what you will."

The second, a publicity photo of a white girl in an off-the-shoulder dress. The third was of Bessie Coleman, in her flying jacket, one hand on the wing of her plane. It was signed, "To Elizabeth —Queen Bess, the Black Sparrow."

Peekaboo saw Mike looking. She glanced at the photographs, and back at Mike. "Have a damn drink," she said.

Chapter 8

Mike wore the rosette to the air show. Annie asked him about the rosette. "The French gave it to you," he said. She asked what for. "For good behavior," he said.

She asked if it had been difficult to get and he said, no, that good behavior in France was different from its like in the States. She asked him to talk about his having been a flier, but his stories were either too technical, or, if not unfit for her to hear, unfit, in his estimation, for him to tell her. So he took her to the Checkerboard Air Show.

The day was cold, which meant to Mike the engines would have increased performance, a good thing, he thought, as they were all flying Jennys, universally shamed as a hunk of junk.

But they were cheap, after the War, and cheaper still to a veteran. And Mike knew of several which had disappeared through actual bookkeeping error from more than one army base Stateside.

"I never liked them," he said. She turned to look at him. Her Irish complexion was always magnificent. It shone to even enhanced effect in the cold. He loved her.

"You never liked what?" she said.

He started to speak, and a plane came in for a low pass in front of the grandstand, the wingwalker braced into the wind on the upper wing.

She smiled. "I can't hear you."

He raised a finger, and took the small paper bag from his jacket pocket, took from it and tore off a small bit of cotton waste, tore it again, in two, handed the bits to her, and gestured that she should place them in her ears.

As the wingwalkers flew off, the barker called the star attraction: the Black Sparrow, Miss Bessie Coleman. The third American woman to receive a pilot's license, the first of African heritage, the first woman of color to receive certification from the Fédération Aéronautique Internationale, the official licensing body of French aviation.

The grandstand was three-quarters full, more than

half of them were black; and black and white were in-
termixed. "Well, that's right," Mike thought, "now
the whites are at the other people's show; and common
courtesy, on the part of both, for the day, overrides race
prejudice. If only I could write."

Bessie Coleman came in from two thousand feet,
slipping the plane down, crosswind, at the edge of
the field. She straightened up, and touched down on
one wheel, and held it on the ground, tail up, walking the plane back and forth between the right main
and the left. She added power in front of the grandstand and took the Jenny up and over.

"No, that's too low for a loop," Mike said. Annie
felt, rather than heard, him.

She looked at him, and then looked back at the plane.

The plane neared the top of the loop. Mike saw the
upcoming maneuver, and nodded. It was not the loop,
but a simple Immelmann. The half loop was followed
by a half roll. The plane, as it went inverted, was rolled
upright, and on the reciprocal heading, as they'd taught
him at Fort Bliss.

The clue that she was about to do one rather than
the other partook, to Mike's mind, of the occult. It was
obvious, of course, that she was not about to loop. She
had just barely enough altitude to complete the loop,

but if the engine failed before the top, she'd fall out of it, or fly in it. But the feeling took him back to France, and to a nonanalytical life.

There the ability to predict the enemy's move meant life or death. Some learned to do it, some did not. The second group died from enemy fire, the first were generally spared to die of mechanical failure.

The Jenny flew off for another pass. The barker spoke through his megaphone.

Mike said, "That's called an Immelmann." Annie smiled, and took the cotton from her ears. "That's called an Immelmann," he said. "We called them 'Jenny Immelmann.'"

She started to ask why, then turned at the barker's direction to "Pay attention to the field before your grandstand." A young man was running out, holding aloft a yellow square of fabric.

"Watch as Miss Bessie Coleman, the Black Sparrow, plucks from the ground this handkerchief, with the tip of her wing, at one hundred fifty miles an hour!"

The young man checked the wind sock, the bunched yellow square on the ground ten yards in front of the grandstand. He found several pebbles on the ground and weighted the square down.

"Hardly a handkerchief," Mike thought. More a bedspread. Certainly not 150 miles an hour, which the

Jenny could achieve only at full throttle in a vertical dive, for the five seconds before the wings came off.

He smiled at the showman's duplicity.

Bessie Coleman came around for a low pass. "Here she *comes*," the showman yelled.

The audience leaned toward the plane. Mike shook his head. "Testing the wind," he said.

"Lower and lower," the showman said. "ONE HUNDRED FIFTY MILES AN HOUR. *THINK OF IT. Yes . . . Yes . . . ?*"

She flew over the fabric at a good three feet. The audience stared. She dropped the wing.

"TO CATCH THE HANDKERCHIEF IN HER *WINGTIP!*" the barker screamed. "THE LEAST *MISCALCULATION . . .*"

Mike looked at the wind sock. "Dead into the wind," he thought. "*That's* right. To do the gag she's going to have to slow it down without cutting the power much."

The crowd expressed its disappointment as Bessie flew over the fabric, leveled the wings, and climbed.

"THE MANIPULATION OF THE AIRPLANE, AT THESE SPEEDS AND IN SUCH CLOSE PROX- IMITY TO THE GROUND, REQUIRES SKILL POSSESSED BY *FEW*, BY *FEW* AVIATORS. THE SLIGHTEST EDDY IN THE WIND COULD BRING *DISASTER*, IT COULD BRING *DISAS-*

TER, MAY GOD FORBID, BEFORE YOUR EYES. HERE SHE COMES."

"Well, yeah," Mike thought of the crowd, "*you're* delighted. You might see somebody turned to smoke. Unlikely, as, if the gag fails, she can go around; if the engine fails, she can put it down, right into the wind; but if she catches a *wingtip*, we're going to see a cute cartwheel."

The crowd hushed as the plane came back for the next pass. "Okay," Mike thought, "she's giving herself a bit of crosswind, to keep the low wing down." He snuck a glance at the wind sock, which he thought of as the Effel.

Bessie came in, five feet above the ground. Fifty yards off she lowered the upwind wing; the plane descended slowly and evenly. "She can crack off the under-wing skid," Mike thought, "plane'll still fly. Ah, that's the trick. She can't catch it with the wingtip, as she'd have to come in with an eighty-degree bank. She's going to catch it in the *skid*."

As she did.

The skid, a half hoop of wood below the wing, caught up the yellow square, which now streamed behind the climbing plane. Bessie waggled the wings. The crowd cheered.

The showman was explaining to them the triumph over death they had just witnessed, but they did not hear. They cheered. The blacks in the audience pounded each other on the back. The blacks and the whites so forgot themselves as to exchange looks of head-shaking wonder, and many shook hands.

Annie, still watching the plane, put her small hand in Mike's. He thought it was the most intimate gesture, and was touched by her trust. "Yeah, I'm a fool," he thought.

"A tear in the wind might put that Jenny in the stands," he thought, "but that girl can *fly*." And he remembered that the maneuver had been named for Max Immelmann, the German flier who, supposedly, had invented it, and personalized it, in supposed honor of his wife, whose name might have been Jenny, and who, it was supposed, might, at times, have wanted to get on top.

Jenny Immelmann, he thought, and split-ass, meaning a high-speed turn. Which was sanitized into Split S, and no one who'd not been at the Front would ever know why. And Effel, he thought, forgotten in the fog of war. The Effel, for the wind sock.

Who was there left to tell the story? *F.L.* for "French letter," meaning condom, which the wind sock absolutely resembled, and the various attempts at jokes, none any good, about the Effel Tower.

"Well, we didn't have to joke about sex," he thought, "we had so much of it. But nothing like the Irish girl." For what he had with the Irish girl was, as Sergeant MacAleister might have said, "pure D love."

The sergeant had been his first instructor in ground school. Mike had quoted him several times to any cub he thought might profit by instruction and not find the quote sententious.

"First thing, call things by their name" was the sergeant's opening advice, on a freezing-cold day at Fort Bliss, when he'd been walking them around the plane. "This here is a JN-4 from the Glenn Curtiss Company, which, in this case, was manufactured, as this plaque clearly shows, Under Contract by the Furness Corporation of Oneonta, New York."

The sergeant circled the plane, and the company circled the sergeant.

"Always call the same thing, *the* same thing," he said. "If you want, on the other hand, to wash your ass out of here previous to what would normally occur, you mention to your flight instructor 'that thing there,' or, should he ask you its name, respond with anything in this world other *than* its name. You will learn its name in these little talks, and in the manual, operator, military, Curtiss JN-4, which you will *never* call a Jenny, and I advise you not to *think* of, lest you fall into that fault, as a Jenny. For that is not its name."

He'd pointed at the half hoop under and just inboard from the wingtip of the lower wing.

"Now, what would you suppose *this* is?"

Several raised their hands.

"You worthless, deaf, and stupid *sonsabitches*. *Did* I not just conclude informing you never to suppose? 'Well, Sergeant, what if,' you may wonder, 'I actually *knew* the answer?'

"Candidates? That's not the question that I *asked*. Don't *ever* fucking 'suppose,' or we're sending you home to Mother. Welcome to the military."

The part at which the sergeant pointed, as Mike, along with the bulk of the candidates, learned, was the "under-wing skid." Its purpose was to prevent a ground loop. A ground loop was "the undesired, uncontrolled rotation of the grounded aircraft in a horizontal plane pivoting on its center of gravity." The center of gravity was, in the JN-4, depending upon loading, between 68 and 82.5 inches aft of the propeller spinner.

Mike had seen wingwalkers hang from the wing skid, hang by their knees, hang by one hand, "miss the grip," and fall as the crowd screamed, only to have the fall arrested by the cleverly concealed parachute, thus giving the observers both the thrill of violent death and the reassurance that it was all in good fun.

Now Bessie Coleman demonstrated a snap roll in eight points, stopping the plane precisely at each forty-five-degree angle.

"Better than I could ever do," Mike thought. "Much better."

The yellow fabric added prettily to the sight as the plane rolled inverted and performed half a loop to return for landing.

"How did she catch the handkerchief on the skid?" Mike wondered. "How would *I* do it?" He decided he would sleeve the wing skid in canvas, and tie fishhooks to it. "That's so obvious and blunt it's probably true," he thought.

"Yeah," he told Peekaboo, "always call things by their name."

"That's true," she said, "that's what the Bible said."

"Is that so?" Mike said.

"*I* don't know it, I've been *told*," she said.

"By whom?" Mike said.

"By the odd minister. Can't say I've seen many a priest since I came up here. They take a vow of poverty. Or maybe I heard it in church.

"I want to ask you something," Peekaboo said.

"Alright," Mike said.

"What was that War *about*?"

"They shot the Archduke Ferdinand," Mike said. "What would *you* do?"

Parlow had long since passed out upstairs, and his girl came down to the whorehouse kitchen for a smoke.

Marcus, the man in livery, watched over the young boy in the butler's pantry, who was shining shoes. Peekaboo and Mike sat at the kitchen table drinking.

"The Everleigh Club," she said. " 'Girls of All Nations.' "

"Was it true?" Mike asked. "Marshall Field's son?"

"The Marshall Field's son? Far's I know it was true. Shot him in the Everleigh Club and carted him home. But, those days, the Levee *was* the Levee . . ." Mike nodded to keep her in her rhythm. "Anything which did *not* happen, was like, if not *sure*, to happen 'fore you turned around. Those were the *real* days."

"You were there?" Mike said.

"Honey, I'd been there, young and pretty as I was, I would've ended up fucked to death, and my jewelry stole by some no-good handsome, *indigent* man, left me for someone he, on the moment, fancied better; weeped myself into stupidity; and got passed down the line 'til I was turning tricks for *rolling* papers; and I thank the Lord he spared me from that common fate. Tell me more about this War of yours."

"That War," Mike said, "wrong with it was, even f'you don't get killed, past a certain point, you're just getting good at it, they called it off. You can't do it for a living."

"Called it a *draw*," Peekaboo said. "Didn't they?"

"No, that's not what they called it, but that's what it was," Mike said.

"Tell you what *else*," Peekaboo said. "Mentioning? The Everleighs? *Most* of the, alright . . . ?" Mike nodded. " 'Girls of All Nations,' Everleigh House? They were colored girls. Some high yaller, she's the Hawaiian, or her eyes got the merest slant to 'em, a Cossack, or something, whatever they are. *Indonesian,* you see? Or Samoan; or, she's *white*-featured, she might be a Hindu, or somesuch, got up in a shawl. *Plus* which, anybody could '*pass*' . . ." She inclined her head, finishing the thought.

"A lot of 'em could pass," Mike said.

"They still *do*," Marcus said.

"*Marcus,*" Peekaboo said, "we got some coffee?"

Marcus left his perch in the doorway to the butler's pantry, and walked to the stove. "*Dora . . .* ?" he said to Parlow's girl.

"Yes, please," she said.

Marcus began to make the coffee.

"*I* could not have passed, of course," Peekaboo said, "but I might, at a stretch, have been a *Hindu.* P.S., all these smart *millionaires,* all over the country, 'Girls of All Nations,' where the Everleighs going to recruit some *actual,* what are they . . . all the different races? White girls, *too,* could do an accent, many of 'em, passed 'em off as a White Russian countess. Fellow wants his dick sucked, he's *already* getting fooled."

"How is that?" Mike said.

"*How* is that? What difference does it make? Some chippie he picks up, buys her a cold drink; or a similar girl, in a costume, fifty, one hundred dollars, the same treatment? He ain't paying for *sex:* b'lieve it or not, what he's paying for? Illusion.

"You want to go upstairs?" Peekaboo asked. Mike shrugged.

"Well, no, you *came* here."

"I'm in love," Mike said.

"Yeah, you told me. *Dora:* who's rested?" Peekaboo said. "What would you like tonight?" she asked Mike. "Hell, *I* know what you'd like: small, slim, and leggy."

"How'd you know what I like?" Mike said.

"Honey, I do it for a living."

Chapter 9

Halsted was the longest street in Chicago. It ran from the Mob enclave of Chicago Heights thirty-three miles north to its terminus in the trolley barns, and two blocks west of the Lake. Lita Grey was born southeast of Chicago. She now lived on the Lake.

On the Lake the new apartment palaces of the stock market money housed those made fortunate thereby and their dependents, among them Lita.

Her ninth-floor corner apartment had a wide east and north view of Lake Michigan. And she delighted to sit in the window seat, drink in hand, watching the water. She most particularly enjoyed the storms.

The February storm battered the plate glass now

and again, with no discernible rhythm, and the wind howled.

She had her long legs drawn up under her. The cashmere throw was tucked beneath and over them, and finished round her shoulders. The shawl was gold, and chosen, as were all her clothes, to set off her violet eyes, her tawny blond hair, and the warm ivory of her skin, that combination regularly referred to in her press releases as "exotic."

A small silver cigarette box and its matched lighter sat on the taboret just to hand. She took a deep sip of her highball and set it down next to them. The wind banged the windows.

"You can say one thing," she thought. "The wind? It's not as if it's 'angry,' or any of that. It's not as if it 'wants to knock us down,' or 'to destroy the works of man,' or anything. It's not even that it doesn't care. We are not *here* for it. And, so, we should not take it personally."

Jackie Weiss's lawyer sat on the couch behind her, his hat in his hand. She saw his reflection shiver as the wind buffeted the window.

"I hope, Miss Grey," he said, "that they're strong enough to resist the storm."

"And I hope *you*," she thought, "someday regain

the ability to speak your native tongue. When you come here on an errand of extortion, which, one would think, would be the happy excuse for that cocksucked-ness which you call your profession."

". . . Miss Grey . . . ?" he said.

"Ruth might of took his hat," she thought, "when she took his coat—but, of course, he is indicating the brevity of his errand: come here, give me an envelope, two weeks, one week, to clear out. Contract with the Chez? My question? None of his concern. Concern more of that bulbous cow Jackie had to climb on top of once a month. Or, more likely, the concern of the North Side."

"Miss Grey?" he said. "Mrs. Weiss has, graciously, I think . . ." In the reflection Lita saw him start to draw the envelope from his jacket pocket.

Ruth Watkins was Lita's colored maid and longtime adviser. Lita and Ruth had determined, in council, that for their démarche to have effect, it must be made not only before even a cursory perusal of the envelope, but before the full announcement of its message.

"Once they go there," Ruth said, "you're arguing about a number, and the only thing worse than that is that they get to say their number first. You must come down, out of the blue, to interrupt their thinking."

"Yeah?" Lita said.

"*They* think. These Jews? Sit around a table?" Ruth said. " 'She's *got* to take ten grand. *I'd* bet she'll take five. Wait, the bitch might hold out for—I don't know *what* she might think she could hold out for. Something must be done!' . . . They kick it around . . ."

"Uh-huh . . ."

" 'All's *we* care about, is not the *number*'—that's *their* strategy—'big or small, what difference?' "

"Tell me why again," Lita said.

"Because, because," Ruth said. "Be assured, it's less than this." She waved her arm, indicating the apartment. "Else they'd just send a note: 'Please keep everything until the end of time.' 'Cause, think about it, what do you have to offer this old hag? She can't fuck you, she can't sell you, she can't eat you, you've got nothing for her, 'cept your nuisance value. Alright. 'Cause? You think about it? One day—had to come—one day, there would be *somebody* Jackie sends with the envelope."

"That's right," Lita said.

" '. . . Honey, thank you for the last twenty-five years, but you're old, your pussy is loose, and I need some *young* thing. *You* understand.' "

"That's right," Lita said.

"But. *That* day, you've got one tactical advantage. *That* day, you could cry and stomp around . . ."

"He *liked* me."

"*Also, could* have been, the old lady died, you throw a headlock on him, drag him to the priest. It's all a matter of time," Ruth said. "That happened? Pride of your youth? 'Ring or no pussy'? I'd bet he'd go. He *don't* go? Later on? He gets tired of you, or his dick gives out? I'd say you're going traveling."

Ruth took a deep breath.

"*Lookit,*" she said. "People are different? *My* thing is: You're like to get beat? Go down attacking. Other fella might know something 'bout his weakness you *don't* know."

" 'It's not about the envelope,' " Lita said.

"The *correct* move," Ruth said, "for them? Is to send the sheriff. So *that,* you're reduced? Trading a blow job for the right to take your vanity case."

"Mink coat," Lita said.

"Baby, let me tell you something. *That* mink coat is, likely, going to the sheriff's wife. F'Mizz Jackie *ain't* got her attorneys here, and, if they've got an inventory, and it's gone? Like, you or me's going to prison." Ruth looked at Lita. "*Alright,*" she said. "*Lita.* Other hand, they call, make the appointment, send over their liar? That's a sign of weakness."

". . . Sign of weakness . . ."

"Yes. That's right. 'Cause he's bringing the envelope."

"And we can't just take the envelope?"

"Where *we* are, we can't *leave* . . . and we can't stay. *No* we can't . . . the *envelope* is like, a fella brings you flowers. You take those flowers, what are you going to have to do?"

"Fuck him," Lita said.

Ruth smiled. "Break down the bargain," she said. "Fella goes in the park, picks some roses, hands them to you, you lay down?"

"No," Lita said.

"Now: flowers he *bought* cost him five dollars. Fella says, I didn't have the time to buy 'em, here's a five-dollar bill. Is *this* a better bargain?"

"No."

"Well," Ruth said, "that's all they're doing with the envelope. Bringing flowers, so that they can fuck you. No. You have to *administer* the situation."

Lita admired her reflection in the window. She smoothed her hair, and adjusted the small diamond brooch near her neck. It depicted a violin, and she mimed caressing it, in indication of its sentimental value. She took the handkerchief from her sleeve and dabbed at her eye. Then she turned from the windows and faced the lawyer sitting on the couch. She looked down at his card.

"Mr. . . . ?"

"Bennish," he said.

"Mr. *Bennish*," she said. "I have in my possession . . ."

"Gifts?" he said. "Gifts that Mr. Weiss may have made you are, of course—"

"Letters."

"—we have no, absolutely no objection to your continued possession of that which—"

"Letters and documents," Lita said. "Transferring to me: ownership of this *apartment*—"

"Miss Grey," Bennish said.

"Ownership—"

"Are you suggesting you have notarized and filed deeds?"

"—of various *accounts*. Of stocks. And bonds."

Ruth, prim in her maid's uniform and cap, stood, hands clasped, in a corner of the room. She gave the slightest nod of encouragement to Lita.

"And a deed—" Lita said.

"Again I ask—" Bennish said.

"—a deed-of-gift. Promising me, on his death, a *substantial* amount of cash—"

Bennish began to shake his head.

"And promising me one half his interest in the Chez Montmartre." She stopped.

"I don't believe you," Bennish said.

"I can produce the documents, if you wish me to," Lita said.

"Why would I not wish it?" Bennish said.

"Because, with them, unfortunately, will come . . ." She hesitated a quarter second, then went on. "Letters from Mr. Weiss to me . . ."

"Oh, *please,*" Bennish said. "If you think—"

"And—"

"Oh be *still,*" Bennish said.

"Don't tell me to be still," Lita said. *"And* from Morris Teitelbaum to Mr. Weiss. And a letter from him *to* Mr. Teitelbaum."

Bennish cleared his throat. He adjusted himself on the couch. "Concerning?" he said.

"Well," Lita said.

"Letters about what?"

"Well, alright . . . Talking about some *boats.*"

"Some boats? Yes?"

"And Mr. O'Banion," Lita said.

"How would that benefit you?" he said. "The release of such letters?"

Lita lifted the cover of the cigarette case. Ruth took

up the little table lighter and lit the cigarette Lita had taken from the box. She performed the suggestion of a curtsy. Lita gave her a dismissive nod, and Ruth left the room.

The man had gone.

"Well," Ruth said, "toothpaste don't go back in the tube."

"Tooth powder does," Lita said.

"Tooth powder does," Ruth agreed, "and tooth powder makes a good silver polish. Speaking of which, ball in their court? They may strike back with a list of 'walk out of here in your shift if you fuck with us.' I don't think they will, but they might."

"If. If they disbelieve I have the letter," Lita said.

"Alternatively," Ruth said.

"What if they rat us out?" Lita said.

"Rat us out?"

"To O'Banion."

"Well, *baby*," Ruth said, "on the spot? You had to improvise."

"Improvise what?" Lita said.

"Improvise about O'Banion," Ruth said.

"No. There *is* a letter," Lita said.

Ruth sat up. "There *is* a letter?"

"That's right."

Ruth said, "From?"

"From Teitelbaum to Jackie."

"What is it?" Ruth said.

"I don't know. *Jackie* was reading it," Lita said. "It's about Mr. O'Banion and some boats."

"How do you know that it's important?" Ruth said.

"*Because* he put it in the *safe,*" Lita said. "I'm not stupid."

Ruth shook her head.

"But what?" Lita said. "They say that knowledge is power."

"*Power* is power," Ruth said. "People say differently don't understand power. *Or* knowledge. Knowledge is what gets you killed." She shook her head. "Alright," she said, "let's *get* it."

"I can't get it," Lita said. "I told you. It's in the safe."

"*Uh*-huh," Ruth Watkins said. "*Uh*-huh . . . Alright . . ."

Chapter 10

Parlow was cleaning his pipe. The stem was cracked, and fit only with difficulty back into the bowl. But he had carried it in France and was devoted to it.

The proof of the front page was tacked up on the City Room wall. The ink still glistened. Mike was looking at it absently. It read *Gangland Shootings*.

". . . the death of Morris Teitelbaum," he read, "co-owner of the Chez Montmartre, following by three weeks the assassination of his partner, Jacob Weiss."

"Let's go," Parlow said.

"I'm thinking," Mike said.

"You're paid to work," Parlow said. "And thinking is not working. Colonel McCormick said so."

"Colonel McCormick," Mike said, "inherited money."

"Yes, he did," Parlow said. "A shitload of it. From the poor sodbusters out there 'busting the sod,' to whom his daddy sold the machines, to sow the virgin plains in wheat."

"Shut up," Mike said.

"The better to make bread," Parlow said. "Whence we find, these ruminations, carried forward, may present *another* hypothetic mystery." He lit his pipe. "In *this* case: what would the Squareheads and Yon Yonson up there do, Old Man McCormick hadn't the talent, make the machines to till the soil or whatever they do, to get the wheat to make the bread, to live in the house that Jack built?"

"*Don't* you have any fucking work to do?" Mike said.

". . . To spread on the surface the butter *they* make from those black-and-white cows one sees on motor trips up north?"

"Gimme a fucken drink," Mike said.

Parlow leaned forward in the swivel chair. He took the long chain from his pocket, found the correct key at its end, and with it unlocked the bottom drawer on his side of the partners desk.

He took out the bottle of rye. He called across the City Room, "*Beano:* two fucking Dixie Cups." He put the bottle on the desk. He waved out the wooden match, puffed again on his pipe, and dropped the match into the last two inches of the French artillery shell that served them as an ashtray.

"War war war," he said. "War in the air, war on the ground. Love in the trenches, and mud in Paris."

"Shut up," Mike said.

"Mademoiselles mad with their choice of heroes to clasp to their diminutive, poxed breasts, and Lester the Little Rabbit knew, as sure as shooting, *this* time, it was *spring*!"

"Shut up."

"Paris," Parlow said, "in the spring. Gave me hay fever."

"You're lucky that's all it gave you," Mike said.

"That's not all it gave me," Parlow said. "Gave me an understanding of culture and art, and their ineffable power, not to 'still,' no, neither to 'assuage,' but to *reveal* the essence of the Soul of Man."

"How long were you there?"

"Forty-eight hours," Parlow said. "But I saw all the museums."

Mike took the sheets of paper from the typewriter. The copyboy dropped two Dixie Cups on the desk.

"Thanks," Parlow said.

Mike slipped the papers into the wire wastebasket.

"That's the wrong way to tickle Mary," Parlow said.

Mike nodded. "Colonel McCormick says that waste of paper is an additional tax levied upon the logging industry."

"I should *think*," Mike said, "the logging industry would be right chuffed at the consequent increase in demand."

"So you *might* think," Parlow said, "if you were a dangerous Bolshevik or Red, interested only in the dissolution of the Social Fabric."

"Don't you *fucking* have work to do or someplace to go?" Mike said.

" '*To tell all is to tell everything*, Catherine said, her staid demeanor belied by her lack of interest in the downward progress of the gown's last shoulder strap, over that shoulder which even the years of tennis and riding could not rob of its willowy aristo form.'

"*All* of these broads," he said, "North Side equestrian broads? Swear that they lost it putting Charlemagne over the last water jump."

"Maybe they did," Mike said.

"Maybe they did at that," Parlow said. "Who are we to say?" He worked his chair to the side of the desk, bent, and took the discarded sheets from the wastebasket.

" 'Sources high and ensconced in the world of our North Side,' " he read, " 'have suggested a possible resolution of their interests with those of the territory left untenanted by the late demise, by lead, of Jacob Weiss, showman and father. Now followed by that of his colleague Morris Teitelbaum.' Who are those high sources?"

"That would be me," Mike said.

"And what was their proposed resolution?"

"Hell do *I* know?" Mike said. "I'm throwing chum to the fish."

"To bring up what?"

"I dunno," Mike said. "Some comment from the Outfit?"

"They said they din't do it," Parlow said.

"Who?"

"The South Side," Parlow said.

"Do what?" Mike said.

"Ice Jackie Weiss."

"Who did it, then?" Mike said.

"Unclear," Parlow said, "but they loved your quip, about 'he died of a broken heart.' You should have been there, they picked up the tab for dinner."

Mike looked at his watch. "Time to go," he said.

Crouch was the city editor, and, like most men dedicated to a cause, he took seriously the signs and trappings of his devotion. These, in his case, were an ancient rumpled suit, a green eyeshade while at work, a Fatima cigarette perennially held between his lips, his eyes screwed up against the smoke, nicotine-stained fingers and teeth, a dirty shirt, and frayed and ink-stained cuffs. He was small, usually unshaven, and had looked every day of his fifty-eight years since his accession to the desk in 1913.

He loved to opine that it was not important to be able to "write." He always pronounced the word as if in quotes.

"The Rewrite men can write sufficiently badly," he'd say. "Leave the adjectives to Miss Fisk, and the sports page. Here's what I'm looking for in a reporter: *observe*; tell me the facts; and if you're *sure*, if you're *sure*, then you connect them."

And since Jackie Weiss's funeral, Mike had been troubled by Parlow's comment about the overcoats.

At Weiss's funeral, he, Parlow, and Poochy had stood back with the gravediggers, behind the chairs, as the rabbi concluded his obsequies. Now the same rabbi was burying Teitelbaum.

"The sine qua non of a journey is disequilibrium," Parlow said.

"I've always thought so," Mike said.

"With this one exception," Parlow said. He inclined his head toward the grave, where they were lowering the casket into the ground.

"Bitch of a time," Poochy said, "getting into that hard ground."

"Nah," Mike said, "we did it in France. Trick is, you make a fire on it, melt it down the first foot, rest of it'll come right up."

"Is that true?" Poochy said.

"Well, you *think* about it," Mike said.

He looked at the sedan, stopped on the road just out of the orbit of the funeral party.

Two men in overcoats got out of the sedan. They walked toward a monument some thirty yards off, but kept their eyes on the small party around the open grave.

Teitelbaum's wife, weeping, was handed a trowel. She looked, vacantly, at the cemetery functionary who'd handed it to her. He nodded at the pile of earth. She took some on the trowel and threw it down into the grave. She stood holding the trowel. After a moment the man took the trowel away from her.

The mourners' breath showed white, and they began, now one, now another, to shift their weight, looking for some warmth in the cold.

". . . Falling like flies," Poochy said.

Parlow nudged Mike, who was still looking, obliquely, at the two latecomers.

The rabbi had finished saying that death was not the end of all things. Mike reflected that this was not the case for Teitelbaum, whose troubles, in the happy phrase, were over, while those of the onlookers, colleagues, and family around the grave were all exacerbated by the demise of him and his partner.

These, Mike mused, usually seemed to fall into one of two categories: "How will I now get by?" and "Who will get what?"

The representatives of the cemetery and its businesses stood back from the grave, The Beautiful, in the person of Mr. Walsh, unmoving in respect. His daughter had been given leave to stay in the red delivery truck, the engine running, her body fighting the cold.

Mike had seen the same two goons before, at Weiss's funeral. Seeing them again, it struck him that the cruel cold had the power to still lust, but none over curiosity.

"That's one for the books," he thought.

The cold had not stilled lust in the two-room flat facing the El. Cold as it was, and the apartment stinking from the gas stove, the stove door open and both burners on to provide a small remedy to the landlord's parsimony with coal.

But the minuscule bedroom alcove gave off the kitchen, and the stove threw enough heat to make them believe in the improvement. And he had two quilts on his bed, and the heavy army blanket, and she wanted him, and God knew he wanted her.

Even today at the cemetery, she looked impossibly fetching, in the thick coat, making her perfect body shapeless, and her father's cap pulled down around her ears, her breath freezing inside the truck's cab.

But today he knew what lay underneath the wrappings, and would know it again, as it was now a possession which, though it filled him with wonder, at the moment no longer inspired curiosity, as did the two thugs from out of town.

"I do not like them coats," Parlow said.

The small funeral party started to break up. Parlow and Mike drew back in respect for the five mourners making their way to the cars, their hieratic cadence warring with their desperate need for warmth.

"I don't like the coats."

Mike turned to the photographer. "Can you get 'em?" Mike said.

Poochy had raised his camera, and swung it slowly to cover the progress of the mourners' group. He mimed satisfaction at the shot he had not, in fact, taken, then, still looking at the mourning group, he let the camera swing back, at his side, and pointed it toward the two men.

They had half-turned from the grave, and were starting back toward their car when he took the shot.

One of the men turned at the sound of the shutter. But he saw only Poochy's back, and the camera down at his side.

They stood in Poochy's cubby in the paper's darkroom, which, by right of adverse possession, had long been acknowledged as the photographers'. Parlow and Mike stared down in the red light as Poochy put the white photographic paper in the developer bath. He nudged it lovingly back and forth with a pair of wooden tongs. "I'll *tell* you what," Parlow said, "even *in* that Eskimo gear—that little button nose . . . ?"

The image started to emerge, and Poochy picked up the print with the wooden tongs and hung it on the clothesline that ran across the cubby.

He leaned back and threw the wall switch, and the red light in the room was replaced with white. The print showed the two men at the grave, far in the background, out of focus, just two shapes, but the one man, through his posture, recognizably angered by the sound of the shutter.

"Yeah, *no.* Guy's a *hunter,*" Mike said. "Heard the

camera, click, click, all through the service. Now? Service is *over*, hears the shutter? 'Not right,' he turns back? Tell me about the coats."

"I don't like them," Parlow said.

He used the end of the tongs as his pointer.

"The hem is too long. The shoulders are too square, the points on the collar are too round, what is it? 'Radiused.' Rather than square. And, in general, they're what is known as 'foreign.' Coats are foreign. Guys' expressions are foreign. Should've snapped the shoes, 'cause the shoes are the dead giveaway. But, in toto, what we have here are two burly and self-confident gentlemen of foreign extraction. *Of* but not *in* the funeral."

"Alright. They aren't *Guineas* . . . ," Mike said.

"No," Parlow said, "they ain't got the coloring."

"Then who *are* these visitors to our shores? Come for the funerals? What do they want?"

"Look where they're looking."

"Yeah, okay, what do they want?"

"Mike," Poochy said. "Maybe they want *you*."

He had asked Annie about the men. Gingerly, careful not to spook her, for he knew she'd take note of his question. As there was no way to ask it casually, he prepared a lie.

"It was cold out there," he said.

She smiled.

"You were in the delivery truck," he said. "Window got so fogged up, you looked like a squirrel or something, in that cold out there, all huddled up in your coat."

He asked her if she'd watched the proceedings, and she said she had now and then, that there was little to watch. And he said he'd seen two men, at the back of the mourners, had she seen them, and did she know who they might be?

She looked carefully at him, and asked if the two men concerned him. "No," he said, "it was said a couple of goons from Detroit were there, to pay the respects of the Purple Gang."

"And if she can tell that's a lie," Mike thought, "then she must love me very much." And he saw that she knew it was a lie, and accepted it, as she supposed he was telling it to protect her.

"And perhaps I am," Mike thought, and hated himself, for he knew *she* was in no danger, and that he was probing for information with which to protect himself.

He went to the Ace of Spades.

"Why you come in here asking *me*?" Peekaboo said. " 'Cause black folks know everything?"

"You bet," Mike said.

"Well, that's true," Peekaboo said. "And you know *why.*"

" 'Cause you've got to be watching," Mike said.

"And one thing *that* I been watching," she said, "is that *you?* You got to know the limits of your special dispensation. You write, about this or that, South Side, the North Side, *City* Hall; you've always? Got one eye on that fine line."

"That's so," Mike said.

" 'That fine line,' does not disappear, just 'cause you go let your dick lead you around. Line's still there, you just too crazed to notice.

"These white people? That girl? These Irish? They ain't got a fine line. Their women? Are goin' to the marriage bed a virgin. That's their rule, and they will cut your heart out. And here's what: your thinking, 'How serious can it be?' will likely be done after they're done, and you know the sad answer."

The whorehouse kitchen was, as usual, hot. The alley window was cracked. Peekaboo and Mike sat by the window. They were drinking the good scotch she obtained not from her regular bootlegger, but as a gift from a customer. Mike came to her, as he did always, as to the disinterested oracle without whose help there is little direction in this world for anyone. He had come to her for her understanding of two men in foreign over-coats.

"Well, Liz," he said, "they were to kill me, that would break the girl's heart. Why'd they want to break the girl's heart?"

"That's assuming that they're with her father," Peekaboo said.

"Well, who *else* would they be?" Mike said.

"*Uh*-huh," Peekaboo said. "That to one side. Let me ask you. You want to marry the girl?"

"They won't let me," Mike said.

"No, well, or *maybe* no," she said. "Let's back up. Father. What's he want?"

"He wants his daughter to be happy," Mike said.

"Oh, good, good," she said. "*Now*, you see, we're getting down, the root of the misconception. From *which* all the difficulties flow. The *father*? Couldn't care less. Irish? Far and away, odds are? He beat her. Why'd he beat her?"

"'To instill into her a sense of right and—'"

"Right and wrong. No. We'll get to that in . . . not *only*'d he beat her; their culture? *I* don't know. It's not impossible he *had* her. He *din't* have her, he wanted to. That's the tale *I* hear repeated. Granted, my samples are limited, but . . ."

"He doesn't want her to be happy?" Mike said.

"Baby, I see the other side of the carpet here."

"You see the girls," Mike said.

"I see the *Daddies*," Peekaboo said. "That's what I see. Daddy. Comes in here? What does he want to play?"

" 'Little Bo Peep,' " Mike said.

"Now you got it," Peekaboo said. "Daddy wants to fuck the milkmaid. Comes in here? What's he want? Girl got up like a schoolgirl, hair in braids. That don't rise unannounced like a summer storm. That's living in there. Every moment he's Back Home in Indiana. Watching his little girl grow up. Her little playmates? Swimming hole . . . ? She doesn't know that? Course she does.

"He doesn't want his daughter to be happy. Married? 'Happy' means she's getting fucked five times a day by her husband, and she loves it. There she is, to his mind, giving up all that cooze his wife's gone dead on. Now? Both of them cheated him."

". . . He doesn't want her to be happy?" Mike said. "What does he want?"

"He wants her? To be two things: gone, and stay gone. Which means, she needs a protector; she ain't washing up back at his house, ten months, covered in bruises and a pair of twins. P.S., her deadbeat husband coming by, sad story, 'they'd be happy if he just had the rent.' Father, this is the last thing he wants. What this means: she's got to marry someone in the community. Community laws dictate: how much the husband can beat her; how often he's allowed, hit up his father-in-law for a loan; amount of time, she gets out, that they have to take her back. He knows these things. *She* does, too. *And* the husband. But. She flies off, marries some *white* boy, out of town, some American, this gives her this license: 'Take me home, Daddy. I didn't know what he *was* . . .' Now, the father? Cannot go over, the boy's parents, haul 'em up before the Church. He don't know where they *are*. Where the *boy* is. 'What are you going to do?' He's fucked. And all the bullshit about 'the girl's responsibility to her people and her faith'? Just comes down to that."

She took a sip of scotch.

"She marries in the group, you see, the fifty-dollar bill now, he doesn't have to loan his son-in-law, who can't pay the rent, he can bring it to *me*, to get some fifteen-year-old *black* girl, dress up in knee socks and moan, 'Daddy, please fuck me.' That's about it."

She filled up his glass.

"So you can: go learn Irish, go to church, whatever they do, but *that's* why 'they won't let you.'"

"I want the girl," Mike said.

"How bad?"

"I can't make a fist."

"You fucking her?"

"Yes."

"That going to last?"

"Yes."

"You sure? 'Cause 'Can This Marriage Be Saved?,' that's all there is."

"No, I'm sure," Mike said.

"Well then, this girl," Peekaboo said, "she knows that. Good. So. Now what you offer her? Most important, is security."

"Not love?"

"Honey, that's what 'love' *is*," Peekaboo said. "Why do you think girls fall in love? I am sure, pick one or some, 'He can: bring me off; buy me shit; protect me and my children; leave me a lot of money.' That's the list."

Mike gave a low, dismissive chuckle.

"I'm lying?" Peekaboo said. "Why do you think these girls come in here? *Stay* here, doing fat white men, 'til their tits fall?"

"Why?" Mike said.

"Why? Because it's their home," Peekaboo said. "And that, baby, is why her father slaps her. *Not* to turn her feet to the path of righteousness, but to get her to leave. 'Cause she can't stay in that house no more. You say these guys are after you?"

"I think they're after me," Mike said.

"Just the two *times*?" Peekaboo said. "Funerals. Is that correct?"

"That's right."

"How do you know they're from her father?"

"They aren't American and they ain't Eyetie, what's that leave?" Mike said.

"Well, you got to do something about it," Peekaboo said. "Maybe I'd talk to her old man. See you can make your case. Weak as it is. Find *out*. And go see Callaghan."

Chapter 11

The jazz band was taking their break. The Chinese restaurant was half-full.

Callaghan was an ex–safe and vault man. He was current with both the gossip of the allied trades, and the side world of the opium market, which indulgence had, as all knew it would, necessitated his setting aside his beloved nitroglycerine before, as one cohort had put it, "it did the same for *him*." He swept his hand around, taking in the restaurant.

"Hop Li, I want a tell you *what*," said Callaghan, "is one super-canny Chink. Somebody told me? His grandfather laid track on the Canadian Pacific, I happen to know, a fact, he has a degree from McGill University, Montreal."

"In what?" Mike said.

"Horticulture, some damn thing," Callaghan said. "*I* dunno. They have plants up there? They must. Although it's got to be one short growing season."

"They have 'wheat,'" Mike said.

"Wheat, of course," Callaghan said. "'The Breadbasket of the World.' Or maybe that's the Great Plains. I got to get out more."

"He's got a degree in horticulture," Mike said, "fuck's he doin' here?"

"I'll tell you," Callaghan said, "and the answer is 'look around.' Forty-five cents for a plate of what essentially is a half cent worth of rice, and not too much of that, a slice of carrot, and maybe this gristle is dog meat. Who the fuck knows *what* the fuck is in these dishes?"

"Health inspector," Mike said.

"Make me laugh," said Callaghan. "'Nother story is? His grandfather? Coolie on the CP, washt up on Dawson, for the Gold Rush."

"Uh-huh," Mike said, "*lookit . . .*"

"'Nother story. Fucken guy, gets rich running a whorehouse. Coolie rail gangs, round-eyed pussy. One white woman. Hundred thousand Chinks."

"How'd he get the white woman?" Mike said.

". . . *I* know? He won her in a fan-tan game. The fuck *I* know."

"All these stories," Mike said, "militate toward the possession of some perverted nature."

"Not at all, and tell you that one too," Callaghan said. "Because I've thought about it. How the Chinks got rich? Came in with nothing, all a sudden, everybody's eating the swill they rejected on the *railroad*. Track boss brought them this shit? They? They would of torn up twenty miles of track." He looked down at his plate and shook his head.

"That's not their way," Mike said. "Also, they would have *shot* 'em."

"Who?" Callaghan said.

"Pinkertons," Mike said. "Also, the Chinese . . . ? Are too smart. Their thing? Keep your head down. Micks, now?" He nodded toward Callaghan. "Your thing is the fire department, the cops, park district, and so on. Politics? What you've got, the *Titanic* iceberg. Most of it is underground; a bit of it, however's, on the surface. 'Nough to let you know the vast amount that's hidden. Your problem? You can't hide it all.

"Irish? Every cop on the beat? Red potato nose and a brogue? You can't hide it. The Chinese? Who knows *what* they do?"

"We know a few things," Callaghan said. He motioned for another drink. The band came back onto the bandstand. The level of conversation in the restaurant rose. The two men in the booth sighed and looked at the band.

" 'Bye Bye fucken Blackbird,' for a sawbuck," Callaghan said.

"No bet," Mike said.

"Three to five?"

"Forget it," Mike said. "It's traditional. And P.S., I like it."

"Everybody likes it," Callaghan said, "that's why it's traditional." The band struck up "Remember."

"See, you just lost fifteen bucks," Callaghan said. "Fucken songs. In France? They sing it the *other* way?"

" 'You took me to find a lonely spot, and after I'd cared to come a lot.' "

"That's right," Callaghan said. "As men deprived of feminine companionship, they turned to buggery, obscenity, or sloth."

"That what the Chinks did?" Mike said.

"On the railroad? Yeah, okay, *Irish?* On the other hand, and one point of contention I do *not* have with the Catholic Church, we go with 'Marry early, marry young, go screw her every night and keep her breeding.' One: it keeps us from insanity or sodomy, *two:* it makes more Irish. Handy, come election time.

"Now, what the Heathen Chinee, they put their

energy in? Building the Transcontinental Railroad; gambling; save their money; and one Australian whore somebody dragged out to the end-o-steel."

"And opium," Mike said.

The young Chinese waitress brought the drink. Callaghan knocked it back and gestured for another.

"And opium," Mike said.

"I heard you," Callaghan said.

"Somebody said I should talk to you."

"Well, yeah, you're talking to me," Callaghan said. "Whaddaya want?"

"I want a tip on a couple of guys," Mike said.

"Who are they?" Callaghan said.

"You tell *me*," Mike said.

He took the photo of the two men in overcoats from his lapel pocket, and passed it to Callaghan.

"*I* can't make it out," Callaghan said. "Two silhouettes in the background."

". . . Best you can."

"Gimme a hint."

Mike spread his hands.

"I mean, do I know? What team do they play for?"

"I think I know, but I don't know," Mike said.

"Who sent you to me?"

"Fella said, 'See Callaghan.'"

Callaghan looked hard at the photograph. "*Because?*" he said.

"I think because you're Irish," Mike said.

"Well, yeah, there's something about these guys," Callaghan said. "They *been* there, and they might be Irish, or Squareheads, or Krauts, for all that." He paused. "Talk to Danny Doyle."

Callaghan stood. The band began to play "Has Anybody Here Seen Kelly?" "Yeah yeah," Callaghan said. He raised his hat to the band in acknowledgment. He turned back to Mike. "Go see Danny Doyle."

Chapter 12

Mike had not fired a handgun since France, and then only in a short burst of target practice, conceived by a fellow pilot as a break in the boredom of a week of constant rain and, thus, no flying.

The pilot had buttonholed a Marine gunnery sergeant into coming by with, as the sergeant put it, a few "helpful hints."

"First of all," the Marine had said, "this here weapon is a forty-five caliber. This weapon is good for blowing the chest out of some guy who is five, ten feet away. Is it more accurate than that? Yes, it is. *You* are not. One a' the fucken Huns, farther away than that? Run. As he is, prolly, going to have a rifle.

"He has got a rifle, there is going to be, of him, more than one. Why would you want to make him mad, or draw attention to yourself? His friends come running; reasoning backward, then, best thing that you could do? *Not* shoot him. You come down, behind his lines? Run. Or hide. They got you outgunned? Throw the pistol away, raise your hands. That's what this pistol's good for.

"The one time you would want to use this pistol is: a guy's attacking you; or you're on the way back to *our* lines, you need to eliminate a sentry, midst of some fire-fight; or otherwise, not calling attention to yourself."

He held his hand out, and a flier took his pistol from its holster and handed it to the Marine. The Marine checked the chamber, found it empty, dropped the magazine and racked the slide several times, locked it open, and sighted down the bore, using his thumbnail in the breech to catch and reflect the light back through the open chamber.

"It's filthy, and a filthy weapon is more prone to malfunction. Why you would want to increase those chances is beyond me," he said. "But, then, we all have our little ways."

It had become the catchphrase of the Aero Squadron.

There was not a botched or bounced landing, ground loop, or other demonstration of inability not greeted by someone uttering the Marine's phrase. It was employed as frequently in reference to machinery: the coy reluctance of the Rhône engine to kick over in the cold; the inevitable jamming of the Lewis guns; the Nieuport's legendary preference for enemy-held territory over which to quit.

The new pilots, on arrival, were already considered dead, because this saved the veterans from both emotional attachments and the effort of reappraisal when, in the first few flights, the new man actually died.

When was the new man accepted?

This was not determined by the group, but by the man himself. He put forward his claim by the first bold usage of the sacred phrase.

"Where's your observer?"

"Yeah. He's in the back, down there somewhere. He's dead."

"We all have our little ways."

The police pistol range stank of cordite, gun oil, and solvent. Sergeant Doyle's "Voice of Command" put Mike in mind of France.

"The Great Mystery," Doyle told the recruits, "will be revealed to you only through practice. They say, 'You can't know what a man will do under pressure.' I tell you, you know exactly what'll do: what he was trained to do."

Doyle sucked in his belly as he addressed the men.

"Those of the older lads, who came through it, may inform you that the pistol is an effective tool with which to hit the broad side of a barn only if *thrown*. Why? They had no *experience*, and were just repeating what they had been told was the case. As *I* was, over there, where the thing was the mark of the officer caste, used as a symbol, to encourage, or in its active mode, to shoot that man wishing to go anywhere other than over the top.

"One had one's trusty Springfield, and was taught to rely upon it; and it, in fact, worked peachy. *However*, Eighteenth and Western, three A.M., when the woman's screaming, there's a shot or two, and some fellow in a hurry crashes out the door and takes off running toward you, with *intent*, it falls to you, then, as per your instructions, to shout, 'Halt! Police!,' giving force to said command by drawing your revolver and loosing off three or four shots into his chest.

"No, we will note, 'three or four shots' do *not* constitute six, or the full complement of your cylinder. You will save the other rounds, lest his partner, done raping the woman and perhaps the man, come, in the interim, out of the house, to find you with an empty gun.

" 'Won't I have *seen* him, Sergeant? This other man?' No. You will not. For, as you draw and fire, your field of vision, normally so broad and wide, will constrict to the width of Queen Anne's pussy, and your world will consist of the man running toward you. It will fill with his chest. It will fill with the second button on his shirt or coat, and it is at this button you must fire.

"How? Aiming, as you were taught in your scant weeks at the academy, and carefully aligning your two sights, then loosing half a breath and squeezing gently? No. For we could school you 'til the cows come home and hand over their wages, but you will not do so. You will instinctively crouch, lean forward, and lose all track of time.

"Well and good. Do *not,* however, lose track of your shots. *Count* them, please. It will save your life.

"To return to the second button of his shirt or coat: Forget your sights. Look at this coat button, *look* at it. 'Til the individual threads stand out. And they will. Stare at it. That's the death spot. You may be distracted by his hands, which may, in fact, hold a knife or a gun. Would you like those weapons gone? The wiser man would kill the fellow holding them. Shoot at the death spot. *Grab* your revolver. *Jerk* it from the leather, *thrust* it toward the target spot, and, when it's there, pull the trigger. One. Two, three shots. 'Mustn't you aim?' Do you aim when you point your finger? 'Jim, look at that fine-looking girl acrost the street.' 'Which one, Mickey?' 'That one *there*,' and there's your finger on the redhead.

"Three or four shots. *That's* what we're going to practice. And then you can look around. And, should you see the second man, why, then, same treatment. Should you not? Why, then, reload.

" 'But, Sergeant,' you say, 'I fired, contrary to regulations. *Before* I had determined that this man was a malefactor. Suppose he was the deranged husband, running from the house to seek help?'

"This is a matter not for philosophy, but of foresight. For you, should that prove to be the case, will then frost the poor unfortunate with the throw-down gun each thoughtful police officer has carried since the world began.

"I think that covers it.

"Everybody, on your way out, put your hand in the box, take six, *six* empty cartridge cases, place them in your right-hand jacket pocket. Off you go."

Doyle motioned for the class to stand, and they stood and filed out the room. The door, when opened, admitted the sounds of a far-off submachine gun, and the *pop, pop-pop* of revolver practice. Doyle turned to Mike.

"Cop, down Chicago Heights, shot down? What's in his pocket? Empty shells, six shells, right-hand jacket pocket. They're *training* them out there"—he gestured toward the range—"to save their brass. *Training inspectors.*" He jabbed his finger again. "Teaching the boys to fucking kill themselves. Chicago Heights cop? Reloading? Under fire. Bent down, picked up the brass as he was trained to do. *My* boys, inspector comes by, 'Show me the brass in your pocket.' 'Yes, sir, here they are.'

"Impromptu checks, make sure they aren't letting the brass fall to the ground."

"Why?" Mike said.

"Why?" Doyle said. "More work for the janitors."

He closed the door to the range and sat on his desk. He took a tin of snuff and opened it and filled his lower lip. He gestured at the wall racks behind him. One held eight Thompson submachine guns, the other eight Winchester riot shotguns. "The procurement of armaments," he said, "offers to the observant many elements of which I am sure constitute Greek tragedy." He pointed at the Winchesters.

"The fucken *riot* gun, which you will remember from your year abroad, is far and away the better weapon for the tasks which fall to our lot. But it *will* kick you in the shoulder. So, the inspectors, charged with the choice, suggest these newest marvels." He

waved at the Thompson guns. "Their professed argument, that since Mr. Brown and the boys have 'em,
Mr. O'Banion has 'em, we should have 'em, too."

"How'd those boys get 'em?" Mike said.

"*My* theory," said Doyle, "is that the manufacturers
gave 'em to 'em. *I* would."

"I would, too," said Mike.

"Valentine's Day? Best advertising campaign in history. 'Rat tat.' Ev' police force in the country, 'We had
better *get* some of *those.*' Like the ladies and the Brand-
New Hat. The thing here being firepower."

"Yeah," Mike said. "You are a proponent of the
tried and true."

"I'm a Marine," Doyle said. "And if there's one
thing that they taught me in the corps, that's *it.*"

"Somebody's stealing the guns, the armory," Mike
said.

"Somebody's stealing *everything,*" Doyle said. "Everyone's stealing something."

He took the bandanna from his trouser pocket and
blew his nose.

"Jackie Weiss," Mike said. "Teitelbaum."

"Hey, now, there's more of them to love. It's just that
most of it's outside their bodies."

Mike said, "What did they shoot them with?"

"Oh, that's your question," Doyle said.

"Can't a fellow veteran stop for a friendly chat?" Mike said.

A voice on the range called, "Sergeant . . . ?" Doyle raised his hand to indicate *one second*. He paused. "The *Chinese*," he said, "invented gunpowder. And used it, just as we do now, to foil the evil spirits."

"The question is, then," Mike said, "what is evil?"

"Well, that is decided," Doyle said, "by the fellow holding the gun."

"*Sergeant*," the man called from the range. Doyle rose.

"At the end of a long day," he said, "why or how were *any* of 'em shot? *My* job, though—and I thank the Lord that I was wise enough never to seek promotion—has the benefit, I come too close to the edge, *someone*, *someone* might take me aside, and shake his head minutely, to warn me from the abyss."

"Which is?"

"Don't ask too many questions," Doyle said. "And *certainly* don't know the answers."

Mike handed Sergeant Doyle a photograph.

"No, I don't know who these fellas are," Doyle said.

He handed the photograph back to Mike.

"I know who they *aren't:* they aren't from around here; and I know *what* they are.

"And, should this become something other than mere journalism, do you have or do you require a mohaska?"

"I have the Luger," Mike said.

"Then remember," Doyle said, "the one phrase you never want to use. It is: 'Wait here 'til I fetch it.'"

He clapped Mike on the shoulder, gently, and walked off.

Mike had obtained the Luger in the mess of his Ninety-Fourth Aero Squadron.

They were at the aerodrome, just south of St. Mihiel. The German had been shot down that day as part of the morning sortie for which Mike was not called.

The German was sitting by the stove of the barn used as the squadron's mess hall. He was shivering from the cold, from fatigue, and from the aftereffects of the adrenaline. And he was overcome with shame. All the American fliers recognized his state; and all knew not that it *might*, but that it most likely *would* one day be them, their disgrace and captivity the marginally better of the two most likely outcomes of their continued flights.

The German felt Mike looking, and looked back at him. Mike knew and the German saw he knew that the only true respect for grief was silence.

Mike nodded, and started out of the mess. He fastened the belt of his leather flying coat around his waist, cinching it tight. He felt something in the large side pocket. He reached into it and removed the nearly full pint bottle of Cognac.

He turned back into the room, and stood in front of the German. The German, again, looked up, and Mike offered the bottle to him. After a moment, the German took the bottle. Mike started to leave, but the German gestured for him to stay.

The German reached into the folds of his flying coat and removed a Luger pistol. He held the grip with his thumb and first finger, and presented the pistol toward Mike.

Mike took the gift and nodded his thanks.

He'd fired the pistol several times, for recreation, while in France. He brought it home, and it resided, with his other war mementos, in his bedside drawer.

He'd often thought about the German, who had retained the weapon through no one could know how many searches, cursory and more extensive, and at what risk.

As a pilot Mike understood: that the German was through fighting, and had kept the pistol for the one purpose only, which was to end his own life.

In his more maudlin moments Mike experimented

with congratulating himself on having saved the man from suicide. The notion was too pretty for him; but, on one drunken night, he had shared the story with Parlow, who said the story made him "want to throw up."

"This Kraut," Parlow said, "who, one, we didn't start it; two, fair fight? He lost? The better man would learn to live with it; three, he's, I guarantee you, back in Deutschland, with a wife already fat, and four kids who stink of cabbage; and four, who *your* children will, most likely, have to fight, because that fucking country, like that Kraut, is a sore loser. And, five, if I want any more of your war stories, believe me, I'll *ask* you, which I won't, 'cause, end of the day, they all sound just like: I loved him, he promised to marry me, he disappeared and left me pregnant, and that's why I'm a whore. Or a lawyer. As the case may be."

Chapter 13

The apartment was cold, as the landlord was only required to provide heat between five P.M. and five in the morning. Mike had often speculated upon who paid what to whom to bring about this ordinance. "But if there were no do-gooders in the world," Parlow said, "they wouldn't be constrained to provide heat at all." Which Mike knew was just a conversational gambit, as Parlow hated the blue-stockinged reformers with a passionate delight. "Their pussies, man and woman, have been stitched up from birth, and I defy the most persuasive Mick ever born to cadge a drink from them."

"But, and I will speak under correction," Mike said, "these same moral adventurers, whose implied hypocrisy you so rightly deplore, are they not also those who favor Prohibition?"

"Yes," said Parlow.

". . . Thus being immune to indictment for refusing a man a drink," Mike said.

"I do not see it," Parlow said.

"As they, in their rightly decried hypocrisy, would likely not only refuse to serve, but probably lack the access *to* spirits."

"They have access to coin," Parlow said, "and I have set my fantasia in a speak or restaurant, and my poor desiccated hero approaching the philanthropic table."

"How does he recognize them, these philanthropists?"

"By their pinched and disapproving mien," Parlow said. "By the awful though expensive cut of their clothes, proclaiming at once their superiority to earthly things, and their financial ability to so hold; by the fare before them, consisting if not of actual raw vegetables, then of some substance equally sad; by the set of the women's noses and the effeminacy of the men."

Mike gestured for another round.

"And, to make an end, by that thin, burnt-out bearing, proclaiming to the sentient world their English derivation and pagan lack of reverence for the Holy Mother Church.

"Let them drink in hell gazing in wonder at celestial images always denied them, of their masters, holy and temporal, and pleading for the chance to mitigate, if not their punishment, their shame, by acceptation of the Holy Sacrament, its blessed balm ever receding as they tread the road of burning pitch.

"Yes, there is balm in Gilead, its name is Revenge."

Mike had, in fact, attended a Mass just prior to, and as a subterfuge enabling, the afternoon's tryst with Annie Walsh.

He sat three rows behind her and to her left, in love with her piety, in love with the very head scarf which she would remove on the apartment stairs, shaking out her hair in transformation from dutiful religious virgin to lover.

Having told her father she was going to Mass, she would not consider the sin of nonattendance. The subterfuge and the unlicensed love she held, when she examined it, as merely a betrayal of her father, who, as a man, was, of course, not entitled to her utter frankness. But though she might affront, she would not lie to God.

Mike understood that the religion's duty did not and was not intended to excuse the subsequent transgression, but that she had chosen to perform it nonetheless, as an obligation. He loved her for her ability to choose. She had chosen to be his lover and to pay the cost, and he loved her strength. He loved everything about her.

They warmed each other in the frozen apartment. After making love she hurried, shivering, from the bed. She took his heavy overcoat from the hook on the back of the door, and put it on.

"Where are you going?" he said.

"Make tea," she said.

She hugged the overcoat around her and ran on tip-toe into the alcove that was his kitchen. She took the matchbox, shook it, and found it empty.

Mike opened the bedside table drawer and took out a book of matches, and a pack of cigarettes. She came back toward the bed for the match.

She glanced down into the open drawer and looked quizzically at Mike. He closed the drawer, sparing her the sight of the Luger. She waited for Mike to answer her unasked question. He lit the cigarette and looked away.

She took the book of matches, walked back to the stove, struck a match, and lit the rear burner. Shook the teakettle, and, satisfied, set it over the flame.

She crouched down by the stove door, opened the overcoat, and flapped the sides to bring the heat close.

The stove was lit and its door open, as in any of the apartments occupied during the day; for though the city allowed the landlords to shut down the furnace, they were prohibited from restricting the flow of gas, and the apartments, in the winter months, stank of the gas and of the stove.

She rubbed her hands, and turned back toward the bed to grin. "No one," he thought, "has ever seen anything so lovely."

He raised himself against the headboard, and gathered the bedclothes tight around him. He sat on the edge of the bed, looking at her.

He saw her, smiling, start to speak, and then she cocked her head, slightly, toward the door. Mike was looking at her when the man kicked the door in.

He was a large man in a heavy coat, holding a large revolver. Mike remembered later that he brought the winter in with him, in that back-of-the-nose smell of weeks below zero, and the Lake, and the outdoors, and that the man smelled of smoke.

"Laborers have that smell," Mike thought. "Hunters, and vagrants. It's the soldier smell, but it's not. No, perhaps it is. The Germans had it."

He had turned to the door. His mind tried to frame the sentence which would explain to her father and her brother and/or their emissary that all would be well, that he was sorry he had taken her virginity, but that they were going to be married, that he had asked to go to her people, but she had said to wait.

The first shot hit the girl as she stood and turned to him.

He thought, "No. She'll be burned, she'll fall on the stove."

He rose to attack the killer, to explain that it wasn't her fault. To stop him.

The man buttstroked him with the heavy revolver, and Mike went down unconscious.

Chapter 14

On the first afternoon he had taken her up to his room, she stepped out of her shift and shivered.

He turned down the sheet and the old army blanket, and put her in the bed. He tucked the covers in around her.

He saw that she was neither afraid nor apprehensive, and wondered how that could be. A verse from a long-ago Bible class came to him; and though he was thereafter sure he had not uttered it, she had absolutely nodded in response. She had drawn his face down to her. He saw it suffused not primarily with love, but with compassion. "She is," he thought, while he made love to her, "the queen of heaven."

The verse, as he remembered it, ran, "There are three things I do not understand: the serpent on the rock, the eagle in the air, and the way of a man with a maid." But the way of the man was clear, and blunt, and simple: he took the woman or he asked her, and that was that; the mystery was the way of the maid, who accepted or acquiesced with a generosity and trust at which a man could only wonder.

Each time after they made love she went to confession. She would dress and take her heavy coat from the hook near the door, and fit herself into it. She would take the flowered shawl from the coat pocket and drape it over her head, transforming herself into a penitent. Then she would nod at him and leave.

After her death, and when they had taken her away, the shawl remained, and the coat remained, as did the clothes she had left folded on the chair, and the shoes underneath it.

He'd thought the police might have taken them, but they were, apparently, not considered germane to the crime.

One of her brothers glared at him at the graveside.

Was it sufficient to say, "We were going to be married"? He thought that any attempt at exculpation would be cowardice and a betrayal not only of the memory but of the soul of her who had been so brave.

At the interment, the brother had looked at him not with what would have been a bearable rage, but with a contempt which, however long he lived, would be among his last memories of Earth.

The brother came to Mike's apartment, but he would not progress beyond the door. Mike took the brown paper package of the girl's effects, and handed it to him, and the man walked away.

But why had she died? And why had they let him live?

Mike had at first believed that the girl's death had been an "honor" killing, and that the murderers, her family, had left him to live with both the anguish of her loss, and his guilt.

But their grief, witnessed at the funeral, was over-whelming, and he saw they would never have done anything to harm their beloved daughter.

But, then, why had the girl alone been killed?

Other than the loss of her chastity there was nothing of which she could possibly be guilty.

She had been killed, then, as a lesson to him. But administered by whom? By those he had offended, cer-tainly, but by whom, other than her family? Whom had he offended?

In the course of his near ten years in Chicago jour-nalism, he had offended anyone the exposure of whose actions caused them discomfort, shame, anxiety, incarceration. His job, as he understood it, was to uncover and to tell the truth about acts most of which someone had a large interest in concealing.

He had revealed facts about the South Side Italians, which is to say Capone; the North Side Irish, captained by O'Banion; the vagaries of the police force; the vice and vice lords of the Levee; and the ever-reliable procession of wife beaters, child abusers, white slavers, dope fiends, thieves, con artists, perverted rich and depraved poor, and, in short, the lifeblood of his chosen and beloved city.

He had, many times, cautioned himself to be careful, and some few times he had even acted upon the advice. But, in the main, he dealt with fear as he had trained himself to do in the airplane. He learned to live with it.

Now they had killed his love.

And as it was not her fault, it was surely his. And now he understood what he had not understood before: the lot of the German flier.

And he remembered the aviator's deepest prayer, not "Do not let me die," but "Don't let it be my fault."

He had gotten the girl killed.

And there was nothing that could make that go away.

———

The rabbit had flown with Mike eight months over the Western Front. "There may be some fellas," he said, "who trust their luck to magic incantations or some-such. I myself rely only upon skill. And this rabbit."

It was celluloid, yellow-brown, one inch long. Is-suing from the top of its head, between the extended ears, was a thick loop of red string.

It had been part of the seal of a pack of opium.

The opium packet was wrapped in thick brown paper, bound with red string, and stamped, clumsily, with Chinese characters Mike could not decipher.

It came as part of the, to that date, most expensive night of his life, in Paris, when he had spent the total-ity of eight months' flight pay on a Chinese courtesan, whose charms and abilities surpassed even the awestruck endorsements of her previous clients.

The room was dark red, the woman's skin ivory; the japanned night table held a bottle of Pernod, a carafe of water, a packet of American cigarettes, the blackened opium pipe, the deck of opium, the appurtenant needle, bowl, and candle. The seal on the deck of opium was black, and pressed into the wax seal was the loop which held the rabbit.

Thereafter he'd flown with the rabbit buttoned into the left breast pocket of his tunic.

Back in Chicago, still in uniform, the blouse was thrown over the back of a hotel room chair. A brunette from the bar went hunting in his clothes for a match. Mike woke up to see her holding the rabbit by the string. "Did this keep you safe?" she asked.

Had the rabbit kept him safe?

What a fool question.

It was, to his mind, a question beyond foolish: it was the utmost blasphemy, not in that it questioned, but in that it named a power, obeisance to whose unnamed and unnameable self had of course kept him safe.

He had survived the War to awake, drunk, in Chicago, listening to the mockery of a power which, obviously, held his life in an esteem higher than he held it himself.

"*I* don't fucking know why I'm here," he thought. "Do any of us?"

And was it necessary to despise every intangible thing in order to think oneself wise, or chic, or whatever the hell people strove to think of themselves for want of other idleness?

"The rabbit," he said, "or, say, the display of same, may indeed have been or be an error of taste. I am newly returned and unaware of How You Do Things Here. I have been away."

He saw that she was moved by his oration, and pitied

her credulity; for it was not that he had suffered, he knew, but that he could speak which won her sympathy.

"Who knows what keeps us safe," he said, "or if we *are* safe?"

Through the next nine years he had carried the rabbit in the ticket pocket of his jacket.

Now Mike stood some twenty yards away from the girl's funeral party. He held back out of respect for the ceremony, and he was held back from his grief.

The Orthodox priest spoke in Gaelic; then he prayed the body into the ground in Latin. The women wailed, the men stood aloof and unmoving.

When the family had gone, the gravediggers appeared. They began to clear the many floral tributes hiding the mounded earth, and shoveled the grave closed. Mike took off his gloves. He took the charm from his jacket pocket, and held it between his hands. They quickly became freezing cold, and he relished the feeling.

He intended to drop the charm in the earth of the closing grave, and was waiting for an inspiration as to the correct moment. He stood in the cold, as close to unbeing as it is possible to be. One of the gravediggers looked over to him. Mike felt his look, and raised his eyes.

He knew the look. It was the perception of a threat. The gravedigger had sensed something just below consciousness that was out of place.

Mike thought, "Of course. He was a soldier." And he nodded at the man. The man held his gaze until he had evaluated the threat. Then he returned to shoveling the earth.

"He sensed me," Mike thought, "as I did not belong. Most here are overcome by emotion. Many are indifferent, but most feel grief. Why did he find me different? He felt my guilt." Mike shrugged. He walked away from the grave, still holding the charm.

He had expected her brothers to come for him.

They barred him from the hospital morgue, standing, by turns, in the corridor. He saw them again at police headquarters, and he knew that they saw him. But they would not come kill him. And after a while he ceased to wonder why.

He was not afraid, for he no longer wanted to live. He thought his murder would be fitting, even if not deserved. And he felt it was deserved. For not only had he failed to protect her, he knew they were correct that he had, somehow, gotten her involved in that which had led to her death.

There was a certain calculus, Mike knew, of rage, and of revenge. The Iberians and the Italians could mature a grudge through generations. But the Irish were a different race.

They didn't shun revenge, but they adored fighting. And would not forgo even the least legitimate of pretexts for bloodshed.

Parlow had taught him the principles: when you cannot find the correct answer, ask a different question.

For the family's lack of vengeance was their own concern. If they acted, they would act when and how and if it appeared good to them to do so. Should they so choose, Mike realized, he would then or soon after be dead, and his travail completed. And if they had forgone revenge, that, also, was their choice, curious as it might be.

He himself could certainly dispatch the one person of whose guilt he was assured. But he embraced his anguish in inaction with a ferocity equal to that with which he had embraced the girl.

Chapter 15

There were the stories one told, and the stories one never told. There were those which killed you if you kept them in, and those you would die before re-telling. Parlow's favorite story had been the Croquet Ball.

The rich and wife-swapping natives of the North Shore had finally outdone themselves, to the shock and horror of the City Desk, who'd previously held that they could not be surprised.

Everyone knew the names, but no one could print them, as they belonged to the clans of the paper's two largest advertisers. But the event occurred, and had to be covered, and it fell to Parlow to express the paper's sympathy, for the death of the two-year-old girl.

He sat and wrote a "They have it all yet they have

nothing," noting the vast lakefront estate where the nurse, daily, led the little tyke (something of a flirt) down to admire the sun, the waves, the seabirds, and the family yacht, *Unity*, bobbing at the dock.

He also fantasized her princess bedroom, full of toys, and the One Sad Doll, laid on the coverlet, awaiting the return of her owner, dead of a cerebral hemorrhage.

Parlow had written as assigned, but in a rage detectable only by his fellow reporters, who understood his claptrap as a self-abasement in disgust at a community whose stupidity and boorishness transgressed the human.

For the unnamed of that number had scrawled a "Meet me in the garden" mash note to the woman of the mansion, tied it around a croquet ball, and heaved the ball through what he believed was the lady's dressing room, but which proved, in the event, to be the nursery.

Yes, Parlow said, the ball crushed the child's skull, but her sainted blood obliterated much of the message, thus saving her mother from the temptation to adultery. Some of the wags at the Port held, per contra, that the little girl was going to hell, having been involved, however unwittingly, in a plot to transgress the Seventh Commandment.

"Yes," said Mike, "we cannot know. We live in a

cloud; but what of predestination, and so on; as, reflect, 'He threw the ball through the wrong window.' "

The Catholics held the child was blameless; the Protestants that we are all damned, and it had just caught up with her; and Mike was asked to pontificate as, since the school fire at All Saints, he had become the arbiter of theological disputes.

His position carried no perquisites save the preemptory challenge "Now let's change the subject." All complied with his rulings, and the subject reverted to the various and endless depredations of those modern Robin Hoods, the city's knights of the blued steel, as Parlow had once written.

But on the night of the croquet ball, the ginned-up repartee between the Prods and the Micks down at the Port wore thin; the girl had died a death beyond the absurd, Mike called for a new topic, and the silence after his ruling kept extending. "Oh, for chrissake," he said. "The kid's dead. Who was, just moments before, alive and gurgling. Now she's in her grave. No one knows she did not 'expire of a cerebral hemorrhage' save her family, her father, you, me, their staff and their friends, our friends, and the gardener, who, no doubt, had to clean the croquet ball and sneak it back into the set.

"The wretch who threw it will, for the nonce, have to fuck his *own* wife. The family of the intended cuckold will, no doubt, petition that god in their employ for a reason for the innocent death, and forsake croquet for contract bridge. Thus the mysterious tide called 'fashion.'"

One Sad Doll was understood to be the work of a good man doing a loathsome job and worrying the wound.

Parlow was not only excused for his One Sad Doll, but subsequently congratulated when a report leaked from the copy desk confirmed that the phrase originally concluded, "waiting with wistful eyes for that embrace which would never again come."

One had only so much sympathy, and that expended on the travails of others was unavailable for expenditure upon one's own.

Further, all realized that the sympathy they were to arouse in their readers was, finally, an effect independent of whatever the actual facts and merits of an action or an incident might be. And to whom could one repair for their verification? To no one, all realized, save to the press, all of whom knew each other to be not only jaded unto death, but distrustful of every human utterance and gesture.

The understanding of this horror was, of necessity, repressed in those doing the job of reporting; it broke through, time to time, in suicide, or retirement from the profession (considered to be the worse of the two similar alternatives). It broke through in their humor and callousness, and it broke out, occasionally, in the idiosyncratic expression of self-loathing, and disgust at the world and all its works. This was the Sally Port's understanding of Parlow's "wistful doll, waiting for that embrace."

Each man at the desk had his own sad story. It was the story he would never tell.

The croquet ball would fade from memory, and disappear with the deaths of those who had heard it. Policemen, Parlow said, are by profession closemouthed to all outside the clan. Upon retirement, however, no one can shut them up. Reporters are your gossips; but when they hang it up and leave the club, they simply shake their heads in wonder and drink themselves to death.

Prior to his bereavement, Mike, of course, *had* been toying with a novel. Its central incident, the only one he had so far addressed, was the mission, over the lines, of a flight of two Allied SPADs, on the last morning of the War.

It was a story he had heard, on the boat home, as others had heard of the Angel of Mons; the Christmas Truce; the Hun and the Yank, bayonets locked in each other, conjoined, dead and frozen in No Man's Land;

and the other myths, truths, and revelations of the Trench War.

The Armistice had been signed on November 10, and hostilities were to cease on the next day: the eleventh day of the eleventh month, at the eleventh hour.

If this nicety were not enough to establish the gulf between the aesthetics of the general staff and those of the men dying in anguish, a further directive was amended. "No unit or individual is to cease from combat until the hour of the Armistice. All plans and objectives contained herein will be executed with maximum effort until the cessation of hostilities."

The order was received, at the Front, with incredulity by the men, many of whom had fought for four years and needed only to hold still for an hour or two in order to return home safe. Some units' commanders chose to disregard the order; some, generally understood to be the careerists, hoping for one more victory, formed their men up and attacked across No Man's Land into the machine guns defending territory which was already, by treaty, to become theirs at eleven A.M.

An army colonel, Mike wrote, was pestered by the newly arrived son of an acquaintance. The colonel permitted the boy to fly his one combat mission in the last two hours of the War.

A veteran pilot, Mike's hero, was told, "Take him

out, let him strafe some empty hillside, bring him back; I'll consider it a favor." The pilot told the rookie, "Do what I do: when I wag my wings, strafe the 'enemy area' that I fire at. Empty your guns, and follow me back to the field."

They took off, formed up, and flew east. The pilot spotted a small, empty wood, some miles ahead. He got the young boy's attention and signed to him to follow his lead. The veteran turned in and strafed the copse, which was not empty, but held a half company of German artillery, sitting out the War's last half hour.

The Germans were lounging against the trees when the first plane dove. Some stood to wave. The plane's fire killed most of the company. The survivors unlimbered their gun and blew the second plane out of the sky.

The veteran turned back to see his wingman's plane in pieces, the dead boy pilot falling free.

Mike's story turned on the loathing of the hero for the colonel, who had let the boy fly, and of the hero for himself, as he, however inadvertently, had caused the boy's death. The story's hero returned to Chicago, but as many times as Mike rewrote the Armistice Day Incident, the story would progress no further.

And then Mike realized that he had gone beyond what was permitted: for his continual revision of the novel's first chapter had, beyond question, called the attention of the Fates, and in response to his summons, they had killed the girl, enlisting his help.

"Well," **Mike** thought, "most of 'em died stalled and spinning in the Jenny, or died when the engine quit, or got shot up by the Hun, or flew it into the ground. An infant got her head bashed in by a drunken fool with a croquet ball.

"And when the Eternal Scorer," he thought, "puts his mark against my name, 'twill matter not if won or lost . . . For all, no doubt, will be forgiven, forgotten, or misremembered, certainly. But what of the plight of the Eternal Scorer?"

No, the great crime, as his mind ran, was the unspeakable nicety of the world that could not simply declare, "The Armistice has been concluded, hostilities have ceased."

"And perhaps in some world," he thought, "the girl is still alive." And the thought comforted him and he believed it, for the half moment, until taken over by the ensuing question, "But how would one get to that world?"

He could not. And it was difficult for him to frequent the Sally Port and its sympathy, however expressed. But he was comfortable at the Ace of Spades.

Chapter 16

Morris Teitelbaum had been shot to death and nobody cared. "News Around Town" noted that his congregation and his widow were dedicating the synagogue's new recreation room in his honor.

Also reported were several nuptials of the working poor and the projected arrival in Chicago of a new British consul. These were at the bottom of page 12. The front page carried a notice of a visit to Chicago of a flight of Italian airmen.

Mike read the front page, and Peekaboo read "Ask Miss Fisk."

"Says here," she said, "way to bring your man home is: go take the kids to work." She shook her head in wonder.

They sat in the whorehouse kitchen and drank. The piano player played "Frivolous Sal" as if stating a philosophic proposition. Mike knew he would be sitting crosswise, on the piano bench, his overcoat and hat on, a cigarette stuck to his lip, and sipping the end-of-the-day rye from the tumbler Peekaboo always brought him to help him home.

The sound filtered into the kitchen, where she sat with Mike.

"Pal," he said, "you're a good commander."

She shrugged. They listened as the man played, dead slow, the perfect ragtime. It was the sound of a broken heart.

Dolly, the last girl down, was at the sink, drinking a glass of water. She let out a long sigh. Peekaboo held an arm out, and the girl put the glass down and came over. Peekaboo gave her a hug. "How you feelin'?" she said.

The girl looked at Mike and leaned down and kissed Peekaboo on the top of the head. Mike smiled at her. "Dolly, you get some rest," Peekaboo said.

The girl retrieved her glass of water and left the kitchen. Mike spoke the lyrics to the music: "A wild Irish devil, but dead on the level, was my gal Sal."

"Well, that's the crackerjack prize," Peekaboo said, "that's the truth. Someone will stick *by* you." But she saw Mike was far away.

The song stopped. Mike heard the man close the keyboard cover. He heard the bench pushed back, and followed the man's footsteps toward the door. He felt he would have given anything for the song to continue.

There was a muttered goodbye as the door opened and closed. He heard Marcus bolt it shut, and then the man was gone.

He looked at Peekaboo.

"There's only one known cure for a broken heart," she said, "it's time; and *that* don't work.

"If it worked, you see, it wu'nt be a broken heart, but just, 'you got your feelings hurt.' So you have to assess," she said, "your remaining assets. Older you get, the more experienced, which is to say heartbroke, or fucked up and fucked over, the more conservative you find yourself, anything good: 'How did I get here?,' 'How can I hold on to it, and what will I do when it's done?'

"Young girl does that, they call her 'mercantile,'" she said. "That's how they act on Lake Shore Drive. Girls *here*? I have to train them, I can, to instill in them the sense well-brought-up *white* girls schooled to practice from birth.

"You, all caught up in 'love,' so on, no wise disposed to consider someday it might end. You do that, it ain't 'love,' which is, we know, a form of madness."

Mike nodded. Peekaboo spread her hands to say, *Well, what* else *would it be?*

" 'Someday, I'm gon' be old,' the debutante may understand, but her mama surely knows it; and she better, she's young and slim, drag some fellow, as the song says, to 'the hitching post.'

"Her mama knows, the juices flowing, she's gon' get fucked in the summerhouse by *someone*—hope to God it ain't the gardener, but some fellow, they gon' make him *pay*. May *be* they in love. That's fine, too. More likely, the girl, her mama, thinking of the future; the boy, now, he's gettin' married, he's thinking of the future, too. The future, him, is, marry the girl, fulfill his duty, he might like her. Like her or not, he's got the money, he's still gon' be coming here, three times a month, he found *that* out on his honeymoon.

"*And* he might have been to France."

Mike smiled.

"Tell me about them French girls," she said. "Go on."

Mike shook his head.

"Oh, yeah, they *perfect*, 'cause they live in memory," Peekaboo said. "You turn it upside down, you never, the Irish girl, got to see her, screaming at you, she's right, you're wrong, and you the madder *for* it. Or getting old, or with the kids, or . . . I say yes. You mourning for something got torn from you; however much you two was in love, it had to, over time, you see, diminish, and 'give way to Worldly Cares.' Some extent. But you can't know that, how could you?"

Mike rose, and put his hand into his pocket.

"That for Dolly?" Peekaboo asked.

"For Dolly, yes," Mike said.

"Yeah, well, you *know*," Peekaboo said, "that girl likes you." Mike took a bill, and handed it to Peekaboo.

"Yeah, I can talk to her," Mike said.

Mike had spent the end of the slow evening and all of the subsequent night with Dolly. Everyone in the Ace, of course, knew Mike's story, and knew of his grief, and they treated him well.

He lay on the bed, in the middle of the night, he kicked off the covers and walked to the dresser. He looked back at Dolly in bed. He nodded at her, and at the bottle on the bureau.

"Yes, please," she said.

He poured two drinks.

He pointed at the compact on the bureau. The compact was open, and it showed full of cocaine. Dolly shook her head.

Also on the bureau was a small framed photograph. It showed ten smiling adolescents, in their Sunday clothes; and, at the end of the line, the black preacher. Each of the children held a rolled diploma—all were smiling. All were black save one slight white girl at the end of the line. The photo was marked *Confirmation Class, 1916, AME Church, Benton Harbor, Michigan.*

Mike looked at the photo.

"You in there?" he said. She nodded.

"Who's the white girl?" Mike said.

"Ain't no white girl," Dolly said.

"Which one are you?" Mike said.

"*You* full of questions," she said.

"Alright, ask *me* one," Mike said.

"Tell me about *your* white girl," she said.

"What have I been doing all night?" Mike said.

While Mike was dressing, Dolly went down to the kitchen, crying. She told the story, and was comforted by Peekaboo, who corrected her complaint.

"It ain't 'men,' it ain't even '*white* men,'" Peekaboo said, "but, you might say, it's human nature. Rare, *rare* is the person, you've known them long enough, you won't see them do something cruel, usually to *you*. Plus, what the hell you doing, get involved with the customers?

"Yeah, *I* learned, early on," Peekaboo said softly, "let them pay, here, to enjoy doing what they resent *there.* But they *got* to pay. Y'ever forget that, gonna be trouble."

"What they resent 'there'—'there' being?" Mike said. Both women looked at the door as Mike entered.

"At they home," Peekaboo said.

Mike stood at the back door, straightening his tie. "And what is it that they resent?" Mike said.

"Curious thing," Peekaboo said. "The men, they're courting you, all the 'yes, ma'am' in the world is insufficient, they get your panties off. Here, they ain't no question. But, this being a Better House, they enjoy, independent, treating the girls with respect. That is the curious thing. Here? They enjoy treating a girl well, *after* they fucked her.

"Yu-huh," Peekaboo said. "People think I'm selling pussy. They wife's *got* a pussy. No. I'm selling something else."

"What brought *that* up?" Mike said.

"First rule I ever learned, *I* was coming up, was make 'em take their hat off. No, that's a lie."

"What was the first rule?"

"First rule," Peekaboo said, "don't sell the same virgin to the same man twice. *That's* why you got to have a turnover in girls, you ever wondered."

"I'm simply grateful for the novelty," Mike said.

"I'd say the girls are, too, but all they see, they're *in* the life, 's the same cracked or mirrored ceiling. Well, each one to her trade." Peekaboo got up and walked to the door; she waved over her shoulder at Mike.

She turned back. "Last time I gave a man advice, he left me broke and bleeding. Kicked me out of the flat I was paying for, n'I *went*. Crawled into the gangway. Milkman found me, thought I was dead. May be I was.

"After you been dead, everything's easier. Isn't it?"

"Yes, it is," Mike said.

"I *know* it is," Peekaboo said. "People say, someday, it starts to turn around. But the people say that, it seems, people it never happened to. People it happened to recognize each other. That's why I say, black folks? Don't need the color on our skin to suss each other out."

Peekaboo walked back to the table and poured herself a drink. "Yeah," she said to herself, ". . . do it in the dark." She moved the bottle toward Mike's glass; he covered it with his hand. She batted his hand away.

"You gonna drink or *not?*" she said. "Don't fuck with me." She poured his tumbler full. He drained it and walked to the back door.

Mike opened the door, and stepped carefully into the small backyard. It was a paved area thirty by twenty feet. There was a low cement bench, up against the brick wall on the alley side. Had anyone ever been discovered sitting there, they would have been branded as an eccentric of a deviance to be shunned.

On one corner of the bench was a heavy brass key. Attached to the key was a purple tassel. There was an oaken door set into the bricks.

Mike used the key to open the door with the precise care of the inebriated. He passed into the alley, and relocked the door from the outside. He tossed the key back into the yard, and walked slowly down the alleyway.

There was the sound of a far-off fire truck, and then another, moving from east to west. The sound rose as the trucks crossed Mike's path, and then diminished. The alley gave onto Twenty-Third Street. Mike turned east, to walk toward the Lake.

Out on the Lake three ore boats were steaming south, to the steel mills in Gary.

Lake Michigan smelled like nothing else on Earth, Mike thought. It must have been the smell of home, for everyone gravitated to the Lake, and it was the Lake they thought of when they thought of home.

He'd once spent a chaste summer night with Annie Walsh on the Point, at Fifty-Fifth Street on the Lake.

Black and white families camped out there, summer nights, and Mike wrote that it was, for the South Side, the Waterhole, where the opposed were pleased to suspend hostilities. And the odd couple, waiting as long as they could, would retire under a blanket, all neighbors respecting the understanding that they were not there.

Annie and he had eaten the picnic lunch she'd brought. And Mike had drunk the wine, and the two cups of coffee in the thermos bottle. She had lain in his arms, awake, until the sun came up, and then he took her home.

That they had been to the Point was understood as both true and acceptable. Had they gone elsewhere, Mike would have been constrained to fabricate an excuse which all in her family would have known to be false. But the unspoken accord of the Fifty-Fifth Street Point extended to its use as an allowable excursion, its special status understood to depend on the truth of its invocation.

When Annie first came to his apartment, she insisted on returning home alone.

He never knew what excuses she made to her family, or if they demanded them or merely accepted, in anger, or in sorrow, or with resignation, her changed state.

For, certainly, she was changed; and, loved, had become even more beautiful.

Now every last thing stunned him into immobility: if it was better to light a cigarette or not, or have a cup of coffee, or go to the office, or leave the office. He remembered being able to decide these things, but not being unconscious of the choice.

In sober moments he recognized that this must be grief. It did not correspond, however, to any previous understanding of the term. He assumed, then, that he had not actually felt grief previously, upon either the deaths of his parents, or of his comrades, or of the enemy in France.

He reasoned with himself that his sorrow over these deaths was one thing, and this was another—that the first was understandable as sadness, an otherwise familiar emotion, merely, in these cases, magnified. But his loss of the girl was, to him, quite another thing.

Alcohol certainly helped.

And Parlow helped, by drinking with him.

He comprehended perfectly the concept that time would heal grief, but had lost all understanding of "time."

He decided to discover the murderers and kill them.

He had killed in France, in the air, which he did not mind at all; and killed strafing ground troops, which upset him.

And he had killed the observer in a Dornier, crashed just inside Allied lines, when he'd landed to strip the German plane of souvenirs.

He'd put down some fifty yards behind the shattered plane, and approached it from the rear, holding his pistol. He saw the pilot had been thrown from the plane and was lying in that rag doll posture never assumed in life.

He'd been walking forward, at once meditating on the transitory nature of things and mocking himself as a poseur, when he saw movement from the corner of his eye.

It was the plane's observer, slumped half out of his cockpit and swiveling the machine gun to point at him. He thought, as he watched, that it was strange that he had not heard the gun move on its rail. He saw the gunner's chest explode, and was surprised to realize that he had shot him.

He had no problem with death, and loved the notion of revenge, as the drunk loves the long-forgotten standby fifth of gin. But the thoughts would not stop. He knew that at some point they might lead him to resolution, but he had no notion when that point might be.

The thoughts, he supposed, were grief. Or guilt, or the impenetrable admixture. For he could not figure his way out of his state. He had been wrong, he knew, in his intimacy with the girl, *if,* which he could not in conscience determine, he had not truly intended to marry her. For it was easy to say after the fact; but, had he actually so intended, why had he not done so?

He had proposed to her. He had understood her demur as a merely formal statement, for he knew she loved him.

The problem to which neither needed to allude was his religion.

He supposed that her family would, if not embrace, likely accept him after a time, and after a conversion to Catholicism. He considered such conversion a price, but a small price for the possession of the girl. And he felt that he would be as true to the Catholic as he had been to the Protestant faith, which is to say not much at all.

He knew that his obeisance to its laws and strictures, whatever they might be, would be complete, if not sincere, and whose business was that but his?

But she was dead, and who had killed her? For,

however he understood it, whether accident or warning, her death must have been intended as a message to him—for who was the girl? Some lovely, some angelic, kind, and perfect being—not only incapable of having done harm, but too young to have accomplished any; unacquainted with evil until the moment of her death.

"Save for the sin of fornicating," Mike said, grasping to adopt some, as he imagined, Catholic formulation for their illicit love. But why the attack? Whom was the attack against?

If it was against himself, why had it failed? And, having failed, why was it not repeated?

Was it against the girl, as a warning to Mike or as a rebuke? For what?

He had spent his still-lucid moments considering the permutations. Her own family, or friends, had they been sent to murder him, would have done so.

He thought he had offended no power in Chicago sufficiently to require his death; not City Hall, not O'Banion and the North Side, nor Capone and the South Side.

But could it have been someone sent from downstate angered by his reportage? Such would most likely have been indicted not only by him, but by all the Chicago papers. Then why would he be singled out?

If it was not a warning to him, nor a penalty he had invoked, why had the murderer come? What good was a warning, or penalty, if the connection to him was unclear?

He'd thought, for the first drunken month, that her family had killed the girl because of its shame. Then his drunken reason cleared to the extent allowing him to see this as a Sicilian, but not an Irish, solution. The Sicilians, he knew, appreciated revenge not only as an art, but as a sacrament. He knew of the young Sicilian swain, in East Chicago, who had been discovered in bed with his fourteen-year-old cousin. She had had her throat cut, the boy forced to watch, and then emasculated, the Sicilians excising his penis, and leaving his testicles. This, it was explained to Mike, was the time-honored formula.

But Annie was Irish; their traditional response was to kill the man, and entomb the girl in a convent.

But if Mike was not the target, it must have been the girl. For what crime? For certainly, it had been none of *hers*. Whose crime, then? Her family? Who were they? Simple florists.

"Dion O'Banion?" he thought. "Why? The Irish are his own, and the folks of The Beautiful, his people. Al Capone and the Sicilians? Why? Because he's a brute?"

Those who considered Mr. Brown merely a brute

had overlooked the truest cruelty of the St. Valentine's Day Massacre: that the seven against the wall worked for O'Banion, a florist, and Capone had had them excised on his biggest day of the year.

The truest cruelty was irony, Mike thought, but where was the irony here?

Chapter 17

The memo had come "From the Desk of Colonel Robert R. McCormick, Publisher, *Chicago Tribune,* World's Greatest Newspaper." It read, *Stolen Limousines Human Interest.*

Parlow twisted it into a spill, lit it, and applied the burning memo to his pipe.

". . . won't draw," he said.

"It won't draw," he repeated, "the stem's broken." He leaned toward Mike Hodge.

Mike was seated across from him in their preferred side booth at the Sally Port.

"The limousines aren't news," Parlow said. "The *pipe* is news. The limousines aren't even human interest—are you listening to me?"

"I am a sick sonofabitch," Mike said.

"Yes?" Parlow said.

"The one thing. In which I could lose myself—"

"Oh, shut the fuck up," Parlow said.

"—in my life—"

"Perhaps I didn't make myself clear," Parlow said.

"—was the Irish girl."

"Yeah. Well, she's dead. So find something else, as it ain't funny anymore. You bore me," Parlow said. "*And I am sure you also, as you put it, 'lost yourself' in the joys of aviation. Up above the 'clouds,' and so on. Taking the lives of those who, but for a geographical accident, might have been your brothers.*"

Two fellows from the *American* came by, and started to slide into the booth. " 'Fireman, save my child,' the broad yells, fourth floor, tosses the baby to the fireman, he *catches* it, how? In his turn-out coat, held with his comrade. Kid *bounces: into* the arms of, who's standing by . . . ?"

"His uncle," Parlow said. "His father. Marie of Rumania and her pet dog Fluff."

"HIS FUCKEN *MOTHER*," the man said. "His *mother.*"

"His mother? Threw the kid, ran down, and caught it?" Parlow said.

"It wasn't his mother *threw* it, it was—"

"His aunt?"

"They said it was his aunt. It was the cooze his father was fucking. The father? Brought the kid along, 'Lay on the sofa, don't move for half an hour.'"

"It *had* been his mother," Parlow said, "*she* tossed him down, you're right, ran down to catch him, she would have been better off, lug the kid down with her."

"They told me, it's his *aunt*, so there it is," the man said.

"Who set the fire?" Mike asked.

"Ah," Parlow said, "there's the *interesting* thing . . ."

Later they sat alone at Hop Li's. "The problem with the Chinks," Parlow said, "is that you cannot *close* the joint.

"Nighthawks," Parlow said, "cops, nurses, newsghouls, compositors, ink on their hands." He inclined his head at the men coming off the night shift. They were generally large and gray, Slavic looking. Many wore coveralls beneath their street jackets. Many still wore the square-folded newsprint hat the making of which was the first skill any of them learned, as youths, their first day on the job.

"Ink on their fingers, ink in their blood," Parlow said. Mike had been silent for the last hour. Parlow drank hooch from the small porcelain cups and smoked his pipe.

Mike looked at him. "I taught her 'The Sheik of Araby,'" he said. "The *real* version."

"The *real* version?" Parlow said. Mike nodded. "That's an honor," Parlow said, "to've been the first to have taught her the song. Yeaaah, you can't close the joint."

"You want to go home, *go* home," Mike said.

"*This* is my home," Parlow said.

"Yeah, I taught her," Mike said, "'The Sheik of Araby.'"

"I'm sure you did," Parlow said.

"Sing it with me," Mike said.

Parlow sat silent.

"Fucken Clem . . . ?" Mike said. "*Valentino?* Did he, for the love of Christ, die in vain? Broads, threw themselves off the second-story window, slit their wrists, the blood ran—n'you won't sing 'The Sheik of Araby' . . . ?"

"Mike," Parlow said, "you want to jump off into your nut bag, imitate a drunk, and so on, your own business. It, however, is a load of bullshit. What are you now, 'abashed'?"

Mike waved his hand for one more round. The waiter nodded and started toward the bar.

"Or, *I* tell you what," Parlow said, "how about you

write 'How many have to die, weep weep.' You want to do *that* one?"

Mike looked at him. "How many have to die of what?" he said.

"The fuck do *I* care," Parlow said. "I have no sympathy for you in the *first* place."

"The fuck you don't," Mike said.

"The fuck I do," Parlow said. "Any girl so sheltered that she never heard 'The Sheik of Araby,' with the filthy lyrics, what business have you to deflower her at *all?* Now you tell me, 'They all have to start *someplace.*' What?"

Mike shook his head.

"This is called grief," Parlow said. "It is, by custom, you remember, suffered in, and only expressed by, silence. So, this bullshit about 'The Sheik' is not your pure D grief, but funny voices. Hiding what-could-it-be?"

"What?"

"You tell *me.*"

"What?"

"You tell *me.*"

"Shame."

"That's right," Parlow said. "Shame that you can't shut up. Jesus Christ. Shut up or *do* something about it. Or blow your brains out. I no longer care."

The new drinks arrived. Parlow and Mike both watched the waiter as he served them. Both admired his absence of falsity in the presence of guilt. Parlow nodded at Mike, to say, *You* see? Mike nodded back.

"*Well* then," Parlow said.

"Shame because I got her killed," Mike said.

Parlow shrugged.

"*Did* I get her killed?"

"How the fuck do *I* know?" Parlow said. "*We* don't know: *who* he was, *whom* he was gunning for, *or* what price glory?"

Mike downed his drink, took Parlow's, and drank that, too. Parlow raised the teapot to refill the cups, and found it empty. "Would somebody, for the love of Christ, just bring the *bottle*?" Parlow said. ". . . Fucken Chinks."

Poochy walked in, reading a newspaper. He put his camera case down on the bar, and waved his finger for a drink. He saw Parlow and Mike and came to their table, pointing at the paper.

"Did you hear about the broad caught the kid?" he said. "Mike?"

"*Poochy*," Mike said. "Poochy. The story you have read is bullshit. The broad, first of all, threw the kid, was not his aunt, but the father's doxy; second of all, no infant's going to survive a four-story fall, however firemen stretch out their overcoat. Third of all, whyn't they use the *net*? And, and, the *true* story, given the above, the wife came, her husband is fucking some girl upstairs, *why is she there, if not to set the fire?* And finally, it never happened."

"How do you know it never happened?" Poochy asked.

"Because," Mike said, "Fitzgerald and Ross, from the *American,* came in all 'reporting' it and so on, didn't smell like smoke."

"You've just broken my heart," Parlow said.

Poochy shook his head in sadness. "Show me one thing that's on the level," he said.

Mike took the paper. "Page eight," Poochy said.

"Page *eight*? You're reading something's on page *eight*?"

"I turned to it by accident," Poochy said.

Mike opened the paper and read. " 'Ex Africa Semper Aliquid Novi.' Who wrote this shit . . . ?"

Parlow leaned over to read the byline. "Fitzgerald," he said.

" 'Out of Africa Always Something New, as Tacitus said. And as we, now, say of *our* own Africa of the South Side—State Street, Thirty-Third Street, our sepia Broadway known as "The Stroll." Early this morning, firemen responded to . . .' "

"It wasn't Tacitus," Parlow said.

"Who was it?" Mike said.

"How the fuck would *I* know?" Parlow said.

" 'Yea, south of that equator which is Madison Street, life, at its fullest . . .' " Mike continued reading. "Nothing about the aunt," he said, "or whoever it was on the fourth floor."

"Maybe they just did it to sell papers," Parlow said.

Mike put the paper down and stared.

"Yeah, *that's* a life, ain't it?" he said.

Parlow said, "Something on your mind?"

"I need to talk to somebody," Mike said.

"And who would that *be*?" Parlow said.

Mike said, "I need to talk to the Italians."

Chapter 18

It was long and widely acknowledged that Parlow knew everyone. He had, as he put it, "a three-cornered connection" with the Italians; he was "an associate member" of the Japanese community, and as such was acquainted with the Chinese through a shared affection for "things Oriental," or "opium."

When Mike first saw the pipe and bowl, at Parlow's flat, he'd said, "Well, *that* explains a lot."

"Show me the man content to slog through life on the natch," Parlow had said, "but, having shown me, let us leave him and find more congenial companions."

In what he characterized as his "sadly infrequent debauches," he had, as he said, "mingled with the great and near great, in that atmosphere of love on the hip.

Love untrammeled, unknown and unknowable to those stuck, straight-up, and confused, upon this shithole."

Mike had said, "This, then, accounts for your lack of ambition," and Parlow had said, "Let us say 'it contributes.'"

Among his boon companions were several users and suppliers from the South Side.

Parlow, on Mike's behalf, had requested an interview with "someone in power" from his friends on the South Side; and Mike was invited to drop by their headquarters, the Metropole Hotel, at four P.M.

In the slack time the waiters were preparing for the dinner crowd. A shirt-sleeved man was tuning the grand piano in the hotel lobby.

Mike was walked to the dining room entrance and frisked quite thoroughly by a small, slim, and vicious-looking man. His overcoat and hat were taken, and he was passed into the dining room.

"Keep your hands on the table," the man said. Two middle-aged men in shirt-sleeves sat at a corner booth, going through a ledger. A third man sat alone in the next booth, eating a pastry and sipping espresso.

Mike approached the banquette, and the older, heavier man looked at him. "Siddown," he said.

Mike sat in the dining chair across from the two men. The older of the two was Jake Guzik, head book-keeper of the Capone Mob. "We know who you are," Guzik said. "We're sorry for your loss. We assume that's why you're here. We understand that you may want, what is it? Information . . . ? Revenge?"

Mike started to speak. The man raised his hand. "And it benefits, of course, no one for you to go around half-cocked."

From the corner of his eye Mike saw the slim man, now standing at the bar, his eyes lightly but definitely fixed on Mike.

"I appreciate you seeing me," Mike said.

"We didn't do it," Guzik said. Mike nodded. "Was that your question?" Mike shrugged.

"Look," Guzik said, "look: do you see what a per-fect position, you understand, your question might put us in? Bring him a cuppa coffee . . . ," he called. The bartender, across the room, poured a cup and carried it, on a saucer, to their table.

"We could tell you *anything*—you fly off, and take out somebody we'd like gone, which, you understand, is for us, a gimme. Or, we point you toward whom-it-may-be, and you take after him in print, making his life difficult. We could do that."

"Why don't you?" Mike said. "Why would you do anything for me?"

"*Because*," Guzik said, "you make people laugh, how 'bout that?

"Who might also respect, some people, that you are a straight shooter, and that you fought in France." Guzik cleared his throat. "And wrote about the All Saints fire."

"Who shot the Irish girl?" Mike said.

"It's a violent city," Guzik said.

"You saying you don't know who shot her?"

"That's the legitimate question," the man said, "given that we had you to the meeting. The embarrassing answer is: that's correct."

Mike shrugged. "Thank you," he said.

"That's alright," the man said. "Two things we hope," he said, "is that you find peace, and that you don't do anything foolish."

The bodyguard motioned Mike back to the dining room door. Mike stood and walked out past Al Capone, finishing his meal in the adjoining booth. Each mimed ignorance of the other's existence.

"Well," Peekaboo said, "they *could've*, easy enough, put you on the send, kill somebody. But they turned *that* card faceup, why?"

"They wanted me to believe them."

"That's right," Peekaboo said. "So the question is: other than what they said was *true*, where's their advantage?"

"I can't see it," Mike said.

"Neither can *I*," Peekaboo said. "Maybe it's true. Unless they just felt sorry for you. I don't know, they confessed to ignorance, which is weakness, what they saying is, 'I been there, *too*.' Which is an offer of sympathy."

"I, uh . . . ," Mike said.

"Well, we know they're sentimental," Peekaboo said.

"Most crooks are," Mike said.

"Yeah, maybe," Peekaboo said. "When it costs them nothing. But show me someone is sentimental about their own, their *own* wretchedness."

"And what is the cure for wretchedness?" Mike said.

"We were down south?" Peekaboo said. "Yeah," she said, "we were down south and they took my brother out. The thing in those days was stump hanging. They would take and nail a man's *privates*, or, as we say, 'dick and balls,' to a stump. Using, it came to hand, a rusty spike. A *railroad* spike . . ."

She looked down at Mike, who nodded slightly.

". . . railroad spike, drive it in with a sledgehammer, an' leave him there. 'N' go off. *Either* leaving him there to die, or, the case may be, his friends come to him, aft they *left,* to cut him loose." She looked at the window, and scratched a fingernail through the frost on the pane.

"*I* always thought," she said, "worst thing was, his friends coming up, man, overcome with shame, how would he take it, accepting their aid, which was to emasculate him, cut him free—*he* wanted was to die.

"And they told me, they come upon him, he was dead . . ." Mike raised his head and looked at her. "We knew he wasn't dead," she said, "as the white boys, killing him, would've spoiled their glee, you see. Of some fitting punishment, some ongoing thing."

"What were they punishing him for?" Mike said.

"Being black," Peekaboo said. "Their pretext being that he was fucking some white girl in town. Li'l white whore."

"Was he?" Mike said.

"Yes. He was," Peekaboo said. "But he wu'nt paying *her. Uh*-uh. And then, to her mind, he *tired* of her, an' she went and had her revenge.

"But I always knew. Either they killed him, his friends, at his request. Or he asked them for a moment, and the knife, and he did it hisself." She picked a tobacco crumb from her lip.

"He was twenty-two years old. We mourned for him. The pastor, n'th' undertaker, wu'nt let us see him, you know, below the neck.

"Well. I'd've killed those motherfuckers. Boys wanted to, the men. Whites would've struck back, of course. That didn't stop the odd road accident. White boy was killed by accident, driving too fast. Out *hunting*, tripped ov'a log, shot himself, all that.

"Whyn'tcha take off your coat? . . . S'hot in here," she said. "You, I know, read all that shit, *Belgium*, and so on, Germans raping nuns."

"I wasn't in Belgium," Mike said.

"Take off your coat," Peekaboo said.

Mike looked around, and then shrugged himself out of his coat, then took off his jacket.

"No, you wu'nt in Belgium, you were in . . . *where* were you in?"

"France," Mike said.

"Oh yes. And saw all of them sporty houses in Paris?"

"Not exactly," Mike said.

"*No?*" Peekaboo said.

"You could have any girl in Europe for a stick of gum," Mike said.

"Princess, and all that . . . ?" Peekaboo said.

"You bet," Mike said.

"Well, how about that," Peekaboo said.

They sat silently for a while.

". . . Drifting away, drifting away," Peekaboo said. "Some do that. *You've* seen 'em, I would guess? Over there? Those, can't put it together again. Or never was together at all. *This,* or the *coke,* or whatever kills them quicker. Someone said, 'They do it to live,' but we know better."

She took a long drag on her cigarette. She put her head back and blew smoke at the ceiling.

"Drifting away," she said. "Or call on Jesus, those who can, 'who washes away all despair.' But you could, as soon, do that with a cut-throat razor. Some girls? Did themselves? This very house."

Peekaboo stared down at the tabletop. She tapped the cigarette ash into the ashtray.

"*I* don't blame 'em," she said.

She poured two drinks.

Mike reached over and threw down the proffered shot of rum. He poured another from the bottle.

"Folks go insane," Peekaboo said, "I heard, many of 'em, over there, woke up one morning, 'Thiz my day to die,' they *feel* it. Is that true?"

"That might be true," Mike said.

"Because," Peekaboo said, "anybody, long enough

life, see things, turn your hair? Straight or curly. *Depending.*

"Many things might be cured, by the Grace of God, and I won't say no; for I've seen it, but I can't say that it touched me, other than, it spared me, come this far, or long, or however you put it, for all the times one would think, 'That's not a blessing.' "

The answer to his grief became clearer to him as he drank himself into a coma. And that answer was to obliterate the question. He holed up in his flat, where he was found by Parlow, from whose care he escaped. He was next discovered, bloody and raving, at LaSalle and Jackson, by a cop. He had assaulted the cop and was clubbed to the ground.

The *Tribune*'s lawyers pulled the necessary strings. The charge of assault was quashed, and Mike was remanded to the custody and bond of Clement Parlow.

Chapter 19

Parlow took him to Yuniko's flat. He came morning and evening, with the doctor, and sometimes stopped by in the afternoon, to sit and smoke a cigarette.

The doctor injected the paraldehyde. After a week, the delirium tremens had passed, but the injections continued. Mike supposed that they were opiates. In any case, they made him drowsy, and he reflected that longing to die gave one a magnificent freedom to not give a shit about any other thing.

There was an old Japanese man in a cardigan. He must have been nearby, for any unusual noise or movement on Mike's part brought him into the room.

In the beginning he administered the alcohol, one

ounce, every two hours, day and night. He always found Mike awake, and waiting.

The man brought thin soup and hardtack twice a day. Most of the food was taken away uneaten, and Mike's body began to stink of the excreted alcohol, the paraldehyde, and of the famine devouring it.

He had obtained some solace from the revelation that his mind, equally, was rotten, but that soon passed, and he was left with the fact.

He remembered a poem, a long-ago, schooldays poem.

"If it chance your eye offend you, pluck it out, lad, and be whole . . . But play the man, stand up and end you, when the sickness is your soul."

He found comfort in thinking the poet, as he had when he was young, a fraud and a fool. For who could advise the tortured who was not tortured himself; and, if so tortured, why had the adviser not taken his own advice?

He could not understand how the girl could have died, and recurred to a problem which, to him, seemed the easier: who had committed the murder, and in retribution or warning for what offenses of Mike's commission?

But, in truth, the two questions were not connected.

Mike realized he had devolved to the second, as it was, at least potentially, capable of solution. But he could reason his way to no solution, given all the time in the world, which his incarceration seemed to him, each moment not being longer than the previous, but quite long enough to last forever.

"An understanding of the process," Parlow had said, "does not exempt one from the process."

"What could exempt one from the process?" Mike had asked. He remembered they had been speaking of lust, or love, but he could not remember which.

He spent the day sleeping when he could. Often, in half sleep, he would hear the doctor speaking low, to Parlow. He remembered a voice which must have been that of his caretaker, speaking in Japanese, and, perhaps, being answered by a woman. But he never saw the woman. He assumed that she must have been Yuniko, Parlow's mistress, and smiled remembering the cub reporter's lesson "Never assume."

Mike relished any train of thought which he might follow, for whatever time, to turn himself from his obsession with suicide.

"Pat and Mike were found dead on the living room floor. The only clues were a pool of water around them, and a cat in the corner. Figure it out." Every cub re-

porter heard it in his first week, at the bar, from an old
souse.

"Never assume."

"Pat and Mike were goldfish," Mike said aloud. He
smiled.

And then the story that he told himself was done,
and his thoughts were not his own. He alternated between outright delirium and obsession. He subdued
himself, occasionally, with the making of lists.

His lists were his bequests. He had few possessions,
but it occupied him to plan their distribution. Each
would be accompanied by a note which would, as if
that were required, further establish his thoughtful-
ness, and, thus, the loss, to the world, of his presence.

He would assign the speech "We never knew how
much he suffered" now to this recipient, now to that
one, then smile, to himself, at his fatuousness. But he
did not stop making lists.

There was a girl he'd wronged, so many years ago.

He'd told the story to Peekaboo, at the end of one
drunken night.

One of the girls was cooking breakfast. Breakfast
was a skillet-fry of the night's unsold meals. There were
always potatoes and eggs, and meat or fish, and it was
highly spiced and peppered. "They, one time," Peeka-

boo had said, "the Nawlins girls, called it pottifer—
I know that's pot-au-feu—but no one else, I ever knew,
just called it anything. One thing I *do* know: to make
it, you have to be a whore."

The girl at the stove and Marcus nodded. "Or have
been a whore," Peekaboo said, "or you can't make it."

The girl ladled out two large helpings into bowls,
and set the bowls before Peekaboo and Mike.

"Thank you, honey," Peekaboo said.

"Y'ever heard of puttanesca?" Mike said.

"No, I have not," Peekaboo said.

"In Italy, they make it with macaroni."

"Uh-huh," Peekaboo said.

"*Puttanesca* means 'whorehouse style.'"

"No, you don't tell me," Peekaboo said.

"That's right," Mike said.

"How about that," Peekaboo said. "What's in it?"

"Macaroni," Mike said, "eggs, bacon, ham, *chicken*,
whatever they have at the end of the day." Everyone
in the kitchen nodded their appreciation of the human
variations on a theme.

"'N' the main thing," Peekaboo said, "is, *spiced*, I
mean spiced; and beer or gin, you have to, burn the
damn thing *out*."

The damned thing, Mike had understood, was the
night. And its exertions and trauma.

Mike had confessed his desertion of what, for the purpose of the story, he had remembered as his first young love. "Honey," Peekaboo said, "*that* girl? Forgot you *long* ago. *One:* that's the way of the world." She gestured, indicating her entire establishment. "*You* see what men are. You think you immune? Being so nice and all, to your self-consideration? Human as you are? She din't get fucked over by you? Wait ten minutes, the next man comes along. She forgot you *long* ago.

"She could go out, a virgin again, marry the bank clerk; you, on the other hand, got to carry it around, all this time, around your neck, like some locket. 'How good I must be, 'cause watch how bad I feel.' That's bullshit of a high degree. Now you can throw that magic charm away. It makes you feel too good."

In the Japanese girl's room he toyed with adding his youthful betrayal to what he thought of as his murder of Annie Walsh. He was diverted to find that it neither increased nor lessened his anguish, which was, he knew, neither grief nor remorse, but madness; differing from them in that it could be neither studied nor manipulated.

A month passed. Parlow and the doctor came.

Mike asked for more substantial food. It was brought

to him, and the liquor was discontinued. When six hours had passed without the ration of alcohol, Mike rummaged the apartment. He found twenty-two dollars in a ceramic jar on a kitchen shelf. He took it and left.

PART TWO

PART TWO

Chapter 20

He stayed sick drunk in the Fox River cabin. His bootlegger, the Polish kid from Milwaukee, came by on his rounds twice a week bringing liquor and food. The food remained mostly untouched. The kid asked Mike if he'd been "over there." Mike said he'd been too young. The kid commiserated that he'd been too young, too. They agreed they'd never know what they'd missed, and there would never be a show like that again.

Mike agreed to anything to get the kid to leave. His conversation was like the excruciating probing of a wound, and after the second exchange Mike always wanted to kill him. He noted that this was a different rage from that he'd felt, time to time, in combat.

He had experienced air combat as calculation. That

a Hun had shot down one of his comrades in no wise increased his determination to kill, nor did it alter his mood: he was there to shoot the other fellow down in the air, or shoot him up, if on the ground, and that was that.

He loathed the engineers of the War, the bureaucrats, the generals, and the press. If the push of a button or some similar mechanism could have consigned them to eternity he would have done it with exuberance. At first, noticing this hatred, he questioned himself at some length: but what about their families, their children, their supposed good deeds, and so on, he wondered. They weighted not at all. He wondered if this willingness to kill was the same as theirs. No, he reasoned, theirs was ideological. They could never, at their most murderous, and with the utmost success of their mindless, careless violent schemes, know the self-righteous bliss which overcame him when he fantasized their deaths.

He had heard, from many, of the German Atrocities, of the infants bayoneted, the children's hands cut off, and so on. He had never doubted that some of the stories were true. "They might be true," he thought, "we are capable of most anything."

But he did not hold it against the Germans that they had had stories told about them. He, encountering a

German, would consider the man like himself. And try to kill him.

They had all heard of the Christmas Truce of '14, and of '15. He'd spoken to infantry who claimed to've been part of it. He doubted their stories, as most of the infantry of the first two years was, of course, dead. But, giving them the benefit of the doubt for the sake of the entertainment, he'd listened to the history of the truce: how first one man on one side, then his opposite number, would emerge from the trench.

How these men, brave or insane, would meet in No Man's Land, and exchange tobacco and schnapps, how the truce would spread to whole battalions, meeting in No Man's Land on Christmas Day to fraternize, to sing, and to trade cap badges, until, as with any fairy tale, at the stroke of midnight . . .

"Well and good," Mike thought.

He knew of two fliers, escaped to Switzerland, and repatriated, who related princely treatment at the German bases where they'd been transported.

"There is the myth of Glorious Single Combat," Mike said, "its most pernicious feature that it's true." Like any aviator, he held in profound respect any maneuver he saw executed well. It did not seem to him incongruous that some of those so well skilled might use those skills to kill him.

Anyone who'd ever flown knew, on takeoff, not only that the flight could be his last, but *would* be, if he was not both diligent about and doubtful of every aspect of the expedition.

To his fellow fliers, death, though not preferable, was not an illogical nor unmerited penalty for lack of skill; nor was it either unfair or discreditable to have run out of luck.

One might fear terrible disfigurement, but there was always the antidote, administered by oneself or one's friends.

A two-place Nieuport had crashed in flames on the field. The pilot's flying suit was burning. Two mechanics dragged him from the cockpit, five yards away from the plane, and beat the fire out with blankets. A third had ducked back into the hut, emerged chambering a round in his Springfield, and run toward the plane to shoot the trapped observer.

And one might long for home, which, finally, always meant Mother, or good loving; past that, Mike saw, "home" had little meaning, nor had it come to mean much more in the years since his return.

He had loved his job, and its proximity to violence, which, he knew, was a drug, and he had loved the Irish girl; and now he was sick and grieving in that impossible grief of betrayal at having your heart broken by life.

The redheaded Polish boy lounged by the woodstove, cleaning his long filthy nails with a splinter. He cleaned each nail at length, and examined the end of the splinter, and Mike thought, "This time I will kill him."

He was talking about several of his uncle's friends, and their methods of jacklighting deer. This led him to a discussion of their wives, and their wives' cooking.

"They took me, my uncle, to eat some of the venison," he said, "at Uncle Wally's house; he wasn't really my uncle, the Polish word is '*pan*,' which means, not like 'uncle,' but closer than 'mister.' *His* wife, I thought her name was Zosh, but that was his *daughter*, I think."

Mike realized that he'd met very few truly stupid people. In his right mind, he thought, he might have treasured this boy as a perfected miracle; but he was sick, and drunk.

Only noticing the kid's shocked, hurt expression did he realize he'd said, "I fucking need to be alone." The kid looked slapped. He took a moment to process the insult, then rose, and left the cabin.

"It can't be the first time anyone told the fool to shut up. Or perhaps he has learned his trick so well that everyone feels sorry for him. Well, *fuck* him," Mike thought.

The murderous objects in the cabin reverted to their intended, peaceable uses: the maul, the poker, the kitchen knife; the room slowly recovered from its adventure as a butcher's den.

Mike was still shaking with adrenaline. "Well, I suppose that I was actually going to kill him," he thought. The rumination gave him a few more moments of continued freedom from his sorrow. Mike now felt a love for the Polish kid, who had distracted him. "It would have been increased," he thought, "if I had actually killed him," which extended the fantasy once again. Mike toyed with it most of the afternoon, until it had cycled down, and he was left, once again, with nothing.

Parlow had joked that his country owed Mike an incalculable debt, as he was the only returned veteran who had not published a book about the War.

"There's nothing you can say about it," Mike said. " 'N' if there was I wouldn't say it."

The explanation, retold at the Port, gained Mike an increase, if not in status, then in appreciation of his sagacity, the general opinion of the old hands being, "This kid, it seems, has been holding back."

And, Mike had concluded, neither was there anything to be said about aviation, which, he'd told the boys one drunken night, was like sex: you had to be there.

He'd deeply regretted the quip, as information of a private nature shared with uninitiates for a laugh.

For the two (and it was no one's business but the flier's) were, of course, linked. And barring a consideration of "mother," or "the girl next door," few of the fliers would have dreaded death but for its unfortunate curtailment of flying, or of fornication with the odd teenage barmaid.

And now Mike's life had been corrupted by the death of his girl. "What kind of men," he wondered, "would kill an innocent girl?" The answer, of course, was "bad men," and he was back where he started, his perseverative thoughts themselves becoming overused, and leaving him with incathectable rage, and loss. "Bad men," and he was, of course, one of them.

For he had truly loved the Irish girl. "Who wouldn't love her? There was no merit in it," he thought. "She was an angel."

He returned, as often as he dared, to memories of their meeting—rationing them in concern that overuse might render them stale.

The compact of their love-at-first-sight had been

concluded, as all are, on the instant, leaving Mike dazed. He'd once had that bright idea the boys at the Port referred to as an *appersoo*—that gangdom could be charted through observation of its florists—and followed the flag. The flag, in this case, was the florist's tag, WALSH'S THE BEAUTIFUL, adorning the larger and more lavish gangland tributes.

Mike had opened the glass door giving on Clark Street.

On his first visit Mike had prepared no story to explain his presence, feeling, as he always did, that to concoct an improvisation in advance was cheating. He would, as always, trust to his inspiration and his luck.

But the various, and obvious, possibilities: My aunt died, I am planning a wedding, or, in extremis, I write for the *Trib*, and we're doing a feature about holiday arrangements, these and their mundane like fled from Mike. He did not remark their flight, but stood tongue-tied, looking at the girl behind the counter, who was looking back at him.

Some time passed and neither he nor the girl had moved. It was the strangest impulse he was ever to feel in life: to walk behind the counter and have her; and she slowly turned, and he saw that she knew it. She lowered her eyes in the most primal gesture of modesty and acquiescence. He began to move toward her. The bell over the door jingled as a customer entered the shop.

Mike turned to the owner. "I'm a reporter," he said, "and I'm doing a story about out-of-season flowers."

The girl smiled.

The elevated train ran close to the second-floor windows of his flat. On her first visit she'd started at the noise. Afterward, she, like the residents, ceased to notice it.

In his reverie it was always winter. His grief did not run to the real memories of swimming at Rainbow Beach, or of fall walks along the Lake, out to the North Avenue breakwater, where they, like everyone else, always stopped to look back at the city, now revealed as beautiful.

He thought of her, unceasingly, naked, and huddled beneath the blankets much too rough for her Irish skin. Of her white body, wrapped in his dressing gown, nestling with him in the bed. She could not do so anymore, as she was dead.

The cycle of regret, self-pity, longing, and guilt could be interrupted only by alcohol; the alcohol was killing him, and he was grateful.

Chapter 21

By a disposition matured by experience, Parlow had come to distrust everything.

The ancient sign displayed in the City Room could still be made out. It read, *Believe little that you see and nothing that you hear.* It was the declaration of his faith; and like any truly embraced faith, its pursuit exacted a price and rewarded devotion. The price was not only that the acolyte acknowledged life as an exercise in folly, wickedness, and deceit, but that this perception did not debar him from participation in that evil world—and that a true knowledge of the world must involve doubt not only of his fellows, but of his own mental processes and reason.

Mike was long past remarking the hypocrisy and

folly of others, but increasingly aware of it in himself. What was there to say at the speaks, at the crime scenes, the lockup, the morgue, the gravesite, the mourner's flat? There was nothing to say. There was drink, and the darkest humor, and there was silence; and if there indeed was a God, the only possible relation to Him, for the reporters, was through the aforementioned observances.

But, as with any strict religious observance, there was a reward. And the reward, for the reporter, was this: that occasionally, he might discover the truth.

Occasionally, through a diligence or intuition always dismissed as luck, he might find out the murderer, the hidden bank account, the absconded husband or wife, the one piece which would make the otherwise random collection of unfortunate facts cohere into a finally human narrative.

The constant practice of doubt as to the material, and disbelief of all human testimony, created, in reporters, as in the judges, the cops, the nurses, and others of the tribe of the night, various instincts.

Having seen lies almost exclusively, the rare instance of the truth was, to them, easily identifiable. Their lives were founded on doubt, but they were not given to denial; their one unassailable devotion was to the truth independent of its acceptability, or in fact, utility. It was to them the One Good. Put on the scent of truth, they proceeded fairly oblivious to blandishment, intimidation, or distraction.

Parlow spoke, now and again, of his old friend "likelihood."

"Mr. Parlow," a cub might attempt, "how did you know to question X rather than Y," or "What inspired you to call the marina in addition to the auto rental garage?"

"Son," he would say, "there's two things: Probability. And likelihood. Is it probable the reverend clergyman screwed and killed this young parishioner? You bet it is. Now, *had* he done so, what is it *likely* he did next? He says he didn't do it. He says he was home alone, in prayer. If so, is it likely that he'd fixed himself a snack? I'd think so. What do you think? Five hours of an evening, all alone? A fellow makes himself a light repast.

"We're in the kitchen. No dishes in the sink. No dishes in the dish rack. Or on the shelf, no trace of water. *No* scraps of food, tea bags, empty cans, in the kitchen wastebasket?"

"It's possible," the cub said.

"Good for you," Parlow said. "However, *this:* Fellow's a smoker. Wire-to-wire. Five hours at home. No butts in the ashtrays. He emptied the ashtrays? No butts in the wastebasket. *This* man was not home.

"Not being home is no crime. But not being home and lying about it means he's covering something up. Is it *likely*, the evening this young parishioner of his, who had been 'receiving instruction,' was killed, coincidentally, our man's out doing something else, *unrelated*, that he needs to lie about? It ain't likely. It's impossible.

"And a man went to the chair because, when he constructed his lie, he forgot to fill his ashtrays. And," Parlow said, "we asked: as he was not home, where was it likely he was?"

And now he asked himself the same question of Mike Hodge.

Mike was not to be found in his apartment, nor in the apartment of Yuniko, nor in the haunts of the *Tribune*.

It was most likely, Parlow determined, he had gone to ground, as will any wounded animal, where he might find safety and comfort.

So Parlow went to the Ace of Spades.

"I have not seen him," Peekaboo said, "but if you find him, you tell him, they ain't no shame to fall off the wagon, and that, spirit moves him, he knows he can come in here, and either be here, as he wants, or drink himself to death, either one. He knows he's welcome here."

Parlow then tried the Golden Dragon. And Hop Li said that, yes, Mike had come in.

"To score?" Parlow said.

"I think he kick that shit," Hop Li said. "He came in to borrow money."

"You help him?" Parlow said.

Hop Li shrugged. "And then he left," he said.

"What do I owe you?" Parlow said; but Hop Li shook his head. Parlow turned to go; then, in an inspired moment, turned and asked, "Where was he going?"

"I ast him."

"What did he say?"

Hop Li shrugged. "He just made this gesture."

Hop Li swung a forefinger around the horizon. Parlow had seen the gesture before.

Chapter 22

Parlow found Mike in the Hunt Club cabin on Fox River.

Parlow tried the door, it was unlocked. He opened it and the stink of the room hit him. Mike sat at the dirty kitchen table. There were three full and two empty bottles in front of him, a dirty glass, cigarettes, and the Luger pistol.

"What the *fuck*," Parlow said, "is your idea of cleanliness?"

Parlow took a chair to the table. He sat down.

"It, apparently," Parlow said, "is a delicate mechanism."

Mike said nothing.

"Did you hear me?" Parlow said. "It's a delicate mechanism. *You* say something."

"What is that?" Mike said. " 'The mind'?"

"Yes, the mind, yes," Parlow said.

The Luger pistol lay on a spread red bandanna, on the table, next to Mike's chair. The bandanna was stiff with gun oil. A rusty oil bottle and two bore brushes sat on the table. Parlow tried the cap of the oil bottle and found it caked shut. The pistol was coated with dust. A new box of cartridges covered a corner of the bandanna. Parlow opened it.

"Oh, very funny," Parlow said, "accidentally shot while cleaning his gun."

Mike shrugged.

Parlow dropped the magazine out of the gun. The magazine was empty. He pinched back the bolt, and saw the single cartridge in the chamber. The toggle bolt was unoiled, and rasped as he drew it back. "Gun's filthy," he said.

"We all have our little ways," Mike said.

"That's sweet," Parlow said. "How they will miss me, who, even in death, assuaged their feelings, by providing an alternative solution. No, he did not take his own life, thereby depriving us of his diverting presence; he would not have done that, no. He shot himself 'by accident,' cleaning a gun he did not get around to cleaning, with a cartridge which, curiously, was shiny-new." Parlow racked the bolt all the way back and the ejected cartridge fell on the cabin floor.

"So my question to *you* is: given the evidence, what the *hell* are you doing?"

Mike took a drink.

"You wanted to kill yourself, you would have done it," Parlow said, "without all this 'pantomime.'" He picked up the corner of the bandanna. "Thus, by induction, you did *not* want to 'end it all.'"

Parlow picked up the ejected shell and dropped it, the extracted magazine, and the gun into his overcoat pocket.

"What if I want to later?" Mike said.

"You want to later? You, you fucken coward," Parlow said. "I never thought I'd use the word. There *is* no later. You had your chance, you were in the throes of grief. You want to later, it would be out of some stupid feeling of consistency. Where's the glory in that?"

"Fuck you," Mike said.

"'I didn't kill myself, consumed by grief, *now* I'm going to do it from a sense of fitness.' *If*," Parlow said, "excuse me, *if*, and this is brilliant, 'it all' was your life. No. You wanted, and I must assume this is what all the alienists get paid for, listening to unloved, rich, fat women, 'You Wanted to End the Suffering!' Is that

226 • DAVID MAMET

what you wanted to do? 'Cause your husband no longer wants to fuck you?

"Sitting here? In your grief. With your German pistol. Your dilemma, then, was not that you wanted to die, but that 'dying,' and here I impress even myself, was the sole escape you, in your state, could imagine from that sorrow you had, at this advanced age, discovered is an inescapable part of life. How am I doing?"

"I wanted nothing more, in my life, than to go outside, and sit against the tree, and blow my brains out," Mike said.

"That is an untruth," Parlow said. "For, had it been true, truly, you would have done it. Show me the error in my logic. You wanted, more than anything in life, to imagine some end to your pain other than that. That's obvious."

Mike poured two drinks, and pushed a glass toward Parlow.

"There are times," Parlow said, "when a fellow has to sober up."

"Why?" Mike said.

"Because the only alternatives are blowing your brains out, which you did not do, and dying of alcohol poisoning, sitting in your own shit and terrified of the bugs on the wall."

On the table were several sheets of paper. The paper

was covered with handwritten notes. Parlow began to read: "He wanted, more than anything in life, to imagine some end to his pain other than the end of life." He read on. "Is 'non-coterminous' a word?" he said.

"It is if you want it to be," Mike said. "Read Walt Whitman."

"I can't. It makes me sick with envy," Parlow said.

"I want you to go away," Mike said. "I don't feel good."

"Of course you don't," Parlow said. "Come on." He took Mike by the arm.

"You forgot the part about where you have to convince me," Mike said.

"Come on," Parlow said. "The room stinks."

Mike didn't move.

"I got the girl killed," Mike said.

"So fucking *what?*" Parlow said. "What? Was she going to live *forever?* She's dead. You're not dead: what's your problem? Put differently, other than the workings of that great healer, Time, what do you want to do? What is your problem?"

"My problem is, I don't know who to kill," Mike said.

"*Whom,*" Parlow said. "P.S.: you've been brought low. And I would say I grieve with you, but, of course, I don't. As we've each got to do it alone. Just like the adolescent boy and sex. The gods have spoken: this is what they said. And now, you're not only twelve days drunk but content in the undoubted revelation of your nothingness in the Great Scheme."

"I loved her," Mike said.

"You were humbled by your love," Parlow said, "you were humbled by her slim white body, you are humbled by death, but real *humility* is nothing to be proud of. And you, full stop, stink."

"I've been drinking," Mike said. "And have neglected to eat."

The cabin had a pump over the kitchen sink. Parlow pumped water into the coffeepot. "Come over here," he said. Mike levered himself up and walked to the sink. Parlow took a chipped navy mug from the sink, rinsed it out, and filled it with cold water. He handed it to Mike. "Drink it," he said.

Mike choked it down. Parlow said, "Now put your head under the pump." But Mike had begun retching. He worked his way to the door, opened it, and stood on the porch, vomiting into the snow. Parlow threw coffee grounds into the pot, and put the pot on the stove. He came up behind Mike.

"There's this to say for a broken heart, it keeps your weight down. And it makes you pale and interesting to the opposite sex. Those of them who might be attracted to a drunk, staring madman. And it's true. I notice—ever the observer—that love or grief—these states which, au fond, seem to be like madness. *Are they like madness?*"

"Fuck you," Mike said.

"Grief appears like madness," Parlow said, "which we saw in the haunted visages, and the demeanors of those returned from the horror of the trenches."

"You never saw any such thing," Mike said, "in the railway depot of Vesy-le-Duc."

"Vesy-le-Duc," Parlow said, "was the second-most-important railway nexus in France, the key *and* the lock to the movement of men and matériel from Le Havre to the Front. I don't care for your attitude and I'm tired of playing 'fetch.' Let's get out of here."

Chapter 23

They drove back through the cold Wisconsin night. The frost crusted the windshield, and Parlow scraped it periodically, clearing a small opening with the edge of a box of matches.

Down toward the Illinois border the box began to decay into wet cardboard. Parlow used his fingernails.

"We got to fucking get warm," Mike said.

Parlow stopped at the small guard station at the state line. He turned the car off. "Gimme a minute," he said.

Mike stared at him.

The guard hut held three Illinois state policemen in shirt-sleeves, clustered around the coal-fired stove. They looked up at Parlow. "Good evening," he said.

"Who the fuck are you?" one said.

Parlow took out his press card. "We're up here covering a story," he said. "My paper assigned me. To write. On the subject of the *roadblock*. And its effectiveness. *My* question is: would it help, or hinder you, professionally, to be mentioned by name as aiding our investigation?"

The hut was full of smoke. The stove gave off that best of heat, like a blanket.

Under the table were five wooden cases. Four unopened, and the fifth with the top pried off. A cop leaned under the table and took a bottle of scotch from the open case.

Mike lay on a cot in the corner; Parlow sat, drinking, at the table, with the three cops, his notebook open before him as he entertained them.

Investigating an arson-murder, he said, an unnamed detective had spied a curious bulge in the paneling of the still-smoldering ruin. One wall panel was slightly bowed outward. The detective had taken his knife and pried around the edges, and the panel had fallen free, to reveal, behind it, a small wall safe.

The safe's door was cracked open, the metal still dull purple from heat. Nestled in the safe were several banded packets of high-denomination bills.

The apartment's two occupants would never be

more dead, and the detective understood it correctly, so Parlow said, as criminally wasteful to leave the money to the firemen.

The safe was too hot to admit his hand so he pried the bills out, packet by packet, with his knife. He was laying them on the desk when he heard voices approaching, and scorched his hands as he stuffed the money into his coat pockets.

Unfortunately, he had just been cleaning his service revolver, and called away from his desk, had stuffed the oily cleaning rag into his overcoat. The rag caught fire, the coat caught fire, the rounds in the service revolver cooked off and blew his leg off at the thigh.

The cops howled. They'd heard the story differently, but Parlow's version was so far superior to their own, no one thought to stop or correct him.

They'd heard the "rookie was looking on" version of the story, and one had heard the variation in which the recovering cop had told it to his wife, which, of course, was patently untrue. No one knew the cop's name, but all knew someone who knew someone who did.

Embellishments included that the rookie had swept the remaining packets of bills onto the floor, under the desk, and had later retrieved them and retired to Florida. That the cop's brother-in-law, downtown, had seen to it that his wound was recorded as "in the line of duty," and he had been fully pensioned. That it took place not in Chicago but in East St. Louis or Gary. That the cleaning rag had been in the overcoat pocket as the cop was setting up to shoot his cheating wife, his partner, a criminal, or a creditor.

Other embellishments held the notion that the revolver had been abstracted from the locker of the patrolman who had, in a divergent story, been romantically involved with the officer in question's wife, the plan being to shoot her in admonition and plant the gun back in the patrolman's locker. A further gloss, passing the end-of-watch, miserable Wisconsin morning, was that the offending weapon had been snuck back into the remarkably porous National Guard armory from which it sprung, there to rest undiscovered 'til the end of time.

But one of the cops had averred that, although the armory would function as an oubliette, it was also the robber's Cave of Treasure. A rookie wondered that, as the cops had guns, and as the crooks had guns, who was there left to sell to? An older cop put his forefinger alongside his nose, the neophyte looked puzzled, while those in the know looked away in disapproval of his indiscretion.

Not included, but understood, was that none of the

incidents, perhaps, had happened, and the stories were true only mythologically, but no less true for that.

The water kettle on the stove whistled. Parlow rose from the chair and stretched.

"Dowd will do it," said one of the cops, and the rookie, Dowd, rose.

"I'll do it," Parlow said. He put on his overcoat. Parlow bundled and held his gloves in one hand, and used them to pick up the kettle. He took the steaming kettle outside.

False dawn added an indisputable and welcome gray to the night. Parlow walked to the car, his shoes squeaking on the hard frost. He poured the steaming water over the windshield, and enjoyed the melting of the rime.

The guard shack was in the middle of nowhere. The two-lane road ran, to the north and south, between sparse trees and flat farmland. Far to the south was a Model A, moving slowly, Parlow saw, to keep itself straight on the icy road.

When Parlow reentered, one of the cops was making coffee on the stove. The open door brought the cold in. The cop at the stove mimed shivering.

"You bet. *Mike,* wake *up,*" Parlow said. "Wake *up.*" Mike stirred on the cot.

He raised himself slowly to one elbow and looked around.

"Wake up, drink some water, *throw* the fuck up, and let's get back to town," Parlow said.

Mike nodded. But he had not been asleep. He was wakened earlier by the cops' laughter and his hangover had kept him awake. And when Parlow had left the hut, the cops had begun a more private conclave, to which Mike had been listening.

The cops had segued from the gun rag in the overcoat to another story of a coat. Some fellow in an overcoat, dead in East Chicago. The rookie asked if it was true that a busboy reported the killers of Jackie Weiss, funny fellas, had worn coats of a "foreign cut," that the report had been suppressed, and the busboy warned not to repeat it, as was the rookie now.

"And, on the *subject*," the rookie was told, "you want to stay *in*, what the fuck are you about, cracking wise about the armory?"

And Mike heard the chastised rookie's concern in his silence.

The car was freezing and the road was slick. A sick dawn was rising over the Lake.

Mike opened his eyes to see the red Burma-Shave

signs on the roadside. He read them one by one as they passed.

HOW COULD . . .
AL CAPONE ESCAPE . . .
FROM AB-SOLUTELY . . .
ANY SCRAPE?

BURMA-SHAVE.

"What were the cops doing up there?" Mike said. "We expecting to be invaded by Wisconsin?"

"Don't take that attitude," Parlow said. "They were no doubt checking for bootleggers. Ain't that a plum assignment. Sit inside in the warm, all day, and drink."

"Why were the fellas funny?" Mike said.

Parlow said, "What fellas?"

"Some jamoke, overcoat, dumped 'im in East Chicago. Funny overcoats. Shot Jackie Weiss. They said, 'Funny fellas.'"

"Yeah. You been away. Overcoats, yes. Funny sleeves—raglan sleeves," Parlow said.

"What are raglan sleeves?" Mike said. "Why are they funny?"

". . . The *funny* thing," Parlow said, "what did they

find in the overcoat? What do you think? Fella in the dunes?"

"I'm too fucking cold to know," Mike said. "The King of All the Belgians?"

"No," Parlow said. "Hard candy."

"Tell me again," Mike said.

"In the pocket; big cloth sack. Tied with string. Hard candy."

"So he liked hard candy," Mike said.

"Thing of it," Parlow said, "the bag? Tied with string. String glued together. Cops needed a knife, cut open the bag."

"Maybe he used it as a cosh," Mike said. "Jailhouse trick: bar of soap in the sock—you've got a cosh."

"He *had* a cosh," Parlow said. "S'pants pocket."

"*Maybe*," Mike said. "*Maybe . . .*"

Parlow leaned closer.

"Maybe he used it as a *doorstop*." "That's the spirit," Parlow said.

Mike began to shiver. Parlow passed him the pint. "You okay?" he said.

Mike shook his head.

On his return to Chicago, Mike found his own flat spotlessly clean. His clothing had all been washed, ironed, and pressed. His shoes were shined. His few possessions had been not only dusted but polished. The celluloid rabbit sat on his nightstand in the middle of a paper doily.

He understood it as a sign, that he had been adjudicated finished with his love affair with chaos.

He lay on his bed and slept for two days. When he woke he made a pot of coffee.

Chapter 24

He returned to the Budapest. The owner half-bowed to him at the door. He was shown to the window table he'd always shared with Annie Walsh. The owner had registered neither surprise, nor sympathy, nor appreciation of a customer's return.

His "courtly reserve," Mike thought, his natural grace and punctiliousness, his respect for the two young lovers, actually was stolidity. "The man's simply a tea shop owner with a quiet manner, I supplied the rest. He bowed me in as a valued, returning guest? Of course he did. He does it for a living. And he showed me to my usual spot? What *else* does he have to remember? He sells coffee and cakes for a living."

The first phrase he'd heard, in basic training, was that those looking for sympathy could find it in the

dictionary, between "shit" and "syphilis." Parlow had
said, " 'Every cynic is a romantic'? *Well.* A romantic is just a cynic for whom, as yet, the nickel hasn't
dropped. You can't get your heart broke if you don't
give a shit. A 'fool's paradise' is a perfect redundancy.
The paradise, whether it's love or success, consists not
in its, no doubt, pleasant attributes, but in the fool's ignorance of their transiency. You can't *live* in paradise,
unless you're a fool. Your time there runs out, join the
cynics."

"What about if you aspire to it?" Mike said.

"To what?"

"Paradise."

"Good. You aspire to it," Parlow said. "What do you
want? Women, money, fame, happiness. You can aspire forever, and you quite well *may*, but, should you
achieve them, you're fucked."

"Why is that?" Mike said.

"Because you've lost the sole talisman in the world
against cynicism."

"Which is?" Mike said.

"Desire."

"Yes, paradise," Mike thought. "Ain't nobody here
but us chickens. The owner's a Hungarian tout, he's

probably German. God bless him, he's got his push-cart, I've got mine."

But he had lost his taste for it, and he knew it.

The perfect coffee and the delicate cakes tasted like dirt. Mike experimented with hating the owner: "He's selling a happy alcove to the widows on the Drive: to break their afternoon of shopping for shit no one needs: what in the world is *happening* to me?"

Crouch had taught him, from his first day on the desk, to "write the police report." The police report was Crouch's version of the "Your Five Friends, the W's," reportedly taught in the journalism schools.

The Five Friends were *What, Who, Where, When,* and *Why.* Mike, once, challenged to recall them at the close of a late morning at the Sally Port, had included the sixth W, *How,* and no one remarked it, 'til the next meeting, when Mike was applauded for his streetwise orthography. The phrase, Crouch knew, was too formal, and too pat—suitable for the gullible who thought they could learn journalism in a classroom, but beneath the dignity of men who "went out there and got their nose broke." But there it was.

"Write the police report," Crouch said. "The sergeant, the lawyers, the judge, the jury, no one cares that 'the crimson blood ran in rivulets.' Tell me that he was *shot.* Tell me *where,* tell me who did it, if you know; tell me that, and only that, which IF YOU DON'T TELL ME, the captain is going to make a *fool* of you at roll call, and kick everyone's ass.

"Write the police report."

Mike smiled at the memory of his first and, he thought, most important lesson in aerial navigation. The fat sergeant had said: "This is a fucken map. This spot *here?* Is where we are. This *there,* is where you want to go. Draw a line on the map? Follow the line from '*here*' to '*there.*' When you get '*there*'? Stop."

His police report, today, he saw, if well done, could not deal with his hopes, his fears, his state of mind, his troubles, or his history. All of these, as Parlow loved to say, would be "adducing facts not yet in evidence."

The *facts* did not include the owner's provenance nor demeanor, nor the appearance nor intention of the women at tea, who may or may not have come from Lake Shore Drive. The facts were: That he was in the Budapest, for the first time since Annie Walsh's death. He had been back in Chicago two months. During that time, it had not occurred to him to enter the tearoom.

He had passed it, on his walks down Clark Street, several times a day, not even remarking its presence. The police report said that *this* day, it had occurred to him, or better, he had entered the restaurant. Now he felt the calm of discovery of the useful question: "*Why?*"

"Alright," Crouch would have said, "yeah, fine, you're brilliant, but you almost buried the lead. 'For the first time since his lover's murder, Mike Hodge, a reporter on the *Chicago Tribune,* entered the Budapest Café, 821 North Clark Street, the site of his courtship.'

"Well then," Crouch would have taught, "thirty words into it, and you have yet to tell a lie. Bravo."

Why had he come to the Budapest? The rule forbade conjecture. But what were the further facts?

The fact was, sitting at the window table, which he'd shared with Annie Walsh, his mind had run to a specific subject. That was a fact. What was the subject? The subject was: how to get from *here* to *there;* how to replace ignorance with actual information.

Of what was he ignorant? He was ignorant of the reason for his lover's death—but could see his way to no solution. He had come into their trysting spot. Why? "In probability," as Crouch would say, "to put a period to it and return to life as before." What was that? What was before him could only be that which had been behind him. Which was a life as a reporter. Well, then. Let him report.

Jackie Weiss was dead. Morris Teitelbaum, his

straw man, had been shot, and that was it. He couldn't see why.

"The trick for writing for the pulps," Parlow said, "is 'Turn it inside out.'"

Turned inside out, two people had come to grief. As they were connected, it was not foolish to consider the connection, the connection was obvious—they were in business.

But what was the outlier? The outlier nagging at Mike's mind was a man in a foreign-cut overcoat, with raglan sleeves, with candy in his pocket, dead in the dunes.

Two men in funny overcoats at the Chez. And at the funerals.

A woman in her forties entered the café. She wore a fur stole and a very expensive coat and hat, and had just returned, Mike saw, from an assignation with her lover.

She removed her compact from her purse. She applied powder and renewed her lipstick. She took a handkerchief from the handbag and blotted her lips against it, and checked them in the compact mirror. She put the compact away, and smiled her pleasure at the waiter's arrival.

Her smile meant, *I am here for a pot of tea, at the*

end of an hour's shopping, and have not come from two hours in an unlicensed bed.

Mike took it in in that fraction of a second. She turned to look at him, angry not at his appraisal, but at his understanding. And when she saw he both knew and did not care, she looked down, her anger warring with her shame. For a moment the shame won out, then she raised her head, exchanged a word with the waiter, then lit a cigarette.

"That's what happened today," Mike thought. "That's all I know. Alright."

Years ago, fresh from the War, he'd asked the old drunk who was, that decade, the sage of the Sally Port: "How do you know when it's time to quit?"

The man had covered the Spanish-American War, the Mexican Adventure, the Great War, and the various Crimes of the Century. And now he was, as they said, "sitting on third base, and waiting for someone to drive him in."

The man was finished, but he had been great. And Mike was young enough to find the transition baffling.

"How do you know when it's time to quit?"

And the man said, "When it feels like fucking your aunt."

But it was not that time. And when he realized it, Mike rose and left the Budapest and returned home.

He called the paper for the files on the Jackie Weiss case, and he began to write.

His return to the life of the City Room was eased by the shouted insults of his fellow reporters. Wisecracks high to low, all pretending to assume he had been absent on a prolonged sexual adventure. The quips ran from the Duke of Wellington's comment that no reasonable man could spend more than forty-eight hours in bed with a woman—the comment having been attributed, the suggestion addended was that Mike had, perhaps, "caught his dick in a knothole." The copyboys, fully aware of their position below any permission for humor, gave him the high sign, and one cub reporter tested his status by jokingly asking to be introduced.

Mike ran the gauntlet into Crouch's office.

"What have you got?" said Crouch. Mike handed him the pages, and sat on the couch while Crouch read them.

"'When last we heard of our stalwarts,'" Crouch read, "'Jackie Weiss and Morris Teitelbaum had decamped for That Better Land.

"'The Chez Montmartre, rialto of these western shores, remains open to all appropriately attired and capable of saying, "Joe sent me," and the rivers flow into the sea. With the exception of our dear Chicago River, which, a marvel of engineering, flows *from* our inland sea, into the Fox River, and, thence, toward the Father of Waters, the Big Muddy. For the latest on our Little Giant pocket crime wave, keep your attention on these pages, obey the liquor laws, and buy American.'

"What the hell?" Crouch said. "What the fuck's *wrong* with you?"

Mike thought a moment, then, "I don't know," he said.

"*I* know," Crouch said. "You either go out and drink *less,* or drink more. *Something.* But don't break my heart come in here with this fucking valentine to your long-lost talent. Because someone at Hull House may care, but I've got to write a newspaper."

Mike started to speak.

"*This* filth? Sounds like someone, trying to write like you, doesn't particularly care if he gets caught.

"Yeah, she was the Irish girl," Crouch said, "and her red bush was the closest that you'll ever get to heaven. And you loved her. But she's dead. And if you come back to work, *work.*"

Crouch lit a cigarette. He looked across the desk, and saw that Mike was lost.

"*Alright,*" Crouch said. "What was the weather, month ago today?"

"I don't know," Mike said.

"Why don't you know?"

" 'Cause I don't care," Mike said.

"Nobody cares," Crouch said. "That's why we don't report it. We reported it *then*. Tell me who was shot in the head *today*. Tell me the Croquet Ball. *You* remember." He took Mike's pages, balled them up, and threw them across the room.

"Go fuck yourself," Mike said.

". . . But, *but*," Crouch said, "and I've noted the insubordination; but you came back here. And here you are. Why?"

"Don't tell me, I'm a 'journalist,' " Mike said.

"That's between you and your god," Crouch said.

"I'm an agnostic," Mike said.

"That's because you were never in a foxhole," Crouch said. "There Are No Atheists in Foxholes."

"I'm not an atheist, I'm an agnostic," Mike said. "And I'm sick to death of 'No Atheists in Foxholes'; by which, and by extrapolation, we might conclude that anyone found *in* foxholes is a deist. For example, a fox."

"Alright," Crouch said.

"And if I'm not a journalist, why am I back here?" Mike said.

"Because where else are you going to go?" Crouch said. "I got something for you."

"Maybe I just don't want to write," Mike said.

"Nobody pays you to *want* to do it."

"Or I've forgotten how."

"Oh, you poor thing, what is it, writer's block? Does the wee thing have writer's block . . . ?"

"I might," Mike said. "What are the symptoms?"

"*I* don't know; I don't understand writer's block," Crouch said. "I'm sure it's very high toned, and thrilling, like these other psychological complaints. I, *myself* (or 'I,' as one used to say, when he could still speak), could never afford it. As I had a Sainted Mother at home, who, without my wages, would have been hard put to drink herself to death. *Further:* I think, *if* one can afford it, *but* one has nothing to say, one should *not* write. This is not writer's block but common courtesy."

"I do not have writer's block," Mike said.

"Good," Crouch said, "for that is a disease of the rich, and God knows you can't afford it."

"I—"

"Like gout," Crouch said. "I beg your pardon, you were speaking."

"I was drunk," Mike said.

"Yes, I understand," Crouch said.

". . . and," Mike said.

"I was at the funeral," Crouch said. "You want to be a sob sister, I'll fire Miss Fisk."

"Miss Fisk is doing a fine job," Mike said.

"You read it?" Crouch said.

"I would rather," Mike said, "do any number of things."

"The women read it," Crouch said. "At least that is what Circulation says."

"They ought to know," Mike said.

"Lovemaking to one side," Crouch said, "take Poochy, scoot down to the South Side; we require bold, clear words and gruesome pictures on the murder of this colored girl."

"Really?" Mike said. Crouch wrote an address on a slip of paper. "Send some cub out," Mike said, "I don't—"

"Yeah, but when I tell you this you *will*," Crouch said. "Who is the girl?"

"I don't care," said Mike.

"She was a maid. She worked for Lita Grey, *maîtresse en titre* to the LL Jackie Weiss."

"No. Everybody works for someone," Mike said. "It won't stretch."

"Well, this might stretch it," Crouch said. "While you were playing Ten Nights in a Barroom, Lita Grey, *late* of East Lake Shore Drive, has gone quite missing. That's right."

Crouch handed him the slip of paper.

"Go the fuck back to work," Crouch said.

Chapter 25

The dead black girl had been identified as one Ruth Watkins. She was already on a gurney in the tenement hall, covered with a sheet. Mike drew back the sheet. Most of her head was gone, and her hands showed evidence of torture.

Poochy, followed by Mike, elbowed his way into the doorway of the murder room. The flashbulb caught the faces of the two attendants, glaring white. The sergeant came over to Mike.

"You lookin' for Reilly?" he said.

"Reilly," Mike said, ". . . this rate a *lieutenant?* What's *Reilly* doing here?"

"He's at the drugstore, talking to Downtown. I heard about your girl. I'm sorry," the sergeant said.

"What the hell. Thank you," Mike said. He looked a question to the sergeant, who nodded him into the room. "Yeah, alright," he said.

The body's position had been chalked out on the loose-weave rug. The flat outline showed one arm stretched forward. The arrow marked inside the head indicated she had been facedown. That she was shot on the floor was clear from the huge bloodstain around the chalked head, and the hole in the carpet. The hole was singed, indicating the weapon's muzzle had most probably been placed against the head.

Mike felt the sergeant moving up behind him. "Guy comes in, girl's in bed," the sergeant said. "Fucked her around a bit. Hit her here and there, took a knife to her hands. She gets free . . . ?" He formed his hand into a pistol, and put it up against the side of his head. "Large caliber," he said. The sergeant nodded. Ruth Watkins had died, then, on the floor, facedown, sprawled out, and reaching toward the dresser.

"Her feet got caught up in the sheets," the sergeant said. "Going for the dresser, tangled up, she falls, guy? Walks right over, *nothing* left of her head."

"Gun in the dresser? Going for a gun . . . ?" Mike said.

The sergeant nodded. Mike walked over to the dresser's half-open top drawer. A small pearl-handled

.25 automatic lay in the pile of neatly folded silk hand-kerchiefs.

"Your guys open the dresser?"

"*I* did," the sergeant said. He turned to the cops in the room. "The fucken gun there, I saw it. I want it to be there, 'til I sign off." He waved his small black note-book. "I got it in the report. Gun was there when I saw it. Better be there when Homicide comes. It happens after *then* . . . *They* take over, their lookout."

Mike looked at the floor. "You find a shell?" he said.

The cop shook his head.

"Who shot her?" Mike said.

"Jealous husband, jealous wife, not a thief, 'cause . . ." He swept his arm around the room, which was intact, and held articles easily translated into cash. "Clock, silver clock," the sergeant said, "radio, for chrissake, couple of furs in the clos—" He raised his voice. "The fucken furs, I saw 'em." He muttered, "Fucken job . . ."

"Not the same as when you came on, huh?" Mike said.

"Aw, quit yer kiddin'," the cop said, in a brogue. "I'll tell you *what*, however, truly, is, kids coming up, you'd think they studied with the *firemen*, what sticks to their fingers, it's a wonder they don't, additionally, sell the bodies to the morgue, spare parts. Or flog 'em for horsemeat, fucken thieves."

Reilly, the homicide detective, appeared in the apartment door. The sergeant went to him, opening his notebook. Reilly surveyed the room, caught Mike's eye, and nodded a greeting.

The evidence technician, on his knees, was digging with a scalpel around the singed hole in the floor. Reilly stood by Mike, lighting a cigarette. He offered one of the pack to Mike, who took one. Reilly nodded at the chalked-out form. "Everybody loves a lover," he said.

Mike lit his cigarette. "Brings you down?" he said.

"Brings me down?" Reilly said. "Communication from Hizzonner, may have come to your attention, 'lack of appropriate response, investigation, crimes against persons, the colored community.'"

"*Uh*-huh," Mike said.

". . . What'd the girl *do*?" Mike said.

"Do?" Reilly said. "How do *I* know? She was a maid, what do I know?"

Poochy stood over the chalked rug. He took a flash-bulb from his overcoat pocket, licked the contact, and snapped it into the flash holder.

"Yeah, *one*," Reilly told him, "and then, that's it."

The evidence technician had taken a small forceps and removed a large, deformed slug of lead from the wooden floor. Mike watched him as he held the slug.

He angled it toward the light, turned it, and looked at it intently.

He shook his head, and shrugged. "*Looks* like a forty-five," he said.

The technician took a small glassine envelope from his kit and dropped the slug into it, then dropped the envelope into his kit. Poochy went up on his tiptoes to take the photograph. The flash went off.

"Ah, for chrissake," Reilly said. He turned away, squinting to clear his eyes. He looked down into the dresser drawer and picked up the small automatic—he turned it and found the initials J.W. set into the grip. He thought a moment, and pocketed the gun. The uniform cops, in deference to rank, mimed witnessing nothing. As they turned away Mike stooped over the evidence kit and removed the envelope holding the slug.

Mike walked slowly past Poochy. "Pop a couple flashbulbs," he said, "and get us thrown out of here."

Mike continued walking toward the closet, where Reilly was instructing the sergeant. The sergeant was nodding his comprehension, when the next flashbulb went off. The detective turned, and started out of the room as the second bulb went off.

"I thought I *told* you," he said.

Mike heard the altercation as he entered the closet.

Three floor-length furs hung on oversized white satin padded hangers. The hangers were embroidered in large flowery script, *Mlle Antoine, Chicago.* Mike opened the coats, each labeled *Mlle Antoine.*

There was a fourth hanger marked *Mlle Antoine.* It held no coat.

Chapter 26

Peekaboo nodded permission at Marcus, and he began.

"White folks," Marcus said, "let me begin with this: see nothing."

"As a journalist I'm well aware," Mike said.

". . . You *don't* realize," Marcus said, "is that black folks see *everything*. And, as importantly, *hear* everything. D'you know that?"

"He can stand instruction," Peekaboo said.

"The girl was tortured," Mike said.

"And if you wanted, *truly*, to understand, whatever you call it, 'human nature,'" Marcus said, "your school of philosophy would be not here, but a barbershop on the Stroll."

"I'm the wrong color," Mike said.

"Yes, and that's insurmountable," Marcus said. "Where we: see everything, *hear* everything, repair to our *Forum* to thrash it about, until it makes sense."

"And return, wiser to the world?" Mike said.

"No," Marcus said. "We *live* in the world. You see, we *live* in the world."

"Where the fuck else would we live? Marcus," Peekaboo said, "that snow gonna kill you."

"*I* don't care," Marcus said. "Of *course* it's gonna kill me. What the fuck do *I* care? Some of the girls here," he said, "break your heart, see them get hooked on the shit, that's sad. The other hand, it makes it easier have someone to *talk* to, and they like to talk."

"Ruth Watkins. Worked for Lita Grey," Mike said.

"The girl, worked for Lita *Grey*, *I* knew her, *through* her brother, 'fore he went away, that is, I knew *of* her."

"*Who* was she?" Mike said.

"Ruth Watkins? She was a *black* girl," Marcus said. "Intelligent girl, got took up, by some white man, so on, worked for his whore."

"How did you know of her?" Mike said.

"I *said*, through her brother. He worked downtown? The Chez Montmartre."

"Doing what?" Mike said.

"He *worked* there running errands awhile some time back. So on. His sister? Comes to meet him, one day, swept up by one of their Sheenies there, for a while, when her brother goes downstate; *white* man?, she takes his sympathy, this and that, he gives her the clap, claims she gave it to *him*, bats her around, what he's going to tell his wife? The altercation, back room of the Chez. Very bad. Coming out, this girl, no place to go, no cash, she's sick, isn't she taken up by this white girl." Marcus stopped. "You really see Bessie Coleman fly?" he said.

"I did," Mike said.

"Where was that?"

"It was right here on Cottage Grove, the air show, 'twenty-*five*?"

"What'd she do?"

"She flew all over the sky and threw the plane around," Mike said. "She snatched a handkerchief off the ground with her wingtip."

"She flying anymore?"

"Not that I know of," Mike said.

"Any black men fly in France?"

"Not for the AEF," Mike said.

"Who then?" Marcus said.

"They flew for the French," Mike said. "They don't see color like we do."

"I know that," Marcus said, "from the tales, the boys came home."

"Some of 'em stayed there, and got married," Mike said.

"Yes, they did. To the *white* women," Marcus said.

"They don't see color the way we do," Mike said.

"Why'd they kill Ruth Watkins?" Marcus said. "Do you think?"

"Well, as they roughed her up, beforehand, it would seem she died because she knew something, wouldn't you say?"

"Or the next worse thing," Marcus said, "they thought she did, but she didn't."

"Yes, that's the bad one," Mike said.

"And the other girl's gone missing," Mike said.

"The other girl?"

". . . She worked for," Mike said.

"Oh, yes."

"Lita Grey."

"Yeah well, they will have done her, *too*," Marcus said.

"What were they looking for," Mike said, ". . . do you think?"

"Well, you *might* have to want to ask that of the cops," Marcus said.

"The cops?" Mike said. "Why?"

"As previous, and I'm sure unconnected, to her death, word is, they pulled her in on a pawn ticket.

Yeah, yeah. *I* would like to see justice done. I don't know what it *is*, but I *would* like to *see* it."

"Pawn ticket?" Mike said.

"Piece of jewelry she was hocking," Marcus said.

"Ruth Watkins?"

"That's right."

"You saying the cops fingered her?" Mike said.

"I wouldn't say that," Marcus said. "It's just she pawned something."

"I don't suppose you know where," Mike said.

"Well, of course I know where," Marcus said, "where does *anyone*?"

Chapter 27

Everyone, Mike learned, went to Levinson's Loan Office, at Twenty-Fifth and State. Mike was the only white in the store, with the exception of its owner, Hersh Feldstein, Levinson's son-in-law.

Hersh and his black customer were separated by the wicket. Hersh had the loupe in his eye and was prying the back off a large gold pocket watch.

"My grandfather gave it to me," the customer said. Hersh nodded.

"Seventeen jewels," the man said.

Hersh closed the watch, and polished it with a jeweler's cloth. He handed it back through the wicket. "I can let you have ten bucks," he said.

"What about I want to sell it?" the customer said.

"Look in the window," Hersh said. "I got a million of 'em."

"Then whyn't you take one more?" the man said.

"You're better," Hersh said, "you want to sell it, take it to the *barbershop,* Remington's, someplace, show it around."

"I showed it around," the man said, "nobody wanted to touch it."

"There you go." Hersh smiled.

"I *got* this watch," the man said.

"*I* din't ask you where you got it," Hersh said. "*I* understand. You got a business, *I* got a business."

"Give me the ten bucks," the man said.

Hersh took the watch back, and began filling out a pawn ticket. He looked up at Mike. "One moment," he said.

Hersh showed Mike the entry in the pawn book: one platinum brooch, shape of a violin, fourteen stones, value fifty-five dollars, fifteen dollars in pawn, Miss Ruth Watkins.

"Why'd you turn her in?" Mike said.

"I run a business," Hersh said, "people needing money come in here with various articles, if I *can* I accommodate them. How would I feed my family, I considered myself the Champion of Abstract Justice?"

"You didn't turn her in?" Mike said.

"Kid," Hersh said, "you ever hear 'Live and let live'?"

"I have," Mike said.

"I work amongst the colored," Hersh said, "we get along, why shouldn't we? I'm not in the business, turning people in."

"Somebody knew she came here," Mike said.

"Yeah, that's not unlikely," Hersh said, "as the cops came by, with the insurance people, every pawnshop the South Side, examining the books."

"Looking for the brooch?" Mike said.

"The entry, it would seem, caught their attention." He showed Mike the card clipped to the page bearing the entry of the brooch: Mid-Continental Insurance.

"They wrote it down?" Mike said.

"They wrote her address down," Hersh said.

Mike shook his head to clear it.

"They come by often?" Mike said.

"I'm walking a *tightrope,*" Hersh said. "My customers tolerate me, the cops tolerate me, everybody tolerates me, many would love to find a reason, ruin my fucken life because I'm *white,* or a Jew, or white and a Jew, or a pawnbroker or all of the above. But we get along. Who's in charge of that? *I* am. And it's just doing business."

"Was this unusual, that the cops came by *with* the insurance guy?" Mike said.

Hersh sighed.

"Was it?"

"The piece was valuable, but not that valuable," Hersh said.

"The piece, the violin, they ask about it specifically?"

"What is it *to* you, finally?" Hersh said.

"I'm doing my job," Mike said. "For the gallant *Tribune.*"

"What is that job?" Hersh said.

"I'd like to find out who killed the girl."

"I would too," Hersh said.

"Why?"

"I liked her," Hersh said. "She was a nice kid."

"Why'd you remember her?"

"She was quite good-looking. Beautifully *dressed*. . ."

"You'd seen her before?"

"Never saw her before."

"You'd remember?"

"I remember everything," Hersh said.

"What was she wearing?" Mike said.

"Lamb coat, Persian."

"She try to pawn it?" Mike said.

Hersh closed the record book.

"She try to pawn it?" Mike repeated.

"Alright, she did. I wouldn't touch it," Hersh said.

"Why not?"

"Oh, come on," Hersh said.

"Specifically," Mike said.

"Well, it had initials in it, they weren't hers."

"What were the initials?"

"As I recall, they were L.G.," Hersh said.

"As you 'recall,' " Mike said, "I thought you remembered everything."

"It was a figure of speech," Hersh said. "She cop the coat?"

"No, I don't think so," Mike said.

"Why'd they kill her?" Hersh said.

"Apparently these things happen," Mike said.

The offices of Mid-Continental Insurance were on the fourth floor of the Monadnock Block.

Mike's press card obtained him an interview with Mr. Everett Shields, head of the Claims Department.

"We very much appreciate your interest," Mr. Shields said.

"I would do whatever I could," Mike said, "to help your company, as our interests, it seems, are the same. Those interests are *human* interests."

Mr. Shields nodded as if he considered Mike's avowal not only true, but laudable.

"We had a *claim*," Mr. Shields said, "upon"—he

consulted the sheet of paper on his desk—"the contents of a *safe.* A wall safe. The residence leased to Jacob Weiss, Three Ten East Lake Shore Drive . . ."

"A *safe*," Mike said.

"The articles *insured* . . ." He gestured to the sheet, giving Mike to understand that the safe's contents were not his to divulge. Mike inclined his head in respect. "We sent our investigator to . . ." He checked his notes. "To the apartment. The safe was *opened*, and *empty.*"

"And you contacted the police . . ."

"We did," Mr. Shields said.

Mike took out his notebook, to proclaim his status as champion of the truth.

He opened it, and laid it down on the desk. He took no notes. The trick had been taught him as a cub reporter, by an old City Desk hand. "The notebook? You're a *reporter;* what does a 'reporter' do? He's *nosy.* The notebook? You don't use it, you have established yourself as someone *so engrossed* that you have forgotten even your profession, so wrapped up are you in their tale." The trick had sharpened his memory and Mike had never taken a note in his life.

". . . and they responded instantly."

"The police," Mike said.

"Yes."

"Was that unusual?"

"It was . . . ," Mr. Shields said. "Yes. Especially that interest in an *old* claim . . ."

"Why?"

"Well. They, as we both know, have more important things to do." Mr. Shields waved his hand at the window, and Chicago beyond.

Mike chuckled appreciatively. "But they're obligated. To solve the crime."

"In theory, yes," Mr. Shields said. "*But . . .*"

Mike sat, not immobile, but still. Deciding to let it come. The El ran by, outside the window. Mr. Shields rubbed his temples.

"It was, yes. We'd made the request, actually, as a matter of form."

"A matter of form, why?" Mike said.

"As the safe's *contents*"—he put his finger on the page—"were of limited value. Our procedure requires a notification of the police. Usually done by the policy's *holder*. But, in *this* case . . ."

"Who held the policy?"

"Jacob Weiss."

"But Jacob Weiss was dead," Mike said. "He's been dead a year."

"Yes," Mr. Shields said.

"Well, then," Mike said. "Who made the claim?"

"I . . . ," Mr. Shields said as he peered at the form, "I'm not permitted to disclose . . ."

"Wait," Mike said. "You said an old claim."

"An old claim?"

"You said the police were interested in an *old* claim."

"Yes, they were more interested in *that*."

"In?"

"In the diamond brooch. *It* was reported stolen a year ago."

"It *wasn't* in the safe?" Mike said.

"Oh no," Mr. Shields said, "it was . . . it was stolen by a Pullman porter." He pointed at the page. "We paid that claim."

"Then," Mike said, "could you suggest why the police are interested in it now?"

Chapter 28

The trinket Ruth Watkins had attempted to pawn had been reported by Jacob Weiss as stolen from his wife's jewelry case on the Empire State, en route from their excursion to New York, back home to Chicago one year previously.

The insurance claim led to Ruth Watkins's demise.

Weiss, Mike and Parlow reasoned, out of town for the week and loveless, had, on his return, emptied his wife's jewelry case on the train, to dump in the lap of Lita Grey. The wife discovered the loss. The Pullman porter was accused and tried, and went to jail.

"Yeah," Marcus said, "*that* shit went missing, nobody in the compartment, *save* the porter. The exception, anyone of sense, the man who filed the claim, and/or, his wife. 'Cause, who stanted to gain? This fellow, William

White, worked for the New York Central all his life, s'if that mattered, four children, then they plant him with some piece of slum, some German-silver piece-of-shit ladies' watch, wu'nt even on the list of the articles supposedly *stolen*, now he's downstate doing five pieces 'cause some *white* man, cheating on his wife, screws the insurance company, pays *off* the cops, plant some evidence on this man; and I will tell you, sure as hell as I am standing here, it came down, Jackie Weiss, Hebe that he is, is also, card-carrying, a white man. Says to the railroad cops, his bitch starts screaming, 'Look here: sometimes, you know, a man needs a little piece of strange pussy.' The one cop? Looks at the other. *They* know where the jewelry went. Cop says, 'Maybe we plant some piece of shit in the porter's pocket.' Jackie Weiss gives 'em a card, says, you're downtown, stop by the Chez, as my guests. *Now,* you see, he's no longer, now, a white man, but, of course, a Hebe, and *they* ain't going to flake the porter for the fucken round of beef, and a couple a'scotch. Jackie, he clears his throat, '*And,* of course' (he says, something like that), 'I appreciate the trouble, and the *paperwork,* et cetera,' peels off two fifties from his roll, looks in their eyes, here's two more fifties, everyone's now relaxed, insurance company's going to pay, William White, as *soon* as it comes down, knows, he's going away. Justice is served."

"How would you know that?" Mike said.

"No," Marcus said, "you ain't been paying attention."

"What did I miss?" Mike said.

"You missed?" Marcus said. "You missed what's going on."

"What's going on," Mike explained, "is anyone linked to Jackie Weiss is turning up snuffed. Doxy and the maid. Paying attention, go on the run, clothes on their back. What do they need? They need money. What do they do?"

"They pawn their swag," Parlow said.

"They've got to pawn their swag," Mike said. "That's all they've got. Whoever's looking for 'em? Trace the junk and find the girls.

"Guys hunting for them? Go to the insurance company. 'What have you got that's missing, Little Love Nest?' 'Nothing much.' 'Oh. What's this *old* claim here?' 'This? Diamond brooch. Got stolen off the train.'"

"Except not," Parlow said.

"He gave it to the girl. Everyone saw her wearing it at the club. She's got to cash it in. Find the brooch and find the girls. How can they find 'em? Send the cops to shake down the pawnbrokers."

"Ah," Parlow said, "I see you've become like the proverbial Young Widow, who, once again, is beginning to sit up and take notice. What?"

". . . They put the cops on the send . . ."

". . . And who is 'they'?" Parlow said. "Mike?"

"The question, then, becomes: who's got the juice to motivate the cops?"

"Where are you going?" Parlow said.

Ruth Watkins was dead, William White was downstate doing the remainder of five years, and Mike Hodge sat in the offices of Domaine Dixon, attorney-at-law.

Dixon was a slim black man in his forties. He was well dressed, his hair processed and marcelled into waves, a trim mustache on his lip. On his office walls were diplomas from Atlee Junior College, the Chicago School of Law, a plaque from the Negro Attorneys' League, and a panoramic photo of the 394th Infantry Regiment, Colored, in reserve, at Douaumont.

"Well, the adversary system," Dixon said, "truly as it appears to come from English Common Law, is a throwback to the pagan, or Roman, trial by ordeal. In *France*, and, indeed, in the Romance countries, the law is in the hands, not of a jury, but of a procurator. His job, supposedly, is to find the truth.

"Our job here, is, each side, each to adopt a *lie*,

which might easily be compared to a weapon, and to see which fiction will prevail before an audience of the uninformed."

Mike smiled. "You writing a book, Mr. Dixon?" he said.

"In fact I am not," Dixon said. "If I were, I might discharge some of these observations. Why do I share this insight with you?"

"Because," Mike said, "you have a guilty conscience."

"Yes, I have a guilty conscience," Dixon said. "An attorney must have either a guilty conscience or no conscience at all."

"What about the Reformer?" Mike said.

"The Reformer," Dixon said. "I suppose." He turned his head and looked down, through the blinds, at the street below, State Street, the Stroll. "Everything changes," he said. "The *Reformer*? Might be the odd dervish, enjoyed getting his spirit broken, or he might persist, and evolve into the Crank, or the Martyr."

He pointed down at the life on the street. "I'm a race man," he said. "I am an American Negro, and I wouldn't change my state for any in the world. The price, for everything of worth has a price, is a broken heart."

Mike nodded in understanding. Though Dixon's head was turned to the glass, Mike knew Dixon could see Mike's reflection. Further, he sensed that Dixon could remark his sympathy independent of sight or sound, through that telepathic sense which blessed the trial lawyer and the confidence man. "He speaks in the rhythmic cadences of a Cicero," Mike thought, "of *course* he likens our jury system to a Roman contest of guile. He is the gladiator. What is his sword and shield? A soft demeanor, a glib tongue, and a total crock of shit."

He'd noted, from his first days as a cub on the *Tribune,* that the two difficulties in reporting were to get the subject to talk, and to get him to stop. Crouch had advised him: "It's the dirty water, when you turn on the tap. Let it run; let it run, eventually, it may run clean."

The advice proved true more often than not. Additionally, Crouch had taught him, listen for their lies. Why do we lie? To obtain something from our listener. What is it? Sympathy, cash, absolution, exemption, *listen* to it. Listen to what they *say,* alright, but the meat of the thing *might* be in what they *want.*

What did Domaine Dixon want?

"He wants me to understand him as tragic," Mike

thought. "He tells me he is a race man. He looks down on the Stroll, performing sad love for his beleaguered people. Alright. But why tell *me*?"

"William A. White," Dixon said, "International Brotherhood of Sleeping Car Porters, husband, *father.*"

"'Deacon of the church,'" Mike bet himself. "He says that, he sold him out."

"Deacon of the *church*," Dixon said.

Dixon continued his biography of the framed man, but Mike had come to the conclusion. Dixon had sold William White out. And he wanted Mike distracted from the betrayal.

"A trinket supposedly taken from his wife's jewelry case, and let me ask *you* something, as I asked the court."

Now, having determined Dixon's role, Mike allowed himself to enjoy the performance. "Smart as you are," Mike thought, "you don't see that boat has sailed. You shopped the deacon of the church out, and sent him downstate. Who paid you?"

Mike cherished the revelation of Domaine Dixon's perfidy, as an unexpected appearance of a beautiful phenomenon of nature—a rainbow, or a red-winged blackbird—common as dirt, but striking when unexpected. "God love you," he thought.

". . . the brooch, worth, let us say, less, *less* than fifty dollars. Why would a man with a family, with children, with a secure position in the community, *why* would he resort to theft? For, surely, he'd had ample opportunity before: the railroad patrons whom he served are, on the most part, wealthy, certainly well-to-do; and travel," he confided, "deadens in many, as we know, a natural wariness. They are secluded, thrown together, many away from their husbands or wives, waited upon by those, *of* my race, supposed to respond to nothing save the traveler's whims. These travelers are easy targets for the thief. But, *but:* William A. White was *not* a thief."

"I believe you," Mike thought, "and I believe that Mickey the Dunce could have got the man off."

"Then why was he convicted?" Mike said.

"He was *convicted*," Dixon said, "one, out of the white animus, excuse me, for the Negro *race*." Mike nodded. "*Two? Two . . . ,*" Dixon continued.

"Like most men who think they understand men," Mike thought, "this man only understands fools." But he had hit his groove, and there would be no new information forthcoming, so Mike was free to nod at intervals, and let his thoughts drift. William White had no money for his defense. Somebody paid Dixon; if asked who, his lie would be "the concerned of the community." But it wasn't true.

Mike had read the transcript of the trial, and Dixon's defense was desultory to the point of malpractice. If he'd been concerned for his client, for the community, or for the race, he would have fought. And if he'd fought he would have won.

Dixon did not take the case pro bono, he was paid; the neophyte errors he had made would have drawn rage from any legitimate backers, so he was not being paid to defend the client, but to accept the damage to his own reputation. He was being paid to throw the case.

Dixon came to a period. He stopped and mimed *That is the sad conclusion.*

"White was the porter of Pullman Five," Mike said.

"Yes, that's right," Dixon said.

"But he claimed he hadn't set foot in Pullman Five, until the theft. He claimed that he was summoned, by the conductor, from the dining car."

Dixon looked at Mike.

"The cook crew put him in the dining car with them, until the con sent for him. He hadn't been in Pullman Five," Mike said.

"It was his *car,*" Dixon said.

"It was, and he made it up, and went for coffee. Jackie Weiss and his wife arrived. White was in the galley. They get comfy, five minutes later, White gets called."

Dixon nodded his respect. "The railroad officer put my client in the car during the time the couple were unpacking," he said.

"You didn't cross-examine him," Mike said.

"What would have been the point?" Dixon said.

Mike walked down the stairs from Dixon's office.

Someone had paid him to ensure William White went away.

Someone had sent a homicide lieutenant to investigate the murder of a Negro maid.

Mike stepped out onto the Stroll. The afternoon was wearing into evening.

In the interregnum, the barbershops, hairdressing salons, and pool hall had just begun to give their charges up to the street. These Negroes had, in the main, come from day—or straight—jobs, as porters, domestics, casual laborers, or were in transition from the Life of the Day, among the whites, to the Life of the Night, in their own precinct and with their own kind.

Many had come home from work to beautify or fortify themselves, and would retire for two or three hours of rest before reemerging into the nightlife of the Stroll.

There were, of course, idlers and street people, hustling goods or services, papers, shoeshines, notions, sex, tickets (real or counterfeit) for various of the night's entertainments, liquor, cigarettes, and drugs.

There were the ropers and doormen for the clubs, out early, smoking and chatting. There were crap games in the alleys, and on the loading docks on the side streets off of State Street.

There were the most beautiful women Mike had ever seen, walking, purposefully, to work at the clubs: cigarette girls, performers, B-girls, waitresses, semipro prostitutes; there was a countercurrent of women having finished work at the shops, the millineries, clothing stores, manicure and beauty salons, tailor shops, and restaurants.

The men, lounging, strolling, entering or leaving the occasions of the afternoon, eyed the women, Mike thought, with a respectful frankness. But the banter, and the competition for the best comment or riposte, ceased as soon as the inhabitants were aware of the white man.

The life stopped in that portion of the street within his orbit, and he left.

Chapter 29

The Kedzie Baths had been there since the beginning of time. Some wag from the *Trib* quipped
they'd found Algonquin arrowheads in the steam room.

The baths possessed the unusually conjoined attributes of being cheap and clean. Mike and Parlow had
discussed the odd and pleasant conjunction. Unable to
agree on a more interesting interpretation, they had
adopted, with some regret, the unsatisfying conclusion
that the baths did a good job simply and well, and that
the world beat a path to their door.

The men found it exotic that anything was done on
the square. "And the outrageous novelty," Parlow said,
"of this new economy, is, look here: you *can't* get a
drink, coke, a blow job from the Chinese girl . . ." He
stopped, searching for the services universally available

at any all-night baths, but absent at the Kedzie. Brought his open hand down to signify that he had not quite finished. "*Hop*," he added, and the list was done.

"The *beauty* being: who do they have to pay *off*?"

"They don't got to pay off no one," Mike had said. The simple audacity of the business plan stunned them. Since the revelation, they'd treated the baths and their own with respect and humble thanks, as they would the sworn protectors of some ancient shrine or monument. That the baths were precisely what they appeared to be they found quietly delightful, their enjoyment tempered only by the rational fear that their delight, if too often or forcefully expressed, might attract the notice of the gods. So, after their preliminary evaluations, Parlow and Mike elected simply to enjoy the anomaly, which, like all things under the sun, would, of course, in time, change for the worse. But it continued reasonable and clean. The men had not shared their discovery widely. It was not their wish to balk others of enjoyment but to limit the corruption inevitably brought about by the irreverent.

Mike had first heard about the baths in Marcus's story of the lipstick stain. It was odd that a man of means would hie himself out to the Kedzie. The address did not suggest luxury. It must, then, he thought, offer some unusual depravity, or accommodation. But the baths, simply, had, from the first, been the resort of the Irish; they went when they were poor, and when wealthy continued their patronage.

Marcus Blaine had been directed to enlist the night-man, George White, in the lipstick scheme. The Ace of Spades, thus, endorsed the man as trustworthy, which was not to say he might not betray or hustle a customer, but that he might be true to the request of a friend.

Mike had taken Parlow there at the end of one shift. They liked the place, and each returned regularly. The position of nightman, Mike observed, was like that of the sergeant major. The culture of a Western army had evolved the perfect mediator between obedience and command. It was the soldier's job to obey. He was recompensed, in part, by his prerogative of bitching; and, more beneficially, by his exemption from thought. He would have to do as commanded, even unto death, but he held no responsibility beyond that. He was, Mike often thought, free.

It was the officer's job both to obey and to command. The orders he received were generally ambiguous; when not ambiguous they were oftentimes contradictory, incapable of execution, or actually absurd.

He was charged, then, with fulfilling what he understood to be the *spirit* of these orders, knowing that success would be attributed to his superiors, and failure (even in the case of the absurd or impossible task) to himself.

But Mike had read Darwin, and so congratulated himself that he, thus, might comprehend All Things by applying the theory of natural selection.

An army needed officers, it needed soldiers. The objective of the first was, generally, advancement; of the latter, preservation of life.

Each held examples of the brave, the dedicated, and the self-respecting; and, as with all humankind, a majority who would, in any situation, take the easiest way consistent with not getting blamed. But the wars must still be fought, objectives must be taken, men's lives preserved or expended with some degree of morality and reason.

What was the mechanism, which, then, *must* exist, to mitigate toward survival of the race? For the race, in war, was, and must be, defined not by genetics, but by nationality.

The naturally occurring mechanism was the sergeant major. He was risen from, and accessible to, the ranks. He was at the complete command of his superiors. But all, officer and soldier, knew that both the officer's objectives and the enlisted men's lives depended on his ability to weigh the absurd against the possible, to correct his superiors without the appearance of insubordination, and to supply to the ranks some promise of consideration in the risk of their lives.

The army functioned, Mike saw, as did the divine right of kings, through the principle of legitimacy. Those above could rejoice that they were not, as those below, slaves; those below could find what happiness they might in resignation, and its attendant lack of anxiety. The system worked to the extent that all accepted it, making the most of whatever benefits they might find.

In what was the system rooted? In culture and human nature? The Bolsheviks had killed their tsar, and installed a new tsar. And would there not arise a new and inevitable class of middlemen, mediating between the excesses of the powerful and the rancor of the mass?

The Sicilians of the South Side had imported their thousand-year-old system of the secret government. The padrone, now Capone, had been the second-in-command to Johnny Torrio, whom he had deposed; and of course, Capone, himself, must be deposed or killed, and, odds on, could *only* be deposed or killed by one he had trusted—by *his* own minister.

The weakness in the Mafia was the absence of legitimacy. Anyone with sufficient ambition could rise through obedience and violence; but there was, culturally, nothing to check his rise. And, so, the leader, as in Sicily, as in Calabria, as in Corsica, was always in danger from those—and, in the main, *only* from those—he trusted. And they were always in danger from him. A misunderstanding, a rumor, a lie, or a whim might mean their death at any time, any suspicion suggesting, to each and all, preemptive violence.

What of the Irish? Ah, the Irish, Mike thought. They benefited from the Eternal Tyrant, England. They were slaves at home, and as free men abroad maintained their unity through loathing of the oppressor, loyalty to their new land, and the construction of networks within the host democracy.

These networks were both overt—hegemony in the civic services, the attendant patronage, and, thus, hegemony in politics—and subterranean: in participation in crime in collusion with, or as a perquisite of, the police. The North and the South Sides, then, ran under two different systems. They could conjoin in Chicago no more easily than they might if Limerick and Messina were put under one government, and separated, as in Chicago, merely by a stream. The Irish and Capone met only in battle, and that, of course, only over their mutual interests: booze, drugs, prostitution, and extortion.

The pool of customers and resources was exploitable by both sides, the Chicago River was a most handy dividing line, but advancement and wealth in crime, as in most any other endeavor, came from blurring the boundaries of mine and thine.

The depredations originated, in the main, from the South Side. There underlings might rise through initiative, bringing, as it were, the head or booty, unrequested, to their chief, and saying, "Behold."

The Irish held more to party obedience and unity. Uncommanded skirmishing and the raid might be viewed as youthful exuberance, but would be censured; and the principle of legitimacy, much as it came from oppression by the hated English, was part of the Irish blood. The ward boss had replaced the clan chief in name, but the principle held: he could not be replaced by clan violence against him, as to do so would be to rebel against the legitimacy of the clan. And, so, there was no violence directed against him; the Irish ruled through the imposition of order: in the wards, at the polls, through the police and fire departments, through the patronage of all city jobs, and through their function as courts of the people.

The Italians ruled through the imposition of terror and uncertainty, and, thus, the extraction of obedience in return for protection.

"The Irish," Mike said, "must win."

"Alright," Parlow said. "Would you tell me why?"

"Because their system," Mike said, "is more suited to their environment. And the *night*man is a phenomenon of Western development."

"Alright," Parlow said.

"He is that sergeant major of an organization based upon legitimacy, and it goes back to Greece."

"That's wonderful," Parlow said.

"The position is a necessary aspect of the *system*, which might be inferred, from its very existence."

"What might be inferred from what's very existence?" Parlow said.

"Like those jokers in Montana," Mike said, "who found this fifty-foot-long dinosaur bone, and some pencil neck in New York claims to've deduced from it an entire dinosaur."

"Well, the bone had to come from *somewhere*," Parlow said.

"I will be god-damned," Mike said, "if I wouldn't have been some sort of a good archaeologist."

"Well, if you want to start," Parlow said, "start now, as those bones aren't getting any younger."

Now Mike sat in the cooling-off room of the baths. George White, the nightman, was at the counter, talking to the cook. Five other men lay on the beach chairs, beneath the Turkish towels. Four were sleeping; one was propped on a pillow, his eyes closed, smoking a cigar.

Mike watched George White, who turned from the counter and looked at Mike. Mike got up, knotting his towel around his hips. He took another from the rack on the wall, and draped it over his shoulders.

Mike had spent two hours in the baths. He had steamed some of the fatigue out of his system. He had showered, and was in the locker room, combing his hair in front of the long mirror. The nightman appeared, carrying Mike's fresh-pressed suit on a hanger.

"Here you are, sir," George White said. He hooked the hanger over the back of Mike's open locker.

"Thank you," Mike said. "I'll hit you when I retrieve my valuables."

"Yes, *sir*," George White said. "I'll be in *there*." And he pointed to a small cubby off the locker room.

Mike dressed and went to settle up at the front desk. He took his valuables from the small wire basket and loaded them into his pockets. He paid his bill and walked back toward the locker room.

George White was in his cubicle, at the pressing bench. He looked up as Mike entered. He nodded, raised the presser, and wiped his brow with a red kerchief.

"Yes, *sir*," he said. "One moment." He took the pants from the press and threaded them through a hanger.

The small room smelled of pressed and steamed wool. It held an ironing board, a valet stand, and a laundry table.

On the laundry table were various bottles of cleaner, labeled *Naptha, Water, Alcohol.* Making a corner with the laundry table was a small desk. On the desk were a telephone and a notepad marked *Kedzie Baths, Since 1898. 2434 North Kedzie, Call Belmont Five Five Two,* and an old studio photograph. It showed several half-naked young girls, posing in front of a vaguely Greek or Roman backdrop.

The girls were naked from the waist up. One dark-complexioned girl had a black wig, cut straight across the bottom; she wore an Egyptian cobra headdress and carried a flail. Another wore culottes, a fez, and curved-toe Turkish slippers. She carried a scimitar.

A light-complected girl with wide, trusting eyes was got up in a grass skirt, and carried a ukulele. There was a Nubian princess, stark naked, covering her genitals with one hand, the other holding a musket, her face covered by a veil. The photographer had titled the piece "At the House of All Nations."

"Yes, sir, I hope you enjoyed your stay," George White said.

"George," Mike said, "why'd they frame your brother?"

Chapter 30

Mike had gotten no information from George. That George was withholding information they both knew well: he was a black man talking to a white, and he was, even at second hand, in the orbit and so subject to the ire of O'Banion's Irish.

Mike had offered to trade a half column on his brother's railroading; but George, with all the guile and talent in the world, could not cleanse or concoct information—even if he had it—that would not, he assumed correctly, redound to his misfortune.

Mike, nonetheless, wrote the half column on William White, "convicted not upon scant evidence, but on no evidence at all, save the district attorney's late-appearing taste for law and order, and upon White's unfortunate proximity to the theft."

He tore the paper from the typewriter and said, "And so on."

"That's certainly true," Parlow said.

"Fucking case, is like the 'lectionary cycle, it keeps going around."

Parlow filled his pipe. "What are we talking about?" he said.

"Jackie Weiss," Mike said.

"Well, *that* takes us back," Parlow said.

"Why don't he go for it?"

"Yes, start with what you know. Now, that's philosophy."

"He's at the Chez, they barge in, he's done, and he knows it: he's got to fight."

"The cornered rabbit, itself, screams at the attacking fox," Parlow said.

"Yeah. But he *doesn't* fight," Mike said. "Why *not?*"

"Maybe," Parlow said, "he doesn't *recognize* the jamokes."

"Yeah, yeah, *sure,*" Mike said. "And where's the girl?"

"What girl?" Parlow said.

"Lita Grey."

"The fuck do *I* know," Parlow said.

". . . Hiding the truer question, perhaps," Mike said.

"Which is?"

"Why is no one looking for her? Which means *some-one* knows that she is dead."

"I believe I *will* have a drink," Parlow said. He unlocked the bottom drawer, took the bottle, and shouted, "*Copyboy!*"

Mike saw his Luger pistol in the bottom of Parlow's drawer. He pointed. "Gimme back the gun." Parlow gave him his gun back.

"Lita Grey's dead, maid's dead, we follow the bread crumbs back, who do we come to?"

"Jackie Weiss," Parlow said. "Morris Teitelbaum, and Jackie Weiss."

"Jackie Weiss," Mike said, "he's done some things, or knows something, or has *taken* something 'they' want. Who is 'they'?"

"Who *are* they," Parlow said.

"Go write for a small magazine," Mike said.

"I would," Parlow said, "but the only good-looking girls there are the men."

"It takes all kinds," Mike said. The boy brought the Dixie Cups.

"Alright, Jackie Weiss," Mike said. "*Assume* it was just an internecine squabble."

Mike poured the drinks and Parlow downed his. "Speak respectfully," he said, "of our beloved crime wave. Many people are killed, and it pays the rent."

Mike's face fell.

"Aw, hell," Parlow said. "I'm sorry."

"Nah, the girl's dead," Mike said. "She's not getting any deader."

But the afternoon, also, was dead. Mike left the paper and went to a businessman's speak on Wabash, where he would know no one.

Mike drank himself sick and returned to the one-room flat. The flat was cold, it seemed the flat was always cold. It was, of course, sweltering hot in the Chicago summers, and Mike, along with the rest of the building, slept out, August nights, on the fire escape or on the roof. But he always considered the heat, though it held sway for half the year, as the exception.

Mike sat in the kitchen. He had removed his shoes and propped his feet up on the kitchen table, but kept the overcoat on against the chill. In an hour, at five P.M., the landlord was required to restore the heat. Sometimes it happened. And sometimes it did not—if the janitor was sick, or absent, or had been instructed to save on coal.

The smell of the gas from the oven filled the room.

The grief he felt was not that of the War. His friends had died, and there was little time to mourn. Their absence struck him as part of a cycle. The cycle ran between shock, sadness, anger, and philosophy. The process continued as one "got on with it"; and the passage of time, consumed in saving one's own life, attenuated the bitterness of one's comrades' deaths, which deaths were now memories.

But his loss of the girl was anguish, and though his attacks of grief became, over time, less frequent, they seemed to increase in intensity. "The problem with death," Crouch had said, "is not that they are dead, but that they *stay* dead."

So Mike sat, recalling the Bible verse that had terrified him as a child, "In the morning you will say, 'If only it were evening,' and, at evening, 'If only it were morning.'" He found it, now, the truest thing he had ever read.

He knew that, at some point, he would form attachments with other women; and he reasoned that it was theoretically possible one might replace the Irish girl in his affections. He found the thought repulsive, but did not know whom or what to curse. Her killer, of course, whoever he might be, but he had, months ago, concluded he would never know—an act of will, the conclusion adopted in the attempt to substitute resolution for insanity.

He sat in the freezing room, welcoming the cold as a counterirritant or a legitimate, by which he meant sane, cause for complaint.

Through the evening hours, his fugue state lessened to the extent that he found himself, by association, puzzling, again, over what Parlow had said was "their own private crime wave," the murder of Jackie Weiss.

Jackie Weiss had been killed. His partner had been killed. His mistress, it would seem, had been disappeared; and her maid tortured and shot.

Crouch had taught him, "Look for the unresolved chord. It's like Wagner," he said, "the fucking thing goes on and on, *I* can't follow it. There are Norse gods and goddesses, and faery spirits of Valhalla, and somesuch, and the thing goes on 'til half the audience is dead, but at the end, so they say, there is one final chord, which resolves the entire Teutonic mess.

"Look for the unresolved," Crouch said. "Any idiot can see what fits; look for what *doesn't* fit."

"Who made the call?" Mike said. "Who called the insurance company?"

He lowered his feet to the freezing floor. He reached down to lace his shoes onto his swollen feet, and he began to pace the small apartment.

Somebody made the claim. Somebody in the know.

What did they know?

They knew the porter didn't steal the brooch; they knew Jackie had given it to his girl. *Who* knew that?

Whoever it was shot Jackie and put the girl on the run, broke. They knew she would have to pawn the brooch, and so, they called in the insurance claim to track her down. And they killed her. And the maid. And they tortured the maid. Why? To *learn* something. What?

Mike took out his notebook, and began to write, *Mid-Continental Insurance Company.* Then he wrote, *. . . the contents of the safe.*

Then he stopped walking.

Perhaps something was in the *safe*, he thought, or *had* been there. But: could the two girls *get* in the safe? The flat was his hidey-hole. Jackie Weiss. He hid the *girl* there, he hid the *safe* there. He's not going to tell the girl the combination, why *would* he?

Mike sat at the kitchen table and shook his head. He took the clean sheet from the typewriter, and began to write.

There was a knock on Parlow's door near nine A.M.

"Who is it?" Parlow said.

"It's the Rose of No Man's Land," Mike said.

Parlow opened the door. Mike came in, carrying two white paper containers of coffee. He put them down on the kitchen table and sat. Parlow locked the door.

Mike took three foolscap sheets and spread them on the table. Parlow looked at the sheets covered with notations.

"Why did they put in the claim?" Mike said.

"What?"

"Nobody wanted the brooch. They just wanted to find the girl. Girl, probably pawned the brooch? Somebody put in a claim, to let the *cops* find her."

". . . Why do they want the girl?"

"Someone," Mike said, "was *after* something Jackie Weiss had."

". . . Alright," Parlow said.

"If we connect the dots, they killed four people to get it. We *might* assume it was something that Jackie kept in the safe. The doxy, the maid, Teitelbaum, equally, were killed to get it."

"And what is it?" Parlow said.

Mike shook his head. "No," he said, "I don't know yet. But . . ."

"But what?" Parlow said.

"Wait, I know a different question," Mike said.

"Alright," Parlow said, "what is the question?"

"Who opened the safe?"

Chapter 31

JoJo Lamarr had achieved what he had of fame due to Mike's notice.

One morning several years previously, Mike had been taking his morning walk, down North Avenue to the Lake, and south to the *Tribune,* on the river. It was dead winter, the Lake was frozen a good distance out. Mike heard a shout, and looked east, to see a man, emerging from the Lake, pull himself onto the ice. On the ice, before the man, was a small, inert form.

Mike ran out onto the ice. The man hefted the bundle in his arms, and proceeded toward Mike. It was the body of a small boy.

The boy was blue with cold, and drenched. The man, JoJo Lamarr, was shaking uncontrollably. He handed Mike the child.

Mike ran, with the child, over the ice and onto North Avenue Beach. A mounted policeman was patrolling the beach. Mike gave him the child, and the cop rode off with him.

Mike yelled, "Call for an ambulance!" And pointed toward JoJo.

Mike walked back to JoJo, who had collapsed on the beach. Mike covered JoJo with his coat, and helped him into the lee of the pavilion.

In the hospital, JoJo was treated for shock and hypothermia. Mike told the story first to Rewrite, and then to the reporters assembled in the hospital waiting room.

The story ran in all five papers on page 1. MAN RESCUES DROWNING CHILD, FROM BENEATH THE ICE.

The least extensive of all the coverage was that of the *Tribune,* as Mike, having first called it in, returned home, to a very hot bath, a bottle of rum, and a nap that lasted into the next day.

The story, as reported, held that Anton Lamarr, taking his morning stroll, had seen the small boy break through the ice; and disregarding all thoughts of his personal safety, ran to the spot, plunged into the Lake, and discovered the boy, now shocked into unconsciousness, lying in ten feet of water.

The papers hinted at, but did not report, that Mr. Lamarr was, at the time, awaiting a hearing on revocation of parole, and faced the prospect of return to Stateville for the remainder of his previous felony sentence. Fourteen years to be served.

JoJo was being arraigned for extortion, and violation of the Volstead Act. His accomplices in this last crime had arranged for bail, and for the attention of a lawyer who would put on a good show. But anyone familiar with the fixers knew that JoJo's services, though of sufficient worth to entitle him to bail and a good show, certainly fell short of the reward of the fix. Of which JoJo was most certainly aware.

On his return to the world, Mike read all of the coverage, and he saw, on the court blotter, that JoJo was due, in a week, to go up before the judge on the parole revocation. Mike went down to see it.

The defense attorney asked for a notice of JoJo's heroism to be read into the record. The prosecution objected, and when the objection was overruled, Mike, and everyone else in the court, knew that JoJo would go free.

That night, at the Sally Port, Mike told his suspicions to Parlow. Parlow said, "It's too good to check," but Mike checked anyway.

He had been schooled to look for the outlying fact, and ask the unasked question. The unasked question was, "Who was the boy?"

Mike found that the child had been released from the hospital soon after his mishap, into the care of one Clarice Mitchell, 251 Luella, City.

Mike went to the address to verify that which he knew as sure as sin: that there was no such person and no such address.

Mike asked the boys downtown where JoJo Lamarr was usually to be found: at the Del Mar Billiards, North Clark Street. Mike found him there, and congratulated him. JoJo, to his credit, reacted modestly: "You have to be bold," he said.

Mike asked, "Who was the kid?"

"The kid?" JoJo said. "The kid, some kid from Cicero, we found him."

"Who was 'we'?" Mike asked.

"Yeah," JoJo said. "*Somebody* might have thought, maybe, they *owed* me something, or was afraid that, if jammed up for a long while, in effect, I might turn snitch. Which I would rather die than *do*.

"So, it may be I went to them. And suggested, 'How about *this*?' As I was stone broke, and they, 'cause, I think, it tickled them, said, 'Okay,' and bought me the kid, they rented him."

"The kid was never through the ice . . . ," Mike said.

"I wouldn't do that," JoJo said. "No. The only, the tricky part was timing. *You*"—he pointed at Mike— "have too much a predictable pattern of behavior. Somebody, wanted to get next to you, or get over on you, he knows where you go and how you get there. Be careful of that."

"Were you through the ice . . . ?" Mike said.

"Yeah, I had to go through," JoJo said. He shrugged. "I dunked the kid, too. But I held on to him."

Mike looked at him.

"Hey, *he* got paid," JoJo said. "*He* got paid."

" '*He* got paid,' " Mike had concluded, that night, to Parlow, and they got sick laughing.

Through that evening, and for some days afterward, one, and then the other, would remember JoJo's tag, "He got paid," and begin to laugh again. But, after the girl's death, in Yuniko's flat, and in the cabin, and at periods afterward, Mike remembered the admonition: Don't be so regular. In your behavior. You don't know who's watching you.

JoJo sat, as usual, in the elbow of the Wabash speak, pleased to be saying sooth to Mike Hodge, who had, after all, made him famous.

"I'm looking for a safecracker," Mike said.

"Safecracker," JoJo said. "A rare breed. Breaks down *into:* the nitro guy, or the peeler, which is to say, strongarm the thing . . . Two distinct subspecialties."

"The fellow with the stethoscope," Mike suggested.

"S'mby, going to sound out the combination?" JoJo said. "*Perhaps,* though many have claimed they did so, but I disbelieve them."

"Why?" Mike said.

"*Why?* 'Cause where'd I hear this story? In the *joint.* So, *one,* whatever you hear there's a lie; *two,* fellow could actually crack the box, a stethoscope? No noise, no fuss, in and out, what's he doing in the bandbox? And I doubt it on another score," JoJo said.

"What is that?"

"Guy is wrong? He *looks* wrong."

"That's right," Mike said.

"Walking down the street? Wrong neighborhood? Five blocks away. He's wrong? Cops are going to toss him. What do they find? A *stethoscope?* It's not, 'I beg your pardon, Doctor,' but, 'Get in the *car.*'

"Tell you about burglary tools," JoJo said. "Don't do it."

"A flashlight . . . ?" Mike said.

"Same thing as the stethoscope," JoJo said. "You turn your pockets out, it's not quite a hard chisel, but what're you doing with it, that you need a flashlight?

You a *coal* miner?" He paused. "It's arguable. But why take the chance?"

"In front of the judge," Mike said.

JoJo nodded, but improved the instruction, "Front of the judge? You're probably goin' *anyway.* They jammed you up for being you. So, theoretically, the flashlight, *yes.* But, *but . . .*" He looked down at his glass, and Mike gestured the bartender for another round. JoJo nodded his thanks. He drained the glass in front of him and pushed it away.

"*But:* 'n' here's the 'A' material: Who needs the flashlight? The moonlighter? He's goin' in there, people are *asleep.* One of them wakes up? 'What the fuck is going *on* here?' Little Billy is asleep in his crib? 'Bang bang *bang,*' homeowner goes. Herr Midnight knows this. Porch climber? Straight folks in the house? There may be shooting. *Cops* figure, 'I found the *flashlight,* where's the mohaska? He might've *pitched* it, but he *had* it.' *So:* flashlight equals, to them, *violence.* Might as well be a gun. Fucken cops hate a gun."

"Yes—they dislike violence," Mike said.

"No. They fucken hate paperwork. No. Our guy? Our burglar," JoJo said, "outs with it, shoots the guy. Fucken guy, now, dead on the parquet floor, cop shows up, 'there goes his weekend.' Who was standing where and 'what the wife said,' all this bullshit. Sergeants

show up? They're going, Lake Geneva, for the weekend, put it to the manicurist. Last thing they want, homicide dicks too, write up these tiresome reports. 'Fuck
it,' they say. 'This is too complicated. Break it down
for me. Your stenographic skills, I want it on my desk
on Monday morning,' everyone's pissed off. You get
caught with a gun? That's why you're going away—you
fucked up their weekend."

"How come," Mike said, "your story, it happened
on a weekend?"

"Happened on a weekend," JoJo said, "as our guy
figured, the householder himself's more likely? Be out
in Michigan City, with the wife or side dish, flopping in
the waves. Increase the odds, our guy goes in there. Eh?
There's somebody there? Don't go in at night. There's
no one there, you go in? Turn on the lights."

Mike nodded. The bartender poured the two new
drinks, and Mike nudged the one toward JoJo, who
nodded thanks.

"They got guys, inside Stateville," he said, "were an
Indian, their name would be Falls for the Tools. All
the time, they're blowing their nose, the cop? Looks at
'em? Don't like 'em? Tosses 'em, what does he find?"

"A flashlight?"

"Much too fucken right," JoJo said. "Fuck the lockpicks. This guy's? Got a *buttonhook,* the cop, end of the month, got to write something? What does he write?"

" 'This suspicious character, long known to this officer as a repeat offender, apprehended while in discourse with known criminals, and in possession of burglary tools, see attached,' " Mike said.

"Correct," JoJo said. "*I.* Would not have, on my person? A paper clip, penknife, *watch key, belt buckle,* P.S., why? As I'm not wearing *no belt.* You get rousted; 'No, Your Honor, I found no tools, but he is known to carry an assortment of forbidden objects . . .' '*Where?*' my lip says. 'Pants pockets? Your Honor, I call attention to the worn suspenders, to the lightweight fabric of the trousers, I defy you to show me how they could bear the weight of these various tools which you allege . . .'

"It's a fucken chess game," JoJo said. "Hardest part is: getting to and from the spot in question, without some alert copper, looks on at some guy beating his wife to death as entertainment, gets all enraged, here am I, going to or from work, I forgot to pay him off.

"*I* say? You got to (and I tell the kids) work in the daylight. *That's* the time you want to go *in . . .*"

"What if they got a maid?" Mike said.

"They got a *maid,*" JoJo said, "*maid* assumes, there, once in a while, *will* be noises, some activity, some part of the apartment or house, either unexplained, or unexpected: lady of the house is balling the tennis instructor, husband came home, *similarly,* some girl, goodness of his heart, he gave her a lift."

"What if the maid comes upon you?" Mike said.

"Maid comes upon you," JoJo said, "look in her eyes, determine if she's, A, straight, or B, wise. If she's A, you excuse yourself; take the pencil, which you are never without, from behind your ear; and tell her, you are measuring for the drapes."

"What if she's B?"

"*If* she's B," JoJo said, "which is more likely, *now* you take the *five,* which you *also . . .*" Mike nodded. "From the vest pocket, where it lives, and hand it to her. Here comes the pencil: 'Sorry to've disturbed you. I'm the man, *as you know,* measuring for the drapes.' You pat your pockets. 'I forgot my card, please tell Mrs. *Mffmr* we will telephone her tomorrow.' Now she's got *what?*"

"The five spot and a story to tell," Mike said.

"Well. That's my gift to her. Eh? I look her in the eye, she thinks, 'Alright, but what if I can't stand up to the *heat*'—'cause, sure as hell, *cops* don't think she's in it? Lady of the house *surely* will."

". . . Because she's black . . . ," Mike said.

"Well, *yeah,*" JoJo said, "which is why she's going to

take the jitney in the first place, 'cause, *I* toss the joint, it's not impossible she's going *anyway.*

"Lot of these broads," JoJo said, "*incidentally.* You see the dawn of understanding, 'This guy wants to *help* me' . . . one or two of 'em, we ended up, space of an evening, very good friends."

"What about, they come upon you in the act?"

"Same way. She's *white,* I got to beg her pardon and leave. It's essentially a peaceful existence," JoJo said.

"How do *you* get in?" Mike said. "The safe?"

"The *safe?*" JoJo said. "I'm not a safe man, but I'll tell you: the daytime, you can't blow it, you can't peel it, *I* don't have the skills, suss out the combination, n'I'm not walking around with picks. I *do* have"—he patted his pockets—"I do have a certain document, lists the various break-in codes, available to all accredited locksmiths, these listed by make and model."

"That's got to cost a mint," Mike said.

"I would assume," JoJo said. "And, of course, a lot of these locksmiths work at night."

"I'm looking for a safecracker," Mike said.

"Yeah, n'I know *why,* I think," JoJo said.

"Why?"

"Because you got a Nose for News."

"What are we talking about?" Mike said.

"Fellow, washed up in the dunes," JoJo said.

"What fellow?" Mike said.

"The box guy. It was in your paper."

"No, you've got me," Mike said.

"Your safecracker, dead, in the *dunes*? Washt up, eaten by the fucken *fish*, so on . . . The guy with the sweet tooth . . . guy with the hard candies."

"Try it on me, again," Mike said.

JoJo shook his head. "The things I do. For a drink. And ten bucks," he said. "You don't know what I'm *talking* about?"

"Tell me a story," Mike said.

"Walter Johnson," he said. "Genius *this* guy was. And most, *most* of the true, ancient thinking, that I came by, I came by downstate, from him." JoJo raised a finger to forestall the question. " '*If* he was a genius, what was he doing stowed away?' He didn't get cuffed 'cause of professional malfeasance, but for icing a taxi-dance girl, which, that year, was against the law. And he was doing the whole thing. Which, *truly*, was hard, for a taxi girl. But he, unfortunately, got artistic, and dismembered her in a fashion sufficiently memorable to attract the notice of *you* fellows, who, in concert, put him away. A more thoughtful man, having chilled her, thrown her in the Fox River, *and* had the misfortune, some *off*-duty cop was fishing, just around the bend, would've told the judge, 'She gave me the clap.' He'd've done? Ten spaces, for manslaughter, be alive today." They sipped their drinks.

"Oh *yeah*," JoJo said. "Your question: Girl comes acrost you cracking the box. She's B or the colored girl, we've dealt with that, *your* question is: she's some legit Swede, or white girl or something, what do you do?"

"That's right."

"Well. What you *don't* fucken do, *ever*, is *scare* her. *Never*. Or, she sees you in the matinee? 'That's him!' And, additionally: 'He tried to *rape* me, and said that Mayor Thompson is a cunt.' You never scare her, you can't *reason* with her . . ."

"Why not?" Mike said.

"Why *not*? 'Cause the broad is stupid. She's not stupid, white girl? Why isn't she out, get a better job than picking up some fat broad's *undies* all day long, saying, 'Yes, mum,' *and not even stealing*. White girl? Comes upon you? She's protecting her *honor*. And, get this, the 'honor of the house.'

"So, Walter: He goes in? He's got two cloth bags, eh? Inside his coat? Little cloth drawstring bag. Two bags. See if you can get it. One bag is empty—*other* bag, *this* bag? Filled with hard candies. Can you finish it?"

JoJo tipped the drink back, and Mike caught the bartender's eye. The bartender nodded.

"Two drawstring bags. One full of hard candies," Mike said.

"Never get it," JoJo said. "*Cops* never got it. It's too good."

"You sure you want to tell me?" Mike said.

"I'm just talking," JoJo said. "I'm just killing time until we get *around* to it.

"End of the day, we're going to get to the part where you get to the favor you want," JoJo said. "I can do it, I will; you know that. Part of the deal, Mike, I assume you assume, everything else, is just two things, I like you, and I talk too much. What is the favor?"

"Why'd they go in on Jackie Weiss?"

"Jackie Weiss, I understand, was dilatory with the vig."

"What if he wasn't?" Mike said.

"Well," JoJo said. "What would lead you to that?"

"What if he was current?"

"Then: the question is: why kill the goose?" JoJo said. "If your information is correct."

"Suppose it *is*," Mike said.

"A*ha*," JoJo said.

"Meaning what?"

"I *wondered*, why you'd want to go fuck round with Dion O'Banion. No aspersions to your courage indicated."

"Yeah. None taken," Mike said. "Am I fucking around with O'Banion?"

"No, I have to think about this," JoJo said. "I have to think about this." He finished the drink and stood up from the stool. "Thank you," he said.

"I give up on the candy," Mike said.

"You don't wanna work it out?" JoJo said. "Okay. The *candy bag,* ah this is so fucken inside . . . *Walter.* Is caught at the box. Door's open, jewels are coming out, the maid comes in. Walter turns, now comes the body language, stooped shoulders, head down, 'You caught me.' He takes the remaining jewels, sweeps them *visibly* into the empty drawstring bag. Ties the strings with a simple, 'resigned' bow—huh? 'Goodbye.' He sighs. He raises his hand, 'Wait,' he turns back to close the door on the safe. Bag with the rocks goes into the coat pocket. He turns back to the maid, in his hand *now,* the *other* drawstring bag. *This* one, full of hard candy. Face down, shoulders slumped, he holds this bag in *front* of him, 'You got me . . . ,' hands it to the maid. He leaves the room, and walks, sadly, down the stairs, sorrowful and ashamed."

"This is the white broad?"

"The maid? Fucken *Lutheran.* Don't matter. What does she *do*? As Walter walks away."

"She looks in the bag."

"She. Looks. In. The. Bag!" JoJo said.

" 'Cause she's a thief?"

" 'Cause she's a *woman*. Give her a bag full of jewels? She cannot *not* open it. Whether she prunes it or not. Got to see what's inside. I walk down the stairs. The elevator."

"What if she opens the bag before you hit the street?" Mike said.

"Well, here's the fucking genius," JoJo said. "And you can forget 'Discoverer of Radium.' The Swedish broad? *Saw* me sweep the jewels into this bag, tie the bag with a simple bow. I *give* her the bag, she goes to open it, she can't get it undone."

"Why?"

"Why? Because, I, previously? I put the candies in my other bag, I took the drawstrings apart, and fucken *spliced* them into each other, *then* tied the bow. And glued it. Now the broad, her problem *was:* what to do about the burglar? *Now* it's: how do I get this fucken knot out of this string, than which *nothing* is more occupying. *Aaand,* and here we get to 'I love it,' I get tossed? The way *in*? What does the cop find? Bag of hard candies, I, my goodness, bought to distribute, the poor kids at Hull House. How beautiful is that?"

"What if you get tossed the way *out*?" Mike said.

"Then I'm fucked. But I'll tell you what. If he's current, I don't think O'Banion killed him," JoJo said.

"Be—"

"Because why would he? I don't get it. Jackie Weiss . . . ? *If* he's current, he's, if he's current, he's getting protection *from* O'Banion, question, why would *anybody* drop him?"

"Fellow washed up in the dunes, bag of candy in his pocket. You know him?" Mike said.

"He'd've had to've studied downstate, with Walter," JoJo said. "What you want, someone bunked up with Walter, long enough, cement a friendship."

Mike rose, left a ten-dollar bill on the table, and handed a twenty to JoJo. He started putting on his coat.

"And, if I were you," JoJo said, "be *careful,* 'cause a lot of people getting killed."

"Yeah, who's getting killed?" Mike threw the line away, and began buttoning the overcoat.

"That black girl, worked for Jackie Weiss's broad."

"What would she have to do with a *safe* guy . . . ?" Mike said. He put a cigarette in his mouth, and took a match from the holder, and scraped it on the holder's side. He lit his cigarette.

"You, I am *sure,* didn't hear nothing from me," JoJo said. Mike dropped the burnt match in the ashtray.

"I think you're bullshitting," Mike said.

"*No* you don't," JoJo said. "What are you smiling about?"

A further five dollars at police headquarters had opened to him the Bertillon files of the parole board of Cook County. Two hours' study had given him the name and photograph of Donald Byrne, Joliet Penitentiary, 1923–1928, cellmate, for three of those years, with Walter Johnson. Mr. Byrne, according to his card, would be forty-one years old, and a comparison of his statistics with those of the dead man in the dunes suggested he would grow no older.

"It's all in knowing where to look," Mike said.

"Who said that?" the clerk said.

"Lewis and Clark," Mike said. "Don't they teach you *nothing* . . . ?"

Chapter 32

Parlow had just entered the Sally Port, and was shedding his overcoat as Mike came in.

"As I put it together . . . ," Mike said.

"For the love of Christ," Parlow said, "let me get a drink."

They walked through the smoky room and Mike ran down the story as he understood it, as if giving it to Rewrite.

"Weiss's safe is cleaned out . . ."

"Maybe the broad got it," Parlow said.

"Lita Grey?"

"Yeah."

"Maybe she did," Mike said.

"Aaand took the mink coat," Parlow said.

"Maybe she did," Mike said, "maybe she didn't, but, *now*? Now? Why is Jackie Weiss on the spot?"

"Because he did something they didn't like."

"Or, *or*," Mike said. "He had something that some-one *wanted;* he, we can assume, had been asked for it nicely, and had demurred."

"A fact not in evidence, but what the fuck," Parlow said.

"They toss the Chez? It ain't there; where *is* it?"

"Maybe at his Li'l Love Nest," Parlow said.

"They break into the love nest, they open the *safe:* some guy? The Candy Man? Opens the safe . . . says it isn't there."

"Alright."

"So how do they treat him?"

"They shoot him and dump him in Hegewisch."

"*Why* . . . ?"

"Because they believe he opened the safe, found what they wanted, and held out on them."

"Right. Now—"

"Good to see you back," Parlow said.

"Shut up," Mike said. "*Now*—" But they had ar-rived at the back booth, and it was occupied not only by the *Tribune*, but by the *American*.

"Whence this ecumenicism?" Parlow said.

In the booth Crouch had just lit a new Fatima from the stab of the old.

The occasion was the presence, in the booth, of a journalist from New York. He was being congratulated on his paper's extraordinary scoop, their page 1 photo of the electrocution of Ruth Snyder.

". . . on the story from day one," he said. "And the betting was two-to-five that she did it. At the outset, then, then five-to-one against execution."

"D'you bet on it?" Mike said.

"I didn't bet on it," the New Yorker said.

"As that would've been of questionable taste," Mike said.

The New Yorker stopped.

The boys were trading Tales of the Unwritten Law. The New Yorker was being grilled on the Ruth Snyder murder. The suppressed testimony, backstage gossip, and police embellishments which were, to the reporters, as Crouch said, "the intoxicating liquor, the ambrosia, of the news, the true news, fresh from the still, before it is denatured."

Snyder and her paramour, Judd Gray, had murdered Snyder's husband. Gray, an undergarments salesman, it seems, was the punch line to a City Room joke which the visitor posed to the group: "Why was Judd Gray like a bad dentist?" Parlow answered, "Because he was filling the wrong cavities."

The visitor's face fell.

"Oh, no," Parlow said, "I stepped on your joke. What have I done. I'm so sorry. And hope you will not understand my boorishness as indicative of the local standard of courtesy. Allow me to buy a round."

Mike slid into the booth opposite Parlow.

"Buy a round," Parlow said. Mike waved a new round for the table, indicating Parlow to pay.

"You fellows will like this," the New Yorker said. "It puts me in mind of a hunting tale."

The table nodded him their agreement: yes, the story was, likely, more than twice-told, but they would be courteous to the chap from out of town.

"This fellow, you see, discovers his wife is cheating on him. Where does she go? To a hot-sheets resort of note. How does he know she goes there? He follows her car. She parks the car, in she goes. Half-seen, through the entryway, she embraces a man even our husband, in his enraged grief, can espy is not himself. He goes to the desk. 'What room did my friends go into, please?' 'Room two oh nine.' Tritty trot, tritty trot, off he goes to buy a gun."

The waiter brought the round of drinks, Mike motioned him to write it down, he nodded and left.

"However deep his grief, our unfortunate cuckold retained that innate sense of self-preservation which separates us from the unthoughtful. He reasons, 'If I, in my state, walk into a pawnshop and demand a gun, the pawnbroker will remember me. Perhaps he won't conclude the sale, perhaps he will call the cops, and so on.' *Better*, he reasons, than trying to evade notice, he will act in a fashion counter to intuition, and purchase a gun openly where he is a valued customer. He'll buy a sporting arm, no one will question him, and, should he walk away from the crime undetected, no one will connect him with it.

"Who would kill his wife, he reasons, with, for instance, a new, purpose-bought expensive shotgun? He goes to his Fifth Avenue sporting goods store. Over the years he has been a valued customer in their fishing department. What prodigies of bamboo and waxed twine, of perfectly balanced reels and flies tied by the greatest artisans, who went blind in their construction—"

"Get on with it," Mike said.

"He enters the store, and is nodded to the elevator. 'Third floor, Mr. Smith? Fishing equipment?' the boy says. 'No,' he says, 'take me up to the gun room.' Up he goes. Delighted to see him and his interest in blood sport, they quiz him. What does he want to shoot? He improvises, 'Birds.' What sort of birds? 'Um, pheasants.' He takes a gun from the rack. 'I'll take it.' 'This is a beautiful Parker VHE twelve gauge, side-by-side, citation grade, its stock of Circassian—' "

"Stop showing off," Mike said.

" 'Circassian walnut. There is no finer gun for upland game. Try it out.' 'I'll take it,' he says. 'The price—' the salesman says. 'It's for a gift,' the fellow says, 'and I'm . . .' He pulls out his watch. 'I forgot my brother's birthday. I'll take the gun.' 'You won't be sorry,' the salesman says. He summons his minions, and instructs them to package and wrap the shotgun, one-two-six.

"The salesman says, '*Now.* What might your brother like to accessorize the . . . ?' 'If he wants something, I'm sure he'll come in,' our man says, 'and you can charge it to me.' He looks at his watch. '*Ammunition?*' the salesman suggests. He brings a box from under the counter. 'What? Yes, yes, two.' 'Two boxes?'

" 'No. Two *shells*,' the husband says. 'Wrap it up.' Husband's looking at his watch. The assistant comes back carrying the unwrapped shotgun. 'Sir,' he says, 'we found a *slight dent* in the forestock . . .' He shows it. 'I don't care,' our guy says. He reaches for the gun. 'Oh no, sir,' the salesman says, 'Von Lengerke and Antoine could not let a less-than-perfect gun leave this store. At that price, no.' 'My brother,' the man says. 'I'm late for his *birthday* party . . .'

" 'Yes, I understand,' the salesman says. He waves the offending gun away, and takes another shotgun from the rack. 'This is the Purdey,' he says. 'Yes, a Purdey shotgun. In the presentation grade. The price is, of course, much much higher, the platinum fittings . . .' 'I'll take it,' the guy says. 'There were only five of them made, we were allowed one. It lists for six hundred dollars. In light of the inconvenience we have caused and of your value as a loyal customer, perhaps you will allow us to offer it to you with a twelve percent discount.' 'I'll take it,' the guy says. He takes the gun, grabs two shells from the box, and walks out of the store. Calls, 'Write it down.' Off he goes to the hotel.

"In the cab, muttering, 'Two one nine, two one nine.' Gets to the hotel. In the lobby he looks at the key rack, yes, two one nine, key still gone, still in the room. Loads the gun. Second floor. Two one nine, two one nine. Finger on the trigger. Kicks in the door. Old fat man, at the sink, in a towel, shaving. Our man looks around. In the bed, fat old lady in curlers, reading a magazine.

"Old guy shaving looks at our guy. 'Mother of *God*,' he screams. 'Is that a presentation-grade *Purdey*?' Our man allows that, yes, it is, old guy puts his hands out, lovingly, 'Might I just hold it?' Our guy offers the gun to the guy. Gun goes off, blows the old lady in two. Blood, shit, and hair all over the walls."

The fellow from New York howled at his own joke. ". . . All over the fucken walls . . ." Parlow looked at Mike.

Mike's own personal "murder by firearm" story had been, over the year, excised from the group's memory. They had passed through the inadvertencies of constant concern for the bereaved; and time had enforced the dictum never to mention a rope in the house of a hanged man, and there were no new inadvertent, hurtful reminders of Mike's loss.

The murder of Annie Walsh was history, and that which was history was not news.

Her death fell, like the school fire at All Saints, into that category of event which was in no wise a fit subject for domination through humor, and so, again, it, being of no use, was put aside.

It had been half a year since Mike had come back to work, and like many another returned wounded, his disfigurement had soon ceased to be remarked upon, and then ceased being noticed.

But the fellow from New York had called it up. And Mike told him, "Your story is bullshit. You want to learn to tell a better story? Go out there and get your nose broke, you fucking ponce."

Mike pushed his chair back and stood.

"And you sold a few papers with that execution shot,

didn't you?" Mike said. "That girl dying . . . No one who saw that photo ever will forget it. But, anyone, actually *saw* a dead body, they didn't cherish the sight, but they looked away."

"*Say,*" the New York man said.

"You piece of shit, you ever see a dead body?"

"I saw a photo of one," the New York man said.

"And what did that *do* for you?" Mike said. "Or was it just 'French postcards'? I'm talking to you. Was it 'news'? Or revenge. The fucking girl getting fried . . . ?"

"Say that it was," the New York man said. "By whom? 'Revenge'? On the part of *whom*? 'By society'? *Yes.*"

" 'Society' didn't suffer in that murder," Mike said. "The *victim* fucking suffered; and whatever society thinks it was owed was paid when she received the sentence *and* died. But she wasn't sentenced to have her fucking picture took."

The man turned his head. Mike grabbed him by the collar, wrenched him around, and slapped him hard.

"Don't you turn away from me, you fucking cocksucker," Mike said.

Mike felt Parlow's arm around him, restraining him. He consented to be walked away.

Parlow whispered, "You're out of your mind."

Mike said, "Yeah. *That's* true." Parlow relaxed his grip.

Mike turned back to the table. "Wait 'til something happens to you," he said. "Then come and talk to me about revenge."

Parlow put his hand on Mike's arm. Mike shrugged it off and walked to the door.

Peekaboo and Mike were two-thirds of the way through a bottle which not only was advertised as, but tasted like, prewar scotch.

"Put that photo of that poor white girl, the cover of their newspaper," Peekaboo said. "I'd call that an act of perversion."

"They killed that girl."

"Your girl?" Peekaboo said.

Mike shook his head. "Ruth Watkins, worked for Lita Grey," he said. "They tortured her. They killed Jackie Weiss, they went to his house, they killed the maid. Opened the safe. Killed the safecracker."

"That ain't *The Trail of the Lonesome Pine*," Peekaboo said. "That's revenge."

"Spanish say, revenge is a dish best eaten cold," Mike said.

"Revenge like lobster," Peekaboo said. "Best hot *or* cold. But they ain't wrong. *White* boy, killed my brother, what can you do?"

"What *can* you do?" Mike said.

"Well, *alright,*" Peekaboo said. "White boy, out driving, some night, wintertime, Li'l Buggy, his best gal. Someone? Waylaid him? Coupla fellows." She gestured, *What can you do?*

"They'd kill the fella, rape the girl?" Mike said.

Peekaboo shrugged.

"What can you do?" she said.

"How they put her back together?" Mike said.

". . . Put her back together?"

"The white girl," Mike said, "after they raped her."

"After they raped her? The white girl . . . Didn't have to 'put her back together.' Left her, all her underthings off, *as if,* or, just as usually, the *case,* her boyfriend'd been fucking her."

"And then they'd kill her *too,*" Mike said.

"'*Too*'?" Peekaboo said. "*Honey:* they'd kill the white boy *second. First* thing, force him to watch. *Rape* her, then kill *her,* n'*then* do him." She looked at him as if to say, *Who brought* you *up?*

"Reason I mention it. My *brother?* Before he died. However he died. He *understood,* spoken or not, *you* understand, his friends would take revenge. And he died *with* that. That's not nothing."

"No. No, it's not nothing," Mike said.

"Now, they *didn't* rape them nuns . . . ?"

"They *may* have," Mike said. "You never know."

"Yeah. Those nuns. Didn't do anything. But that's the way of the world."

She rose wearily. "Yeah, *you* know," she said. "You got to do what gon' make you feel better, sugar." She sighed.

"The white girl, in the buggy," Mike said. "How'd it come down? Set it up like she killed the boyfriend?"

"That's right," Peekaboo said. "He was trine, fuck her, she fought for her honor—he's trine break her neck—so she killed him."

"How did she do it, with a throw-down gun?"

"Mike," she said, "poor black boys? Ain't got no money for a *throw*-down gun. Follow me: White boy was trine to rape her? She stuck her hat pin in his heart."

"What about if she wasn't wearing a hat?"

"Well, then, there you *are . . . ,*" Peekaboo said.

The telephone was silent. The last expected customers had gone upstairs, the cold weather bid against the chance of a late-night walk-in. Peekaboo told Marcus to "start putting it away," and he left the kitchen. Mike stood, looking out the frosted window.

"Down south, Texas, down to Shreveport," Peekaboo said, "lots of them, Creoles, seem to me, mixture, Spanish and the French. And Negro. You'd think, some of 'em, passing, but I never saw them. Too proud, God bless 'em, to pass. And they *could,* you know? But they set themselves, or kept themselves, off, so's you could tell. Not by they skin, which sometimes you could, nor either by their clothing, if you look at it, for, most the time, they was just *well* dressed, but, if you looked hard, you know, and sizing them up, you'd see they was better dressed, better looking, better figure, the men *and* the girls, than if they was white.

"Because they were *proud;* and I don't blame 'em. One I know. White man, insulted him? Called the white man out. *White* man said, 'I don't fight no nigger,' which was certainly convenient. The *Creole?* Caught him in the street, whipped him worse than you would a dog. White man, whimpering. In the dirt. *I* got to think: that was the best revenge. And *that* wu'nt eaten cold, and you know it's true.

"Étouffée, now, got to be hot. You could woof it down, you come in, bucket of beer, and so on, but it should be hot. I knew them could cook it, *most* of them, light you up hot as you could wish, *spicy?* That's what cools you off, a hot day.

"S'inn on the balcony, ices? As they say, you on the right road, but you going the wrong way."

"Mint julep," Mike suggested.

"Alright," Peekaboo said. "But, the worth of *that,* of course, the bourbon, help you sweat it out. As, look here: the *heat,* you know, is what keeps us alive; filled with all these degraded notions, finally, come down to philosophy. Poor Creoles, if you understand, far superior to white *or* black, these grandees, something, brought down *by* the knowledge. Like here, you see, peddling one race to the other, black girl, slave to the white man, white man, slave to his dick, you know otherwise tell me. *All* about heat."

She reached behind her, to the rolltop desk, she took a package of cigarettes and shook one out, lit it, and put the burnt match in the ashtray.

There were five black imitation-leather ledger books, with red imitation-leather corners. Next to them were several rough-sharpened lead pencils, their edges squared by a knife. The knife lay next to them. It was a small office knife. On the celluloid handle was printed BRANDT'S RESTAURANT SUPPLY, 221 SOUTH DEARBORN. CALL DEARBORN FIVE, 113.

Peekaboo exhaled the cigarette smoke. She sighed, and turned back to the rotogravure section of the *American,* rolled into a cylinder and stuck into a pigeonhole of the desk. She removed it, and it opened to the fashion page. It showed two stylized line drawings, a man and a woman, dressed for spring.

". . . And they killed that poor *black* girl," Mike said softly.

Peekaboo looked up from the fashion section. Then she looked down.

"Overcoats getting longer this year," she said.

Chapter 33

Mike walked into the City Room. Parlow was back in their corner, feet up on the desk, reading a proof. Mike stood over the desk, still in his hat and coat.

"Says here, 'Sir William Frederick, assistant British consul, to visit fair city,'" Parlow said.

"How can you read that shit?" Mike said.

"It cheers me."

"Where did you get those fucking boots?" Mike said.

"I bought them," Parlow said. "From a bootery in London, much as *anyone* would."

"I need a drink," Mike said.

Parlow removed a half-pint bottle from his overcoat pocket.

". . . Where also, I purchased this overcoat, Harris Tweed, hand-woven by the poor but honest 'hand weavers,' of Ireland, or wherever 'Harris' had elected to light."

Mike shook a cigarette out of the pack, lit it, inhaled, and shook his head.

"What is it?" Parlow said.

The Woman's Department of the *Tribune* sat in the northwest corner of the City Room. It housed the desk of the sob sister, generically called "Ask Miss Fisk," who also doubled as the gossip editor, and the layout tables for "Styles and Fashions."

Mike came through the door of the Woman's Department. The young man who, that year, was Ask Miss Fisk, looked up from his typewriter.

"What's a raglan sleeve?" Mike said.

"It's a sleeve cut on the bias," the young man said. He demonstrated by slashing the edge of his hand diagonally across his shoulder.

"It was named for Lord Raglan, who, in the Crimean War, lost his arm. It, generally . . ." But Mike was involved with the bound copies of *Fashion Annual* shelved on the wall. He opened them, one after the other, to Men's Outerwear, and placed them, open, on the layout table.

"Why do you ask?" Miss Fisk said.

"They wear them *here*?" Mike said.

"Yes," the young man said. "They're coming back." Mike, shaking his head, paged through the volume for 1926.

"What?" Mike said.

"They were adopted, as a novelty, some years after the War."

". . . By the *veterans*?" Mike said.

"No, not at all," the young man said. "No. Generally by the rich. After the War, who would have seen them in their travels."

"Would see them *where*?" Mike said.

"In England, in Scotland."

Mike showed a line drawing to Miss Fisk. It showed a fashionable man, in an ankle-length overcoat. Mike pointed to the shoulders.

"Raglan sleeves," Miss Fisk agreed.

"Cashmere, camel, vicuna . . . ?"

"*Vicuña*," Miss Fisk said. "It's an expensive—"

"No no no," Mike said, "this was cheaper. It was *rougher*."

"What? Where?" the young man said. "Yes, they were adopted for the *drape*, the fabric, coming from the collar, fell—"

"He came through the door, *yeah, no,*" Mike said. "These, these these, fit like a *box.* The fabric . . . It looked like? The fella on the Front? You sleep in the coat, a year, nothing else has that look. It was *rough.* The fabric. But, but, it was worn out in the weather, fella, sweated into it, slept in it. *Heavy* material."

Mike stared at the line cuts of the fashionable coats, and shook his head.

"Who did?" Miss Fisk said.

"And the *collars* are wrong." Mike pointed to the book. "It was like, a farmer—not a farmer, a . . . He wore it like a *work* coat." He stopped.

"What?" young man said.

"It was his only coat. It could have been his father's coat," Mike said. "It was made, it wasn't 'fashionable,' it was made. For a man who'd only have the one coat. To last him. And the collar was rounder."

"What do you mean?" the young man said.

Mike took a sheet of paper and drew the coat and the collar. "You know," Mike said, "how the fella looks? When he comes in? His clothes look like that, and you know how they smell, from the rain. He's been out in the wind.

"And you know," Mike said, "their *hands.* And the look, when he's been out there?"

Miss Fisk looked at the line drawing. "Like a worker," he said. "Some Englishman, a casual worker, or . . ."

"That's what it was, that's what it was," Mike said, "that they'd been *soldiers* . . ."

"Or an Irishman," Miss Fisk said.

"What?" Mike said.

In the Newspaper Morgue Mike sat over a book, with Parlow, at the desk. The girl from the Morgue, who insisted on calling her department "Research," had brought the new book, and left with the old. The new book, which was *Jane's Small Arms of the World*, edition of 1919, had been opened at random, and Mike was slowly paging through it.

Parlow looked over Mike's shoulder. " 'European handguns of the Great War,' " he read. "What did *you* carry?"

The pages held schematic drawings of handguns, and their specifications. Mike leafed quickly through the section on automatics.

"What did *you* carry . . . ?" Parlow said.

"Please be quiet," Mike said.

"I never learned the trick," Parlow said, "I—"

Mike turned back several pages and pointed. "This," he said. "Seven point six five, Fabrique Nationale, semiautomatic . . ." Mike turned quickly through the chapter.

"I'm still reading," Parlow said.

"There's nothing to know," Mike said. "It was a thirty-two-caliber short—my gun."

"What was it good for?" Parlow said.

"You crashed, you used it, to put the plane out of its misery."

"What a romantic life," Parlow said. Mike turned through the pages showing the Colt and Smith & Wesson revolvers. "Smith & Wesson, and Colt," Parlow said, "are not European, as every schoolgirl knows."

"Shut up," Mike said.

"Crouch is looking for you," Parlow said. "What's that?"

Mike had stopped and was looking down at a line drawing of ungainly revolvers.

"The *Webleys*," Mike said, "were *used*, if you must, by the British, to whom we gave or sold them; and by the French, who, having forsworn the sword, required some arm of honor, to surrender to the accommodating German."

"Ah," Parlow said.

Mike continued through the subsection "Revolvers, British." He stopped.

Parlow read, "'Webley revolver, point four five five.'" He looked at Mike.

"It was something like this," Mike said.

"*British*," Parlow said. "But you said the caliber was forty-five. Forty-five. Which even I realize is different from four five five."

"That's right."

"So why are we looking at *this* gun?" Parlow said.

Mike took the lead slug from his pocket.

"This's the bullet that they shot the black girl with," he said. "Measures out at four five five."

"And what did they kill your girl with?" Parlow said. He pointed at the book.

"No," Mike said. "No. It was *like* this . . . *Something* like this." He shook his head. "It was, it had a shorter barrel, almost no barrel at all. The . . . the, it was a *vicious* . . ."

"Would the Americans bring one back, as a souvenir of war?"

"Very good," Mike said. "I . . . Of course it's possible, but it's unlikely."

"Why?" Parlow said.

"Because of the ammunition. Four five five. I've never heard of it being sold here."

". . . But—"

"*Yes*, someone might have brought one back as

a souvenir of war, or as a *paperweight*"—he nodded toward Parlow, in compliment to Parlow's noncombatant status—"but any, saving your presence, who would prize a war trophy would, likely, prefer something of the forces with whom we were at war.

"But it was *like* this gun," Mike said. "It was *like* this."

". . . But the caliber of the bullet was wrong . . . ," Parlow said.

"What the hell do you know about it?" Mike said.

" 'Fucking noncombatant'?" Parlow suggested.

"No, no, I'm *asking* you," Mike said.

"Well, you could amend your *tone*," Parlow said, "after all."

Parlow took his pipe from one jacket pocket, and his tobacco pouch from the other. "Many fine people have never shot someone," he said. ". . . Or been shot. Jesus Christ, I'm just a *fellow*, alright? *And* your friend. You want to put that in the balance, for the love of . . ."

Mike took his pipe and snapped it apart at the stem.

"Why don't you straighten up," Parlow said, "and kick that shit."

"And why don't you buy a new pipe?" he said.

". . . Alright," Parlow said softly.

". . . You understand?"

"Sure," Parlow said.

"What can I do to make amends?" Mike said.

"Buy me a new pipe," Parlow said.

There were the places one reserved for special meditation. In grief, in love, in the life crises or change, Chicagoans always went to the Lake. The bar, and not the cemetery, was the place for grief, the club or bordello for comfort or its counterfeit. And most men had a special place, held in reserve, for the practice of actual deep cogitation. Mike's was the Mallers Café.

The cafeteria was on the second floor of the Mallers Building, twenty feet from the platform of the El trains. The platform had been built as part of the boondoggle of the Elevated project. The dodge was the encirclement of the downtown business district by an elevated rapid transit system.

It was sold to the voters as an aid to their retail shopping, and was financed by huge bribes, given by the merchants to the City Council. The City Council took the money and donated the right-of-way, in perpetuity, to their choice of street traction companies. The fortunate companies were chosen according to the decimal system, and the City Council got rich by robbing both Peter and Paul.

The stop across from the café had its own second-floor connection to the great emporium of Marshall Field. His son had been killed in a shootout at the Everleigh Club. Mike, as a good Chicagoan, cherished the chicanery of the street traction business, the City Council, and the whorehouse shooting and the subsequent attempts at cover-up.

The trains came by every minute or so, and no one noticed them. The clientele was generally on a time clock, wolfing down the "coffee and," midmorning, or the quickest lunch, before heading back to work.

The building was Chicago's Jewelry Exchange. Every floor held several jewelers, appraisers, vendors of fixings, gold or silver dealers, rare coin operations, and engravers. Most in the cafeteria were these small-business owners or the employees. Time spent in the café was time in which they would not be making money. So they ate quickly and silently, the American-born—the minority—nosed into the sports section, the immigrants reading the editorials.

Mike sat over a third cup of coffee. "Yeah," he thought, "*look* at it: that one's got a heavy date tonight, this guy's screwing his secretary, what's he worried about, did she miss a month? That fellow's a carthorse, working himself to death, most of the day, the underlying thought: 'For *what?*' Here's a fellow with ambition, well, he's young enough. There's a guy, what is he doing? Plotting. He's plotting. I'd bet on him, not even knowing the deal: he's a thug."

The coffee had gotten cold. Mike, reluctantly, rose to leave. He paid at the counter, walked out. On the stairs, he reached for his cigarettes, and found the pack empty.

The El clattered overhead, up Wabash Avenue. Mike stood on the east side of the street, thought, "Wabash is always in shadow, but you never notice it. Why don't we notice it? Because in summer it's a bit of a break from the heat; in winter, the El tracks protect it, just a touch, from the snow; and finally, because it's alive, and interesting." There were clerks and shopgirls, most of them hurrying, as the stores were, in the main, beyond their pocketbooks. There were professional men, doctors and lawyers, businessmen going to lunch, or the club; there were the shoppers, most of them men, leaving the women to the great emporia one block west, on State Street.

The loudspeaker outside Lyon & Healy music blared "The Sheik of Araby." Two young boys listening sang the antiphonal responses.

I'm the Sheik of Araby . . .

". . . without no clothes on."

Your love belongs to meee . . .

". . . without no clothes on."

At night when you're asleep . . .

The boys straightened up and began to walk slowly away; some yards behind them walked the uniformed cop whose notice they'd seen they'd attracted.

"Yes," Mike thought, "some bogus excuse from school. But you know it won't stretch *that* far. Good for you."

The cop stopped, content that the boys had moved on.

"Yeah, it's a great show," Mike thought.

Mike strolled south, and found himself outside the window of IVAN REISZ, TOBACCONISTS, 1885.

The store smelled delightfully of pipe tobacco and Havana cigars. The owner was a white-haired German. Before the War he had sported a Kaiser Wilhelm mustache. Mike had been in France during the transformation, and the old man was now clean-shaven and, to Mike's eye, looked naked. He stood at the pipe counter, polishing a beautiful meerschaum. He put on his customers face, and half-nodded at Mike.

"A pack of Camels," Mike said. "And I need to buy a pipe."

The owner reached behind him for the cigarettes.

"One moment," he said, and walked to the back of the store. Mike looked down at the various pipes under the counter glass. The owner returned with the cigarettes.

"Let me see *that* one, please," Mike said, and pointed.

"Is it for you?" the owner said.

"No," Mike said. "It's for a friend."

"He likes this style?"

"Yeah, that's the one he smokes."

The owner lifted out the pipe and handed it to Mike. "A *bulldog*," he said. He waved his hand over the pipes display. "We have the bulldog *bent,* the *straight,* which is *this* one . . ."

"No," Mike said. "This'll do it."

The man nodded. He took the pipe, and hunted in the counter below for the box.

The salesman put the pipe into its box. The box was marked *Alfred Dunhill: Bulldog.* Mike declined the offer of gift wrapping, of pipe cleaners, of tobacco. He paid for the pipe and his cigarettes and left the store.

"Yeah, I made a fool of myself with that idiot from New York," he thought. "And Parlow. I'm losing my mind."

He knew that Parlow understood his outburst, and would accept the gift less as an apology, and more, correctly, as thanks for his understanding.

"Yes, but it can't be the *old* pipe," he thought, ". . . the bulldog."

As he walked he reviewed the New Yorker's story. It was not that it was bad, he thought, and who cared if it was improbable; but it was offensive for a stranger to apostrophize the gun violence yarn in the place of its birth.

"If it were one of the lads," Mike thought, "I could appreciate it, but a fellow in spats had no right to tell a story involving guns. *And* he had his fucking facts wrong."

He stopped to light his cigarette. The El ran overhead, and Mike turned toward the window to shield the match. The window held a selection of sporting arms: the handguns displayed flat, and the long arms mounted in a star radiating around the company's trademark, Von Lengerke and Antoine. *V, L, and A.* Sporting goods. Mike went inside.

He told the floorwalker, "Gun department." The floorwalker directed him to the back of the store. The salesman was displaying a rifle to a customer. Mike took the pipe box from his pocket and opened it. He took the leaflet covering the pipe from the box and read, *Congratulations. You have just purchased the finest briar pipe made. Alfred Dunhill, of London, warranties this pipe against not only defects, but wear, and dissatisfac-*

tion. If at any time you find yourself less than pleased, return the pipe for a full refund. We thank you for your purchase, and your . . .

The salesman said, "May I help you?" Mike looked up. He closed the box and put it down upon the counter.

"I wanted," Mike said, "to ask a question."

"Yes?"

"About a shotgun."

"What sort of game do you wish to hunt, sir?" the salesman said.

"No," Mike said, "I'm actually, I'm just curious." He saw the salesman conceal his disappointment. "Well done," thought Mike, "you work on commission, selling to the high end, here comes a bloke with a crushed hat, and what if a hot prospect walks in?"

Mike took a card from his pocket and handed it to the man. "The *Tribune* is thinking of doing a service feature on the"—his mind raced for a quarter second—"guns of the cognoscenti."

"Ah," the salesman said. He looked at the card. "*I* know you, sir," he said, "and I know who you are, and I appreciate your work."

"Thank you," Mike said.

"And *I*"—he leaned closer to Mike—"although I don't know this would interest you, have been mulling over an article about language and firearms."

"Really," Mike said.

"Yes, although you might say, as it would deal with antique arms, the current interest might seem lacking. *But . . .*" The man espoused to Mike the history of expressions, part of the language, whose origin, seemingly lost, was rooted in the Age of Black Powder.

" 'Hang fire,' " the man said, " 'flash in the pan,' 'chewing the rag,' 'shot his wad,' which was 'shot his rod,' being the ramrod, the loss of which, having been shot, rendered the arm unable to fire . . . 'Lock, stock, and barrel.' " The man ran down and Mike agreed that his observations might indeed make good copy, and that he might forward his article to his editor, Mr. Crouch, City Desk, *Tribune.*

The man thanked Mike.

"But, on no account," Mike said, "mention that we spoke, for my endorsement would, with my editor, do your chances harm." The salesman nodded. "Envy," Mike said.

"Thank you, I understand," the man said. "And take *this*," he said, "as a coincidence." He pointed to the pipe box on his countertop.

"What of it?" Mike said.

"It's a *bulldog*," the man said. "The bulldog shape, *pugnacious—*"

"Is there such a thing—" Mike said.

"Pugnacious, aggressive, squat—"

"Fine," Mike said, "but *is* there such a thing as a presentation-grade Purdey—"

"Also, the name of a revolver. I beg your pardon?"

"I beg your pardon," Mike said, "I fear *I* interrupted *you*. You said the name of a pistol. What is it, please?"

"The Bulldog," the salesman said. "More accurately, a revolver."

He took a stack of sales catalogs from the counter, and opened one. "Webley Arms," he said. He turned to the line drawing of an ugly squat heavy revolver.

"Webley Bulldog," he said, "or, more accurately, Webley R.U.C."

He turned the drawing to Mike, who recognized it as the handgun the man had used to murder Annie Walsh.

The salesman was still speaking when Mike looked up. ". . . never see them over here," he said, "as the caliber, four fifty-five, is unobtainable. In Europe, however—"

"R.U.C.," Mike said. "What does that mean?"

"R.U.C. Royal Ulster Constabulary," the salesman said. "Black and Tans. Keeping down the IRA. And here's another instance for your article . . ."

The salesman turned and took down from the gun rack a submachine gun.

"Thompson, forty-five caliber, commercial grade and the best protection you can buy." He opened the bolt; showed the gun, empty, to Mike; and laid it on the counter.

"John Taliaferro Thompson invented the gun, in 1914. Known, currently, as the tommy gun, most assume, incorrectly, in compliment to Mr. Thompson. No. The first recorded use is Irish. For they, in the Time of the Troubles, adopted the gun to assassinate the Tommys, which is to say, the British soldiers."

"The Irish," Mike said, "where did they buy the guns?"

"Oh, no, they couldn't buy them," the salesman said. "There was, and is, a strict embargo. No. They stole them."

Chapter 34

Mike was getting Sergeant O'Malley drunk.

The Piper's Kilt was the cop bar for the Forty-Third Ward. The eight-to-four was on, and the two o'clock hour granted no immunity to any on duty, being neither at the top nor at the bottom of the watch, nor sufficiently adjacent to noon to explain a working officer's presence at the bar.

The odd patrolman came by, casing the bar for superiors, his survey aided by the least perceptible "yea" or "nay" nod from the bartender.

The presence of the sergeant in the back booth would have been sufficient to dissuade the incursion of the rank and file, but Sergeant O'Malley had been drinking for an hour, and was drunk.

"Oh yeah," O'Malley said, "the North Side got

the Thompson gun, what was it, 'twenty-two or
-three."

"Before Capone . . . ?" Mike said.

"It wasn't Capone, then, it was, yes. It was *Torrio.*
O'Banion and them—"

"You guys didn't have it?" Mike said.

"Will you let me tell it?" O'Malley said.

"Did you have it?"

"They came through," O'Malley said, "my recol-
lection. Some of the, the National Guard, downstate?
Somebody, I think, was impressed, its operation, or
a couple of bucks and a hooker, salesman threw in, it
might have been, ordered a few, one, two, for 'evalu-
ation,' what there is to evaluate, escapes me, it is the
most perfect instrument of peace since the Holy Sacrament; but, *but* bureaucracies turn slow, like a ship of
the line. You in the navy?"

"No," Mike said.

"Marines?"

"No."

"Yeah. The *navy?* Was the white guys, mainly, I
think. I was a Marine—that's where they put the Catholics."

"A lot of Irish."

"God bless 'em," O'Malley said. "Father Durning,
St. Malachy's? Lot of the force are members, for the

early Mass, it being convenient to the House, 'opined,' that the unpleasantness, as he said, blotting the name of our fair city, could be eradicated by referral to those same Catholic virtues shared by both the Irish, which we comprise, the North Side lads, and the Outfit, with whom, for all their dark Italian ways, we also share a faith."

"That's a fine sentiment," Mike said.

"We thought so," O'Malley said, "and it furnished food for philosophic contemplation."

"What did you conclude?" Mike said.

"The consensus was the sermon was well said, and poetic, but it lacked the common sense that God gave geese. As, accepting that the Eyeties and Sons of Eire are of one faith—which I am, finally, no wise inclined to fully grant, though the two rituals may share some outward trappings—who fights more fiercely than the members of a family?"

"Well done," Mike said.

"Witness the eternal and the bloody wars of the goddamned Protestants, over their points of doctrine discernible to no one at all but the fanatic, or those who, speaking in their favor, just enjoy a fight. The Prods are clustered, in their comfort, along the Lake, looking down on the lesser races who, in which we are united, struggle to eke out a living catering to their otherwise illegal needs, those who are mobbed up, or, as in our case, endeavoring to regularize, if not to diminish, the depredations of the aforesaid.

"Fellows, I believe, acting freelance, or, as we said in Ireland, as factors—or middlemen—flogged the few trench guns to the National Guard. It was some of these, I believe, which went missing into the hands of O'Banion."

"How do the dots connect?" Mike said.

"The *Jews*," O'Malley said, "who would sell you the shirt off *your* back, who wholesaled Our Savior, who run the pawnshops, the bucketshops, and who are in league, in the main, with the North Side, were, I believe, the middlemen, who were, on speculation, hawking the trench broom, or tommy gun, to the police forces of the Middle West."

Mike nodded.

"But, *but:* in 1922 the police, they were not buying. *How,* then, the gun makers reasoned, to draw attention of the law enforcement community to the true merits of this piece of genius?"

"Give it to the crooks," Mike said.

"Mike, for a Protestant, you have an agile mind. Yes. Now see *here,* for I will ask you, can you quote from that captain of industry Philip D. Armour? And tell me what it says upon his cans of lard?"

" 'We sell every part of the pig except the squeal.' "

"The Sheenies, likewise, whom he must have observed, understand that it is the gleanings of the field in which the profit rests. That is your profit. Our arms middlemen, coming through, could, it is true, appeal directly to the forces of crime. Of course. *But:* first, the public outcry, of which you I know have heard, having, time to time, created it, would turn *against* the arms manufacturer.

"No, no, the arms must be sold to a legitimate purchaser, and *then* stolen. This, you will see, apes the acumen of Philip Armour, for the merchants of death not only thus immunize themselves against the accusation of aiding the lawless . . ."

"They collect a commission on the guns they sell," Mike said.

"Yes, *and, and,* after the guns go wandering off with the lawless, they create a demand for their like in the police community, and increase their sales commissions there, too."

"It pays to advertise," Mike said.

"Indeed it does," O'Malley said. "And now both sides are armed with Colonel Thompson's gun, and the opposition of crime and the law is less and less likely to resemble Pistols at Dawn, and more and more the Chinese New Year. Why did you ask about the Thompson gun?"

"Because they used it to shoot Nails Morton's horse," Mike said.

"The poor beast," O'Malley said. "And wasn't it an act of irony."

"How's that?" Mike said.

"Because who was it stole the original guns from the armory," O'Malley said, "and flogged them to O'Banion?"

"Who?" Mike said.

"You disappoint me," O'Malley said. "Who would arrange it but the Sheeny businessmen who were the salesmen in the first place? They arranged it."

"Why did they go to O'Banion rather than to Capone?" Mike said.

"Well, everyone trusts their own," O'Malley said, "when it is in preference to trusting a stranger. The Jews, they went to the Irish through Samuel 'Nails' Morton, a man of their faith. Didn't they? . . . All them guns."

O'Malley stood.

"Where are you going?" Mike said. "You got to rush off? Have another drink for the love of God."

O'Malley sat. "You trine a get me drunk?" he said.

"After the *first* guns . . . ," Mike said. He filled the two glasses.

"Alright. The *profusion*," O'Malley said. "Well,

now, as with any luxury product, its distribution may have outdistanced its inventory control. Torrio, and them, could obtain them through purchase and barter with associates here and there, and back east, closer to the factory. Which, I am not saying, but, if I were they, I would have left but minimally guarded. And let nature take its course."

"And O'Banion?"

"*Well*," O'Malley said, "he had his entrée, some might say, more directly, through the arsenals of the patriotic lads in blue." They both drank. The bartender laid the check on the booth table, and Mike waved him away.

"Patriotic to *who?*" Mike said.

"What?" O'Malley said.

"Patriotic to *who?*" Mike said.

"Why, to their *country*," O'Malley said. "*Sláinte.*" He drank.

"*All* the guns," Mike said.

"What?" said O'Malley.

"'*All* the guns,' you said. How many were there? That went stolen?"

"Well," O'Malley said. "I'm going to have to look into that."

Chapter 35

Mike met Danny Doyle at dusk on North Avenue Beach, at the end of the breakwater. The Gold Coast stretched behind them. In the clouds to the south they could just make out the orange glow of the steel mills in Gary. The wind was, as usual, cruel.

Danny had come in civilian clothes; he wore an overcoat, a cloth cap, and gloves, his face and neck swaddled in a thick blue muffler.

Mike had been sitting on the last bench, looking at the Lake. He rose as Doyle approached, and noticed that Doyle had so correctly interpreted the invitation as to have come out of uniform.

"Yeah, fine," Doyle said, "and let's walk, or we'll freeze to death."

They began to walk down the breakwater and back toward the beach.

"You got," Doyle said, "a romantic streak, which, being neither a Jew nor an Irishman, I got to say has to come from your nurse dropped you on your head out of the cradle." Then, having run out of small talk, he stopped.

"I want to know about the IRA," Mike said.

"Well, Jesus, Mary, yes, and Joseph," Doyle said, "*you* don't want a lot."

They kept on walking.

"Lot of people were in France," Doyle said. "You could ask some other one of them, other than *me*."

"Tell me who to ask," Mike said.

Doyle shook his head in disgust.

"My *mother*," he said, "I was growing up? She told me two things: 'Whatever you have to do? *Never* get a good girl in trouble.'" He turned his back to the wind and lit a cigarette. "And 'Never trust a Protestant.'"

He turned to Mike.

"The best way I can *help* you," he said, "and I *will* help you, and, I swear to you, this is a gift: we never had this conversation."

Doyle walked away, down into the underpass to Lake Shore Drive.

Sir William Frederick, the secretary at the British consulate regretted, was in Chicago only for a short stay, and would be unavailable for interviews, "as his time was not his own."

Mike hung up the phone. He walked down to the Newspaper Morgue and pulled the files on Sir William. Then, after what he felt was a shamefully short debate, he went home and affixed to his lapel the rosettes of the Croix de Guerre and the British Distinguished Flying Cross.

The desk clerk at the Palmer House knew Mike, and tipped him the room number. Mike knocked on the door. He was admitted into the first five feet of the suite's anteroom by a bodyguard. A well-bred fellow at a desk looked up annoyed and said, "What is it?" in the poshest, most dismissive accent Mike had ever heard.

His eyes went to the medal rosettes on Mike's chest, and he rose, coming, unconsciously, to a modified attention.

"I beg your pardon," he said. "May I help you?"

"My name is Captain Hodge," Mike said. "I would like three minutes with Sir William." He passed the man a card.

"Could you tell me the nature of your inquiries?" the man said.

"I'm sorry, I can't," Mike said.

The secretary excused himself into the next room. Mike and the bodyguard each looked at nothing. Half a minute later Mike was passed into the inner room.

The sitting room held a fireplace displaying neat birch logs, a white baby grand piano, and a large, ornate desk. The bodyguard stood against the wall, halfway between Mike and Sir William.

Sir William rose from the desk, still looking at the card. He put the card down and removed his spectacles. He wore a business suit, and, in its lapel, the single-wing emblem of the Royal Flying Corps.

"*Captain* Hodge," he said.

"Once," Mike said.

"No, you don't actually keep the rank over here, do you?"

"Regular army, they might; though they usually don't under colonel. On retirement. Mere captain's nothing to brag about."

"Well, no, but one *does*. You introduced yourself as 'Captain,'" Sir William said. He indicated, with the most deniable of questioning looks, Mike's rosettes.

"Yeah, I'm ashamed of myself," Mike said.

"Because they're false?" Sir William said.

"No. They're mine," Mike said, "but my exploiting them is an insult to the glorious dead who fell to ensure, for us all, the future."

"Would you like a drink?" Sir William said.

The bodyguard poured the whiskey. Sir William and Mike settled into their seats before the fire, and Mike was pleased to see him utilize the apparent conclusion of his interrogation to ask the telling questions.

"What did you see of it, whom did you fly with, who pinned the medals on" were easy, beautifully thrown away, and answered as if casual small talk between two acquaintances. And Mike was growing pleased that, after what was, in effect, the grilling, the bodyguard left the room to request the vetting of Mike's story. Nothing would be done until someone had vouched for him, so Mike spent the time chatting Sir William up.

"I think that you flew with the R.F.C.," Mike ventured, in imitation of a man who had done no research.

"Oh, what? I suppose I *did*," Sir William said, in his part of the charade, and they both laughed.

The phone rang. Sir William answered it. "Yes?" he said. He listened for a moment, then said, "Thank you," and hung up.

"Captain *Hodge*," he said. "Captain Hodge. Someone, it seems, has vouched for *a* Captain Hodge."

"That would be me," Mike said.

"Who was your squadron commander, in France?"

"Hubert Devere," Mike said.

"Do you recall his wife's name?"

"He didn't care for women," Mike said.

Sir William nodded, and refilled their glasses.

"How might I help you?" he said.

"I want to know about the IRA," Mike said.

Sir William took Mike to lunch at the Drake Hotel. The restaurant looked out over East Lake Shore Drive.

"My real war was South Africa," Sir William said. "It perhaps is rougher *here*."

"At least the territories are defined," Mike said. "I understand over there was a bunch of hide-and-seek."

"No way to fight a war," Sir William said, "save that it was *their* way, and they won."

"Well, perhaps one could learn from them," Mike said.

"One could," Sir William said. "One has. The Irish have. Mow down a bunch of innocents, throw a bomb, 'o'er the Border and awae, wi' Jock O'Hazeldean.'"

"What can be done about it?" Mike said.

Sir William nodded. "The *Irish*? You can do this," he said. "Have a drink, and thank the Lord it's not your fight."

"It's *your* fight," Mike said.

"Yes."

"What will come of it?"

"In truth?"

"Yes."

"In truth? It will bring the Empire down." He shrugged.

"Now," he said, "your wars here, your gang wars, mimic, interestingly, the border squabbles of Europe. Imported, whole, from Sicily, as I am told; and, as I know to be the case, from Ireland."

"What can we do about it?" Mike said.

"Here," Sir William said, "the clan fights within itself, for place and wealth; and, as a clan, against the Other, for territory.

"Each fights, additionally, against what the learned might call the host mechanism."

"The dominant culture," Mike suggested.

"Perhaps," Sir William said, "save, what does it dominate? It is dominated, by those groups which can fight and disband. The borderers. Like our friend Piet in South Africa, the various gangs, here, can pick their fights. We have only the choice of accepting or rejecting each particular battle."

"Napoléon said, 'Who dictates the terms of the battle, dictates the terms of the peace,'" Mike said.

"Indeed he did," Sir William said. "And, like the rest of mankind, he did not take his own advice; and his grand army died in the snows of Russia."

"And here?" Mike said.

"Here, the snows are the riches of your merchant city. Which will tempt, and *convince* the immigrants that the easier way to power is that indigenous to the locale. In South Africa, our friend Piet hid behind rocks and potted us, just as he shot the gazelle.

"Your immigrants here steal and kill; they have the local franchise for sin, and they sell liquor and drugs and women, on license from City Hall. Reformers might call it kickbacks or bribes but it is, finally, merely a license.

"The politicians who oppose them, those who cannot be bribed, if such there be, are, currently, killed. In time, and one may, perhaps, see it already, the Irish, and the Italians, will ask: why not *become* the politicians? And they will.

"They, then, as one soldier to another, will have taught themselves the foremost lesson: study the ground. Then they will not only possess the sin franchise, but every other fungible good, service, and permission."

"What will you do with the IRA?" Mike said.

"Currently, currently, all we can do is kill them. If and when we find them."

"Can you prevent them?"

Sir William shook his head. "We can interdict their *arms*, now and then. They'll go elsewhere, of course, but their arm of choice is, currently, yours . . ."

The waiter came by with the coffeepot.

"Yes, I think so," Sir William said. "You?"

Mike said yes. The waiter poured the coffee and left.

". . . the tommy gun . . . ," Sir William said.

"And they buy them here?" Mike said.

"They can't buy them here," Sir William said, "as there is an arms embargo. They steal them here."

"From whom?" Mike said.

"From your army."

"I'm looking for an Irishman who may be in the IRA," Mike said.

"Should you come across him, I'd hope you'll tell me," Sir William said.

"Can you help me?"

"I would if I could," Sir William said. "Which isn't quite true, and, as one soldier to another, I owe you the truth. And it pains me to refuse you. I perhaps could give you a lead, but it would be a violation of my oath of office. The IRA are involved in the theft, from your armories, of these guns. They are here. I would advise you to steer clear of them. They will not hesitate to kill you. They'll kill anyone."

Sir William patted his lips with the napkin and rose. "*Well*," he said. "Now: here's a tip, however, f'I can do you a good turn."

The good turn concerned the missing automobiles. The coach-built North Shore touring cars lifted, Sir William said, and driven to East Chicago. They were loaded on freighters, and traveled up through the Sault Ste. Marie locks, the St. Lawrence, and trans-ocean to be sold in Europe, mainly in France.

A British contingent of "observers" was due to raid the next outgoing freighter, the first of the coming month. The actual raid and subsequent arrests being conducted by the Washington Bureau of Investigation.

The two men rose and walked across the restaurant.

"Why would you care who's stealing some cars?" Mike said.

"Oh, no. We don't," Sir William said. "But it does get us onto the docks. Which, we have friends who tell us, are the same docks from which our Irish friends are shipping their guns."

Chapter 36

JoJo had called, with, as he said, "a lead into the thing." He asked Mike to meet him at the Chez. Parlow insisted on coming along. Mike asked why.

" 'Cause I don't trust the little snitch," Parlow said.

"Snitch he may be, but he's a noncombatant," Mike said.

"Well, it may take one to know one, so take me along," Parlow said.

The sign read UNDER NEW OWNERSHIP, which meant, of course, "under the same ownership," which meant, of course, Dion O'Banion and the North Side.

The Chez Montmartre was now called the Place Pigalle. The bad liquor was still served in coffee cups; the crap and poker games in the back room were still gaffed; the girls were new, but interchangeable with the girls of old, and they were kept in place still, under the supervision of the North Side.

One could, as before, get a passable drink; edible, overfussed food; a girl; and a floor show. The floor show's quality depended, as always, on the biological imperatives of the manager.

"I know they've got to get laid," Parlow said, "and, owning the barrel, they will shoot the encompassed fish, the chorines, which, while not sport, is, at least, sex; what, though, is the connection, which you must allow exists, between the mugs' taste in broads, and the broads' universal lack of talent?"

The singer nestled in the crook of the piano. She sang "Bye Bye Blackbird" as if it were a dirge for all the good in the world.

"She's not even *attractive*," Mike said.

"She is if you're Jimmy Flynn," Parlow said. "And look at it: This girl, mirabile dictu, he doesn't even have to pay her, take her clothes off. She's stark naked anyway." Parlow nodded at the girl, who was now circulating on the floor, tweaking the necktie of this and that nightclubber, planting a kiss on a bald head, trailing across a shoulder what passed, in courtesy, for a languid hand. The singer came to the bridge.

"No one here can love or understand me / Oh, what hard-luck stories they all hand me . . . ," she sang.

"Best bridge ever written," Mike said.

"I won't argue with you," Parlow said.

The titular ownership of the Chez had passed through Teitelbaum's widow and back to O'Banion and his consortium. There had been talk, the lads said, that Lita Grey held the philosopher's stone which would transform her from the Discarded Woman to the Ruler of It All, but that talk had disappeared with Lita Grey.

"She opened. The Pandora box," JoJo Lamarr had said. "How do I know? As it consumed her. You guys, famously, saw that in France."

"What did we see?" Mike said.

"The Krauts would put a live grenade under their bodies when they died; you guys come around, turn 'em over, or looking for souvenirs, *bang.*"

"I'm sure that went on," Mike said.

"You ever get any souvenirs?" JoJo said.

"I got a love bite from a fifteen-year-old Belgian girl," Mike said, "and a souvenir of the Black Forest: paper knife, with a picture of an elf."

"*Uh*-huh?" JoJo said.

"What was in Pandora's box?" Mike said.

"Well. The secret that can get you killed," JoJo said. "The Black Forest, they make up the fairy tales?"

"The Grimm Brothers," Mike said.

"Yes. The Brothers Grimm," JoJo said, "all the tales of dark forces, and beasts, and so on."

"What are we selling?" Parlow said.

"How did the *guys*," JoJo said, "make up those stories?"

"They invented them," Parlow said.

"Yeah. I understand. But what does that *mean*?"

Mike looked at Parlow, who raised his eyebrows, meaning, *That is either the stupidest or the wisest question I've ever heard, I'll be damned if I know which.*

"They just wrote down a lot of words that occurred to them," Mike said.

JoJo nodded.

"What are you selling?" Parlow said.

"But I can't be happy," the singer sang, " 'til I make *you* happy, too." The audience broke into applause. The singer half-curtsied. The band swung into a two-step, and various men walked their women onto the dance floor.

Mike saw the thief's retreat from the direct question. "Brings you up here?" Mike said.

"Brings me up here is: a *drink*, and a glance at the

bare titties, neither of which, you been downstate, one can never get enough of."

"I'm sure that it was very trying," Parlow said.

"I heard something," JoJo said, "which, I immediately thought, would interest you." He looked at Mike for a moment.

". . . *Alright,*" Parlow said. "Excuse me." He rose and left the table. JoJo watched him walk across the room to the hatcheck, where he began chatting up the hatcheck girl.

"*I* knew that girl, I knew her *father,*" JoJo said. "But I can't remember her name."

"Why'd you want to meet here?" Mike said.

". . . He was a cop? A fireman? A something. In Hegewisch? A cop. He got tossed, he worked as a chauffeur in Hyde Park. His name was, no, his name was . . ." JoJo looked nervously over Mike's shoulder.

"Oh *shit,*" Mike said. "Aw, come *on,* JoJo. You're putting me on the *spot*? Are you fucking putting me on the spot?" Mike looked around the room, but saw no muscle beyond the one eternal bouncer at the door.

"Why would I do that, Mike, I wouldn't do that, and if I did that, why would I do that *here*?"

"Well, then, what the hell's the name of the charade?" Mike said.

Mike felt a light touch on his shoulder. He looked around to see a fellow in a tux.

"Mr. Hodge," the fellow said, "if you would come with me."

The singer finished and bowed herself off, followed by the four barely clad dancers. The MC took the stage.

"Will you look at the sense of *humor* on these broads . . . ?" he said. "*Give* 'em a hand."

The audience applauded as requested.

"*Thank* you," the MC said. He adjusted his tie. "Always delighted to see the cognoscenti of this great and glowing town. It is a rare treat to see this many lovely faces not demanding child support. Drink up, you geniuses, for if you can get smashed on water and iodine you're sittin' pretty and you've got a hell of a short memory. How 'bout those girls, huh? Who wants to take 'em home to Mama . . . ? I'm marrying one of 'em. I got quite a shock, I know her as Louise, on the marriage license, they tell her, 'Put your real name.' Turns out, she was christened 'Third from the Left.'"

Mike was led through a curtain just off the stage. He squeezed by the last of the dancers. They were lifting off their headdresses and placing them on the rack just offstage.

Mike smelled the sweat and powder from their dressing room. The chorus hurried down the narrow corridor, stripping themselves naked as they filed into the dressing room. Mike was directed down the corridor and up a narrow staircase.

The room was paneled in black walnut. An enormous chesterfield took up one wall. Jimmy Flynn sat behind the partners desk once occupied by Weiss and Teitelbaum. He stood as Mike was passed into the room.

He said, "You want a drink?"

"No thank you," Mike said.

Flynn said, "Then sit down."

Mike sat on the couch. Flynn walked around the desk. He took the partner's chair and turned it, and sat facing Mike. He rubbed the top of his head for a moment.

"*Look*," he said. "Instead of the preface, here it is: your, your *work*, it gets back to us, is taking you into an area, you don't want to go."

"Alright, what are we talking about?" Mike said. " 'Cause you don't want me, I presume, just, hang up my hat, and move to Michigan, or die, or something, or why'm I here?"

The man did not speak.

"Give me a hint," Mike said. "*You* know who I am."

"I know who you are," Flynn said, "and you have the reputation of being an okay guy, that's right."

"Well, then, why don't you . . . Let me start again," Mike said. "If you don't mean to shoot me: tell me what you *do* mean, and perhaps we'll work something out."

"I'm in a hell of a position. Nobody wants to hurt you," Flynn said, "this fucking thing has hurt you enough. Look . . ."

Mike left the office, and began down the stairs leading through backstage and out the front. The chorus was on, singing and dancing to "The Oceana Roll."

"To see the smoke so black, come from the old smokestack / It's floatin' up to heaven and it won't be back . . ."

Mike turned away, toward another staircase at the far end of the corridor. The floor show was heard, filtered, through the sets and flats stacked at the rear of the stage. Mike had been "given the warning," and he needed to sit down.

A half-open door gave onto a small carpenter shop. The shop was empty. Mike went in and sat at the carpenter's bench. The cheap Masonite board above the bench was covered in chalk drawings of props and scenery. Elevations and plans were pinned into the board, as were several yellowing publicity photos of the chorus.

" 'This fucking thing has hurt you enough,' " he thought. " 'This fucking thing has hurt you enough.' "

He had been, politely, asked to back off his investigations into the deaths of Ruth Watkins and Jackie Weiss. They were connected, as far as he knew, solely by proximity to jewelry belonging to the late club owner.

And the request came from the Chez, Mike reasoned, so the two murders must have been connected to the Chez. Very well. But were they connected to *him*?

In what had the "thing" hurt him enough? Only in the loss of Annie Walsh.

An old man's voice said, "What are you doing here?" Mike turned to see the man, quite obviously the stage carpenter. He was a black man. His coveralls were ancient, and washed, over the years, to the consistency of silk; a flat carpenter's pencil sat in his coverall pocket. He wore a clean blue shirt, buttoned tightly at his neck and wrists, and a four-in-hand string tie, not seen since before the War. He might have been in his late sixties.

"What are you looking at?" he said. He spoke with a trace of a Southern accent and with formality, as a man who had previously had a different life. A teacher, perhaps, Mike thought.

"I beg your pardon," Mike said, and rose.

"What are you looking at?" the man said.

"I was looking at nothing," Mike said. "I came down from the office, I got turned around."

"Who are you?" the man said.

"My name is Hodge," Mike said. "I'm a reporter."

"Are you here about her?" the man said. He nodded his head toward the Masonite board.

"Did you expect someone to come about her?" Mike said.

"She's *dead*," the man said. "I told the police." He was anxious, and lied badly.

"I'm not here about her," Mike said. Whoever she might have been, Mike thought, the man was doing a pathetic job of protecting her. Mike turned away, to spare the man his lie. He found himself looking at the publicity photos of the chorus girls tacked to the wall.

"She's *dead*," the man said. "She's *dead*. And she didn't *do* it." He motioned Mike away from the photos.

"Alright," Mike thought, "somebody's dead and her picture's on the wall. She's dead. And she didn't *do* it. Who is she?" He used the photo grabber's trick. The City Desk sent them to the homes of the bereaved, to steal a photo of a deceased or accused in the confusion. If there were multiple choices, the picture grabber would ask, "Do you have a photo of your son?" If there were photos of several likely candidates, the picture grabber would exploit any opposition, saying, "I just want to know, which one *is* he?" He'd move his hand over the photos. When he reached the right one, the defiant or reluctant family member would look away. "Works every time," Poochy had said. "Every time."

Mike leaned back toward the chorus girl photos; the carpenter turned with him. He scanned them, left to right. At the last-but-one, the carpenter lowered his eyes. The photo showed a reed-thin flapper, half-naked, miming abandon in a pose indicating some sort of free-form dance.

"She didn't do it," the man said.

"She didn't do what?" Mike said. "She didn't do *what?*"

"She didn't take anything out of the safe," the carpenter said.

Mike looked at the photograph. It showed a white woman in her early twenties, with a crooked, winning smile and wide-set eyes. Mike had seen the image before in the Girls of All Nations photograph. She was the "Hawaiian" girl with the ukulele.

The photo was inscribed, "To Pops, Affectionately, Lita Grey."

Chapter 37

There were two fat businessmen in the parlor of the Ace of Spades, and three girls hanging over them. Ralph, the piano man, was giving the parlor "Frankie and Johnnie."

Now Johnnie he was a bull-dagger
He said to Frankie his femme,
"See all them lovelorn old lezzies,
"We won't never end up like them."
He was her man, but she done him wrong.

Frankie went down to the barroom,
Just for a packet of snow.
She asked the bartender for Johnnie
And he said, "Well I just don't know."
He was her man, but she done him wrong.

Peekaboo came downstairs. The businessmen half-rose in an imitation of courtesy. She smiled, and walked toward them.

Mike was standing inside the parlor door. Peekaboo gave him half a nod as she went about her business.

"You folks made up your *mind*, or you want me to turn the house upside down, send *out*, if you must have more refined or exotic tastes, *Topeka*, than we got here." The businessmen laughed. Peekaboo continued her banter.

Ralph sang:

"I don't want to tell you no stories
"I don't want to do you no harm
"But I saw your Johnnie 'bout an hour ago,
"With a little Chink twist on his arm."
He was her man, but she done him wrong.

Marcus came by with a tray of drinks for the businessmen. He looked at Mike, who shook his head no. Marcus laid the tray down on the low table and bowed himself out.

Peekaboo used the interruption to move the party along. She made the choice for the men, with the usual "I know who *you're* looking at," and seeing she had established the pairing, then made her adieux and walked toward Mike.

He started to speak. "Doing business here, sugar," she said under her breath. He nodded.

Ralph sang:

Frankie went down to the corner,
She didn't go there for fun.
With a nose full of snuff,
And inside her muff,
She carried a Colt forty-one.

Mike followed Peekaboo into the kitchen.

"Ruth Watkins," he said.

"Yes, I know who that was," Peekaboo said.

They flanked the kitchen doorway, Peekaboo surveyed the parlor. "Out-of-towners don't go upstairs *now*," she said to herself, "I got to either throw 'em an exhibition, some brand-*new* idea, r'charge 'em rent on the couch." She sniffed and rubbed the back of her hand against her nose.

Frankie she kicked down the doorway.
Johnnie said, "Frankie, please."
Frankie said, "Johnnie, you might as well pray,
"You're already down on your knees."
He was her man, but she done him wrong.

The businessmen guffawed, as at an off-color joke in a men's club. Thelma capitalized on the moment to pull them to their feet. Peekaboo nodded approval.

The girls helped the two businessmen toward the stairs. Florence, the odd girl out, stayed behind, and Ralph gave her an understanding nod.

Peekaboo and Mike faded back into the kitchen as the procession climbed the stairs.

Frankie she pulled out the pistol,
Shot 'em both deader than sin.
Sat down and lit up a reefer,
Smoked 'til the cops came in.
He was her man . . .

Peekaboo closed the swinging kitchen door.

"Ruth Watkins," Mike said.

"And I'll tell you: why she came to grief," Peekaboo said, "was, just as, you touch fire, you're going to get *burnt, she* was associated, wound up all tight, with the white girl. Who, no doubt, sold her out."

"How would the white girl profit . . . ?"

"*Uh*-huh . . . ," Peekaboo said. "N'it may be, both, they was both Leslies, many of them are," Peekaboo said.

"Many of whom?" Mike said.

Peekaboo walked across the kitchen, cracked the door into the parlor, and looked for a while at Marcus cleaning the rug with a carpet sweeper.

"Many of *whom*?" Mike said.

"Many of whom what, lover?" Peekaboo said.

"Many of them, you said, were dykes."

"That's right," Peekaboo said.

"Many of *whom*?"

"You know, the one thing I learned, *early* on"—Peekaboo sighed—"was: what gets you killed, more than the next thing, is the inability to let things *be*."

"Yeah, well, I can't let it be," Mike said.

"And why is that?" Peekaboo said.

"Because I got the girl killed," Mike said.

"Now, tell me again, just how you did that?"

Mike rubbed his face. He shook his head, as if to clear it.

"*Come* on," he said.

"No, how 'bout *you* come on," Peekaboo said. "How 'bout *you* come on, with this fucken, it ain't *grief,* anymore, it's a *habit,* and if life don't go on, then it baffles me what *does*."

"You ever lie to a man?"

"That's *all* I do," Peekaboo said.

"White or black?"

"Don't make no difference," Peekaboo said. "That's *all* I do."

"You ever lie to me?" Mike said.

"What the hell *I* care, if they were dykes or not, that ain't *my* lookout, and, thus, I got no need and so no desire to know. About *anybody*."

"D'you know the girl, Ruth Watkins? *Lizabeth*," Mike said. "Did you know her? Well?"

"I got to tell you. To stay out of it. Please."

"Why? To protect me?" Mike said. "To protect me?"

"To protect *her*," Peekaboo said.

Later they sat alone, in the parlor, in the dawn. The house was closed, and Marcus had closed the pocket doors, shutting them in before the dying fire.

"Two things I learned, this life, only way to *help* someone, is not free. Usually it gon' cost someone; most times, that person is *you:* You got to give them something, whether it's money, or 'reserve,' *you* know, or even, you have to be cruel, *for* them. It hurts you. To *not* fix 'em up, or buy 'em a drink, or lend 'em money, go and do it for themselves. You got to be content, they *think* you cruel. Or *fire* s'mbody, everyone thinks: 'That hard bitch, they just trying to make a living.' May *be*, at the cost of, costing someone *else* their job, closing the place *down*, something.

"Sometimes, you know secrets. Human nature is, turn it into gold, or attention, or a pass from the cops, rat out some competitor to the Flying Squad. Sometimes, the price is: *someone's* going to get hurt. Only question is, who? You din't *ask* for that choice, but you got it.

"What I *do*. For a *living*. I keep secrets. Men pay me for that. I pay the police. They pay City Hall." She shrugged. "And here we are at the kitchen table."

"She was passing," Mike said, "Lita Grey."

Peekaboo glanced over his shoulder at the sound of the door, and Mike turned to see Dolly insinuating herself into the room. Peekaboo looked at her hard.

Mike saw it and Peekaboo saw that he had.

"Why don't you give it up?" Peekaboo said. ". . . *Mike* . . . ?"

"Because I got the girl killed," Mike said.

"What if I could *tell* you something, you'd give her up?"

"As a favor?" Mike said.

"Black woman can't do a white man a favor. She's gon' pay for it. But I might offer you a trade."

"Where is she?" Mike said. "Lita Grey."

"I don't know," Peekaboo said, "and that's the truth; but I can give you something, *in trade for,* you stop looking. You game?"

Mike said nothing.

"You *game?*" Peekaboo said. "I tell you what. I'm gonna *give* it to you, you decide."

"What is it?" Mike said. But Peekaboo didn't speak. "Alright," Mike said, "what *is* it?"

"You din't get that Irish girl killed," she said.

Mike walked to the window.

"You din't have nothing to do with it," Peekaboo said.

"I don't understand," Mike said. "Who got her killed?"

"Her father," Peekaboo said.

"No," Mike said. "No, you'll have to explain it to me."

"It's in plain sight," Peekaboo said, "like most things that you want to hide. It killed Lita, and it killed Ruth, and I'll tell it to you, if you say it's over, if you let it *be* over. That's the deal. Is that the deal?"

"I didn't get the girl killed?"

"No."

"Then *what?*" Mike said. "And how do *you* know?"

"The Irish?" Peekaboo said. "Love to tell each other stories, 'mongst themselves? How smart they are, all night long. Just one dumb Negro fetching towels. And you hear things *when* you hear them. *If* you do."

"What did you hear, and how did you hear it?"

"I heard it," Peekaboo said, "through George White,

the Kedzie Baths; and tell *you* 'cause you stood up for his brother."

Then she told him the story.

And the story was that O'Banion and the Irish had been running guns to the IRA. Weiss and Teitelbaum were in charge of the routes and the transport.

They had operated on the principle that the best way to hide something is to make a show of it, and had moved the guns from the armory to storage and onto the ships in The Beautiful's red flower van.

Teitelbaum and Weiss had gotten cute, and were skimming guns from every shipment to sell at their leisure. They were discovered and killed. Mr. Walsh, the owner of the flower vans, said that the job had now become too dangerous to him, and to his beloved daughter. So the IRA shot her to remove the objection.

"And what about Lita Grey?" Mike said.

"Lita Grey got caught up in it, Ruth, too," Peekaboo said, "and that's why they're dead. There you are, and that's the deal."

Chapter 38

B ut the deal was no deal, Mike told himself, because Peekaboo lied. And he told himself that, even had she told the truth, he would have betrayed her; that she was correct in her assessment of a favor between blacks and whites. And that he did not give a fuck.

For from the corner of his eye, he had seen Dolly turn minutely away when Peekaboo said she did not know where Lita was.

And so, he went to find Lita Grey. And he knew where to find her. He'd learned in Dolly's room: from the photograph of the black adolescents of Benton Harbor, Michigan.

He found Lita in a one-room flat, in the least run-down block of the Negro section of Benton Harbor. Down the street from the AME Church where she and Dolly had attended confirmation class. Many of the block's inhabitants were, or worked for, the town's Negro professionals.

The pastor had the house just north of the church. The town's two black dentists, three black doctors, all five members of the Negro Bar, lived on the same block of Pine Street.

The grandest homes had a coach house in the back. Most of these had been converted into garages; and many had had the coachman's, or chauffeur's, quarters on the second floor turned into apartments.

Hers was one room, its entrance off the corridor, carved out between the other three flats, and running from the landing of the staircase through to the one bathroom.

She had violet eyes, tawny blond hair, and ivory skin, and was now known as Nella Adolphe. She had been born Berenice Mancuso, and had performed, in Chicago, under the name of Lita Grey.

She was twenty-eight years old, and fear had helped her to look forty. She was dressed in a simple, prim, ankle-length gray dress. Over it she wore a brown cardigan, a thin, threadbare coat, and a head scarf.

She preceded Mike up the stairs, and ushered him into her room. She started to close the door behind her, and then stopped.

"We have to keep it open," she said. She motioned at the window, giving onto the main house.

"Our housekeeper, there . . . *I* think she's got nothing to do but spy on the tenants. And *especially* . . . ," she said, and ran her hands in front of herself, indicating the female form. "So she can see me," Lita said. "So, I'm going to stand here."

The low light came in through the window. Mike stayed at the open door, his hat in his hand, his coat on.

"And we don't get too much *heating* in here," Lita said. "Which is a change, from, even in Chicago, you know, it was, those apartments were warm—"

"Uh-huh," Mike said.

"—on Lake Shore *Drive*," Lita said. "Hey, but that's a sad topic. Maybe you could advise me, or help me to come back?"

"Maybe I could," Mike said.

"How could you *do* that?" Lita said. " 'Cause I'm safe *here*, I think. But . . ."

Mike nodded.

"And I only have two ways to make a living. That I know of," she said.

"How do you live here?" Mike said.

"I *work*," Lita said. "For a dentist. And I'm a receptionist. They killed Ruthie."

"Yes. They did," Mike said.

"It's terrible. To lose someone," Lita said.

"Yes it is," Mike said.

"Then, you know what I mean," Lita said. "But . . ." She looked out of the window. "And, *you* know, I think that I got Ruthie killed."

"How was that?" Mike said.

Lita sat on the bed and began to cry.

"How was that?"

" 'Cause I mentioned. That we had that letter. In the safe.

"Ruthie knew we had to get out. The problem, only place *she* could go, downtown, with our own. But they knew where to *look* for her, so . . ."

"But they didn't know where to look for *you*," Mike said.

"So, inn't funny," Lita said, "once again, who had the advantage."

"Yes, that's funny," Mike said.

Lita stood, and looked out the window.

"Who'd you tell them that I am?" Mike said.

"I said you were an insurance adjuster. And I have to show you some 'receipts' that I had in my room."

"I said that I could help you," Mike said.

"How could you help me?" Lita said. "To come *back*?"

"Perhaps," Mike said.

"How?" Lita said.

"I . . . ," Mike said. "I'm going to ask a favor of someone. Who might set you up."

"Back in Chicago?" Lita said.

Mike shook his head.

"*Somewhere*," she said.

Mike nodded.

"*Doing . . . ?*"

Mike said nothing.

" 'Cause I can *sing*," she said.

"Yes," Mike said, "but if you *sing*, you might get noticed. Maybe Cuba?"

"*Cuba*," Lita said. "Cuba. Thank you."

"Will you tell me? What was in the letter? In the safe?" Mike said. "You read the letter?"

She nodded.

"What did it say?"

Chapter 39

The Newspaper Morgue was, of course, never closed, but in keeping with its title, it always seemed, to the newsmen, indelicate to frequent it during the day. But now Mike sat and studied. The topmost file showed the murdered safecracker, where Poochy had caught him, in transit from the Black Maria to the East Chicago Morgue.

There was the fellow, dead, on the stretcher, fresh enough from the water, and recognizable as a human being. What was left of his face was pinched and long. He had sparse, thin hair, badly cut.

"I want to see the photos of Teitelbaum's funeral," Mike said. Poochy dug down and retrieved the file.

Mike leafed through the rabbi at the graveside, the floral tributes, the widow weeping.

"I want to see the shot you snapped of the guys in back," Mike said.

Poochy found the print and Mike stared at it. "Blow it up. As big as it goes," he said. "I want to see their faces. If we can."

He waited while Poochy enlarged the photograph. And then he had it enlarged again, until it showed only the blurred forms of two faces.

They were the faces of the two hard men in the overcoats. The man on the right, in sunlight, turned to the camera, like a hunter, half-hiding the face of his partner. He was the safecracker who'd washed up in the dunes.

Mike took the magnifying glass and looked for a long while at the other face, just half-seen. Just planes and shadows. And it was the man who had killed Annie Walsh.

Mike turned to see Parlow standing over his shoulder.

"They're running guns."

". . . Alright," Parlow said.

"They were stealing the guns from the armory, and shipping them to the IRA."

"The cops know?" Parlow said.

"Many of the cops," Mike said, "you'll note are Irish."

"Of course," Parlow said.

"The cops and the North Side."

"Of course."

Mike held the magnifying glass over the photograph. Parlow looked down at the face.

"They weren't after me," Mike said, as if repeating a catechism. "They just wanted to kill the girl."

"Who'd done what?" Parlow said.

"They were sending a message to her father," Mike said.

Mike put the magnifying glass down. On the table next to it were ten or twelve clippings. Parlow read, " 'Continued Thefts from National Guard Armories.' "

Mike picked up a newspaper clipping.

The headline read SAMUEL "NAILS" MORTON, WAR HERO, KILLED IN LINCOLN PARK. The clipping showed two photos. On the right was that of a man in a riding habit, sprawled, dead, on the grass. The photo on the left showed a horse, crumpled, dead, in his stall; against the stall, prominently displayed, was a Thompson gun.

". . . Read all about it," Parlow said.

"The *tommy* gun," Mike mused. "Nails Morton? Alright? Thrown from his horse. O'Banion? Comes in, machine-guns the horse to death."

"Tit for tat," Parlow said.

"Of course; and they leave the gun, as 'tainted,' alongside the horse's body."

"It's lovely. It's medieval," Parlow said.

"Yes, and it's wasteful," Mike said. "Jackie Weiss, Teitelbaum, *somebody* says, 'Our fellows leave these machines lying about? I'll bet I can find someone who'd cherish them.'"

"Jackie Weiss was in it with Teitelbaum?" Parlow said.

". . . They got cute. Guns go missing? Irish? Where do they look first? At the outsiders. Outsiders, in this case, as per usual, are the Jews. *This* case, they're right."

"You figure this out at the whorehouse?"

"No," Mike said. "I just wrote it on a piece of paper."

Mike took his jacket from the back of the chair. He put it on and began to load the contents of his pockets, resting on the library table. He took his cigarettes and lighter, his reporter's notebook, and a fountain pen, and put the small celluloid rabbit into his lapel pocket.

"Where you going?" Parlow said.

"I am going," Mike said, "to close out accounts."

He took the photograph of the two men in overcoats. Parlow pointed, meaning, *Those men?*

"This one," Mike said, "is dead, the safecracker . . ." He ripped the photo in two. "And *this* one," he said. "*This* one . . . ? I want to see his face again."

"What was in the safe?" Parlow said.

"The hell *I* know," Mike said.

But he did know. The Teitelbaum letter had been in the safe.

It cataloged the conspiracy of O'Banion's North Side Jews to rob the IRA. And it contained the names of the recipients of the stolen guns, which were being sold to the Jewish mobs of Detroit, the plans for their transport, and a statement of accounts.

Ruth Watkins had observed Jackie's secrecy concerning the safe, and, one night, supposedly amorous, and supposedly drunk, had walked up behind him as he worked the combination, and embraced him as he turned the dials.

Ruth knew the combination, Lita knew of the letter; after Weiss's death they pooled their information. They opened the safe, read the contents of the letter and fled.

Lita had told Mrs. Weiss's lawyer she possessed the letter, and that confession had led to the safecracker's attempt. He reported the safe empty, as, indeed, it now was; but he was not believed. He was killed, and Ruth Watkins was killed. The letter had gotten them all killed by the IRA.

Lita had kept the letter. She offered to sell it to Mike.

They settled on three hundred dollars, Mike's life savings.

He'd had the money wired to him, and met Lita that

evening, outside the railroad station. He gave her the money, and she handed the letter to him.

When his train was called, he stood and walked toward the platform. Across the waiting room, the sign read COLORED ONLY. Lita Grey was sitting there, a suitcase beside her. She did not look up.

Chapter 40

The Hawthorne Hotel was the Cicero headquarters of the Outfit.

The smoke shop, off the lobby, was the Outfit's withdrawing room; those awaiting audience sought Capone's underlings there, to present, each, his particular case. High management, and sometimes Capone himself, came to the smoke shop to savor that camaraderie, though now confected, which had suffused their early, struggling days.

The smoke shop had a barber chair, a long counter behind which the glass-fronted shelves held the choices of tobaccos, and a window seat in the barred window. There was always a minimum of two bodyguards stationed in the smoke shop. One's post was in the window seat, looking out; the other's was in the doorway, keeping an eye on the lobby.

Mike walked from the train station to the hotel.

He saw the bodyguards on each of the four corners of the intersection, and did not see but knew of the sharpshooters in the buildings opposite. In the lobby he made out four heavies, stationed prominently.

He was greeted by a manager in a morning coat. "May I help you?" the man said.

"I have a message for Mr. Brown," Mike said.

"We have no Mr. Brown here," the manager said.

"That's a shame," Mike said. "Perhaps the Mr. Brown *I* speak of hasn't checked in yet."

"No, sir, I would *know*," the manager said. "And we're all booked up."

"Well, he may be staying somewhere else," Mike said. He turned away, then turned back. "But, perhaps you could do something for me," he said.

"What would that be, sir?"

"I wonder," Mike said, "if you'd oblige me, by holding on to this."

Mike made a slow demonstration of his gesture, reaching, elaborately, toward the top outside pocket of his overcoat. He saw the manager look anxiously around the lobby. Mike put the first two fingers of his right hand into the pocket and extracted a small envelope. He held it toward the manager, who looked over Mike's shoulder.

Then, "Of *course*, sir. Thank you. When will you be calling for it?"

"Oh, in a while," Mike said.

"Would you like me to put it in the safe?" the manager said.

"Oh, no," Mike said, "it has nothing but sentimental value. But, I'd appreciate it if you held it. Behind the desk would be fine."

"Of course, sir," the manager said.

Mike nodded his thanks and turned to leave.

One of the heavies had detached himself from his post and positioned himself in front of the revolving door. He nodded Mike over toward the smoke shop.

Mike walked into the smoke shop.

The bodyguards there hustled him through a door in the back and into a small parlor. One stripped the coat down to immobilize his arms. He frisked Mike roughly, tore off the coat, went through the pockets, and then wrung it between his hands. He found nothing. He did the same with the suit jacket.

Finding nothing again, he pointed to a chair in the corner. Mike sat.

After what Mike judged to be a quarter hour, Jake

Guzik came through the smoke shop door. He held the letter Mike had brought. Mike had seen him last across the table at the Metropole.

"Yeah, here you are again," Guzik said. "What the fuck are you doing here?"

"I brought something for you," Mike said.

Guzik held up the letter, as a question.

"Yeah? As you'd think, we *know* this," he said.

"No. That's not what I have. That's just the calling card," Mike said.

"Which proves what?" Guzik said.

"Which proves," Mike said, "my good intentions."

"Well, then, let's hear it."

"I'd like to talk to Mr. Brown," Mike said.

"You're talking to *me*," Guzik said. "S'close as you get, and only 'cause you made him laugh. Once. But listen to me: you're *close* to it, and closer than this is: you're either on the payroll, or you're dead. Do you understand that?"

"Yes. I do," Mike said.

"So, what're you, some fucken ponce, gets his thrills rubbing shoulders?"

"No," Mike said. "No. You were kind enough, one time, I came to you about my girl."

Guzik mimed bewilderment. "Didn't we *do* that? Aren't you done?"

"No," Mike said. "I want to talk to him about the Duesenbergs."

"The Duesenbergs?" Guzik said.

"That's right."

Guzik looked around. "No, I don't know what you're talking about."

"I'm talking about the shipping business," Mike said.

"You *writing* about this?" Guzik said.

"I'm not fucking writing about it," Mike said, "and far be it from me. I *know* about it."

"You know what?"

"I know you're shipping various articles to England."

Guzik shook his head sadly. "*You're* playing with fire . . ."

"And I know something you don't know."

"And what is that?"

"That the English, and the Bureau of Investigation, are planning to hit the docks, East Chicago. First of the month."

Guzik said nothing.

"They're going in, to stop you shipping stolen cars to England."

"The Brits and the Feds, what do they care about some cars?"

"They don't," Mike said. "While they're there, they're hoping to stumble on some Irish guns."

Guzik said, "Why the charade?"

"They're protecting a source. You've got a leak," Mike said. "That's what I came to tell you."

"Who is it?" the man said.

"I don't know," Mike said.

"You don't know, but you know *this*," Guzik said.

"I'm a reporter," Mike said.

"No, I don't like this one fucking bit," Guzik said. "I don't like it." He looked hard at Mike. "*Fella*," he said. "No one wants to hurt you."

"I understand," Mike said.

"But I don't know why you come in here. To 'do us a favor'?"

"No," Mike said. "I want something in return."

"What do you want?"

"I want a tip on a guy," Mike said.

"A tip on a guy, that's all?" Guzik said.

". . . And I want a hunting license."

The Bureau of Investigation raid had proved abortive. They found no stolen cars; there were no stolen weapons.

Those on the scene had reported consternation, and

then fury, on the part of the local authorities; and much cursing, on the part of the Federals, most of it linked to the name of Capone. Vows for his imminent demise, and rage at his cunning, and suspicion, on the part of the Bureau, and British consul, of the Chicago police, who, after all, were Irish.

The story reflected credit on no one, save the Capone Mob; but the story had limited currency. The raid was witnessed by few, those few prudently silent, and when it was discussed, in the various pubs of the East Chicago docklands, actual witnesses stayed mute, and the talkative concealed their ignorance of the true nature of events with an assumed wise discretion—the knowing wink was answered by the sage nod, and life went on.

The raid established Mike's bona fides with the Outfit, and the Outfit, in this case, made good their part of the deal.

Mike was given the name and address of a certain Irishman who had, indeed, participated both in the trans-shipment of arms, and in the execution of those deemed to have impeded it.

His name was Samuel Kerry. His current habitation was a flat just south of Division Street, on the Chicago Sanitary and Ship Canal. He walked his brindle bull terrier there every morning, at dawn.

Mike had observed him doing so for the last three

mornings. Kerry would stand in the entranceway of his tenement, looking through the small glass panel in the door, left and right. Should a car pass, he would retreat into the entranceway.

Cars at that time of the morning were infrequent. Few local residents owned autos, and dawn was no time for deliveries. But he was unvarying in his routine.

Should there be no cars, he would emerge from the entrance, the dog on the leash, and turn his head as if scenting the air. But actually, listening for the sound of a motor.

Assured, he would set off with the dog.

On his walks he would turn now right, now left, now directly across the street, and past the facing tenements, through the gangway, and out onto the towpath of the canal.

Or he would double back, through the walkway abutting his tenement, out the rear, into the alley, and then, again, left or right, in an unpredictable pattern.

But his dog got him killed.

For, at the end of the walk, whatever route he'd set out on, he always stopped just under the Division Street Bridge and waited for his dog to relieve herself.

And on the fourth day, Mike was waiting for him.

The Irishman, now out of the wind, unsnapped the leash and let the dog go. He reached into his overcoat, and extracted his tobacco pouch and his pipe. The match flared as Mike stepped out from behind the abutment.

Mike held the Luger in his hand.

He looked at the man lighting the pipe.

The man who, when Mike had last seen him this closely, had been murdering Annie Walsh. The man stood still. He was not cowering, he was not resolute. He just stood there.

"You're too regular in your habits," Mike said.

The man did not move. The match continued to burn.

Mike thought, "*Finally?* He's just a man." And he no longer wished to shoot him.

He shot him anyway.

The Irishman fell backward into the canal.

Mike tossed the Luger in after him.

The dog ran, yelping, down the towpath.

Mike kicked the ejected shell into the canal.

THE
RETIREMENT
PARTY

Chapter 41

A Chicago couple shattered the National Dance Marathon record by doing the Charleston for twenty-two and one half hours.

An unidentified man in nailhead denim was fished out of the Chicago River, wrapped in chains locked to a Duesenberg hood ornament.

Leopold and Loeb, two deranged boys, had kidnapped and murdered a school chum. It was, for a year, "the Crime of the Century." Clarence Darrow had been hired for the defense.

He first pled the two boys Not Guilty, citing extenuation of a kind previously unrecognized in law. They were, he said, "deranged by privilege," and, so, entitled to the same consideration the court might extend to poor youths undone by want. Also, no boy under eighteen, Darrow argued, had ever been put to death.

The case absorbed the press, every day, every paper, every edition, for the year. The editorial pages took up, as per political bent, the questions of extenuation, motive, retribution, justice, and deterrence.

The *American* held that mercy should trump justice, and that the boys were young. The *Daily News* opined that no one disputed their age, which was a fact, nor their crime, to which they had admitted, but that the law allowed the mitigation of premeditated murder only in cases of insanity.

Three weeks into the trial Darrow changed his plea to Guilty.

The Sally Port discussed it long and hard, deciding his move, though entertaining, would have no chance of success. For, the guilt having been stipulated, all that remained was the question of punishment, which would now be decided solely by a judge, and how, the facts being what they were, could the judge decide other than for death? This, all complained, though interesting, made no strategic sense.

Yes, Darrow argued, they had committed the crime, and no, they were not insane, but, though guilty, they should escape execution because, the reporters thought, of some hodgepodge of excuses which, when reduced, amounted to this: they had been ruined by overprivilege.

The round table's surprise at this boorish attempt to flout both custom and reason was surpassed by their shock when the judge accepted the plea.

That Darrow refused to plead them Not Guilty by Reason Of was, even the *Daily News* conceded, his right. And he could, if he wished, put that case before the jury. But this baloney, it was held, was a monstrous disregard of all law and tradition.

Every speakeasy, chance meeting, dinner party, elevator ride, wedding, or funeral was occupied, in whole or part, by the crime and the chaos it released. How could the rich boys kill? Why did they kill? Were they insane, or merely pure evil? Why had Darrow, in retirement, taken the case?

He, known as the Patron of Lost Causes (and, some added, Lost Cases), had, by his own report, fought all his life for the underprivileged, the unwanted, and the underrepresented.

He had defended murderers, anarchists, jury tamperers; and had, himself, narrowly escaped conviction for jury tampering, in the case of an anarchist bombing in Los Angeles.

He was known to have said that the strength of the prosecution, in any case at all, was superior to the strength of the defense; that as the prosecution could hire expert witnesses from a bottomless purse, the defense should be entitled to the use of any monies available from any source. And as the prosecution had, as its minions, law enforcement agencies by no means reluctant to extort confessions, so the defense, though it could not administer beatings, might use the power of the purse to sway this or that juror or jurist to the side of Truth.

But Chicago was set against Leopold and Loeb. And Darrow and the families concluded that to plead them non compos mentis, and to put the case before a jury, would result in their death by electrocution.

Yes, the better solution, they determined, was to throw themselves upon the Mercy of the Court. But what of the bogus pleas that, while *not* insane, they had been marred in some other, unknowable way?

Did this not come down to the argument that it was obvious that they were unbalanced, as they had committed a crime? And, then, of what use the law?

At least they so reasoned at the Sally Port. Where Parlow had made a decided hit in quoting Kant to the effect that one should always act as if the postulate inferable from one's actions could be adopted universally.

The boys at the Port cheered when Parlow made his speech. Crouch said that he, as an altar boy, had once *been* the first postulate. Asked if he had served Mass correctly he responded in the affirmative, and all agreed that, according to Kant, then, all was well.

The case itself was fairly clear, and, so, though enjoyable as gossip, was not troubling to the reporters.

The two Jewish lads had been spoiled rotten. They had written a ransom note to the parents of their school chum, demanding ten thousand dollars. Previously, and, it would seem, in the name of safety, they had taken the boy out to the wetlands in Hegewisch, and murdered him.

Unstated in the police reports, but common knowledge among the reporters, some of whom had been at the coroner's office, was that the boy had been genitally mutilated and sodomized before his death.

The tenor of the room held unanimously that that was not fit for consumption as news, but split as to whether or not those facts, if known, should ensure the boys' execution as monsters, or excuse their crime as unquestionably psychotic derangement.

Darrow and the judge had made the argument moot.

They would be tried not only as minors, but as minors suffering under some unnameable curse: they deserved not execution, but understanding. That was Darrow's plea.

But why had the judge agreed to consider it?

Parlow, of late, had spent a good deal of time in the courts, and had followed the Leopold and Loeb case closely.

After Darrow's three-day speech, which Parlow characterized as "Sarah Bernhardt Come Again," the judge had sentenced the youths, each, to life plus ninety-nine years, sentences to run consecutively.

They went, in chains, to Stateville.

The questions raised by the trial took their place among life's other imponderables.

The Capone organization was on the run. A new sentiment of reform, and a new mayor, had prompted Al's decampment to Florida.

Various shootouts, in his absence, decimated much of the Irish mob; these and attendant reprisals now occurred to the city not as a crime wave, or gang wars, but recurrent, unavoidable disruptions, to be borne like the weather.

The present became part of the past, digested as history, hearsay, legend, or misinformation.

The Ace of Spades had been closed down by the

new reform. Rumor had it that Peekaboo had moved south.

Mike spent the better part of a year in the cabin on the Fox River writing his war novel.

Crouch was retiring from the paper.

Parlow had wired Mike pleading with him to come down for the party, and Mike had come.

Parlow had met him at Northwestern Station. He took Mike's bag and walked him to the taxi stand. They rode toward the hotel.

"Best thing," Parlow said.

"What?" Mike said.

"*Darrow?* The kids? Set his fee. The families . . . ?"

"Yeah, I know," Mike said.

"Everyone, rich Yids, purchasing *justice* . . . ?"

"Alright."

"Bar Association . . . ?"

"Set his fee," Mike said, "I know. One hundred . . . ?"

"Hundred thousand dollars," Parlow said.

"That ain't news," Mike said.

"The families? Refused to pay it."

"This, also, ain't news," Mike said.

"*Why?*" Parlow said.

"Why what?" Mike said.

"Why'd they refuse to pay it? . . . Figure it out."

"They're cheap?" Mike said.

"Rolling in dough," Parlow said. "Rolling in dough; one. *Two*, they're *Jews*, last thing in the world they want, everyone to say, 'The Jews stiffed him.'"

"*Three?*" Mike said.

"Three," Parlow said, "is, *ostensibly;* Darrow? He got their boys off." He sat back and smiled.

"Ostensibly," Mike said.

"You bet," Parlow said.

Mike thought for a moment. "I give up," he said. "But I like it."

"The asked, but unanswered, question," Parlow said. "What was it?"

Mike shook his head. "Wait."

"Nothing's a mystery but the one thing," Parlow said.

"*Okay,*" Mike said. "And not the kids . . ."

"No."

"What could it be but the kids?" Mike said.

"Figure it out."

"No, I give up," Mike said.

"It's the *judge.*"

"Okay, tell me," Mike said.

Parlow smiled. "Why does the judge go for this cockamamie 'They ain't nuts but they ain't sane' defense? You been away too long."

"Somebody paid him off?" Mike said.

"Yeah. Welcome back," Parlow said. "Darrow, the families, paid the judge off. Stand up there, take the gaff, listen to Darrow cry about 'human mercy,' and sentence them some private asylum."

"But he sentenced them to Stateville. For life *plus* ninety-nine."

"And why'd he do that? When he was *paid*?" Parlow said.

"I . . ."

"Never assume," Parlow said.

"Ah, fuck, you got the better of me," Mike said. "*You* didn't figure it out, you *got* it from someone."

"That's fair," Parlow said.

"Well, what's the story?"

"Story is: Darrow? Goes to the judge? Figures, 'What can it *cost*?' Judge says, 'One hundred thousand dollars, they go to the nuthouse in Switzerland.' Darrow goes to the families. He tells them, 'One hundred thousand, cash, the judge will go along.' They get up the money, crocodile briefcase.

"Darrow, crocodile briefcase, now, on the way to the judge's office? Has an inspiration. Whacks himself on the forehead. Takes out *fifty* grand, gives the judge fifty, says, 'Judge, the Jews? That's as high as they go.'

"Judge, alright. Is philosophical. *But.* Alright? Down

at the Monadnock Club, next day, he's sitting in the steam, with the head cashier, LaSalle National Bank. 'Curious thing,' the man says. 'Judge, I know you can't talk about the case, *but,* fellow from Leopold's office comes by, picks up, how about this, a crocodile briefcase full of cash. Full of cash.'

" 'Why'd you tell *me?*' Judge says. 'I *tell* you,' the cashier says, 'as, as a public citizen, it occurred to me, maybe they were trying to fund an escape. You can buy a lot of escape for a hundred thousand bucks.' "

Mike began to laugh.

"Fucking, the judge? Is sitting up there? Sentencing time? He's the only one knows the true story. Families, Darrow, the boys, *they* think they're going to Switzerland . . ."

Parlow started laughing. He pounded Mike on the knee.

The car had stopped outside of the Red Star Inn, the site of Crouch's retirement party.

Mike started to get out of the cab.

"Hold on," Parlow said. "The fucking *families* now. Want to have Darrow killed. They apply to Capone. He tells them, 'Yeah. One hundred thousand dollars.' They pay *him;* he goes fishing in Florida."

The doorman of the Red Star Inn opened the cab door on two men howling with laughter.

Acknowledgments

This book would not have been written without the enthusiasm and encouragement of Pam Susemiehl. I am indebted to David Vigliano, without whom the book would not have been published.

DAVID MAMET is a playwright, essayist, screen-writer, and director. His scripts for *The Verdict* and *Wag the Dog* were nominated for Academy Awards. He received the Pulitzer Prize for his play *Glengarry Glen Ross*.

HARPER LUXE

THE NEW LUXURY IN READING

We hope you enjoyed reading
our new, comfortable print size and found it
an experience you would like to repeat.

Well – you're in luck!

HarperLuxe offers the finest in fiction and
nonfiction books in this same larger print size and
paperback format. Light and easy to read, HarperLuxe
paperbacks are for book lovers who want to see
what they are reading without the strain.

For a full listing of titles and
new releases to come, please visit our website:

www.HarperLuxe.com

FOL
FEB 1 5 2024